WAR
STORY

Books by Gordon McGill:

WAR STORY

ARTHUR

WAR STORY

Gordon McGill

DELACORTE PRESS/NEW YORK

Published by
Delacorte Press
1 Dag Hammarskjold Plaza
New York, N.Y. 10017

This work was first published in
Great Britain by Michael Joseph Ltd.

Manufactured in the United States of America

First U.S.A. printing

Typography by Jack Ellis

Library of Congress Cataloging in Publication Data
McGill, Gordon, 1943–
    War story.
    1.   World War, 1939–1945—Fiction.   I.   Title.
PZ4.M14377War   1979   [PR6063.A2177]   823'.914   79–28169
ISBN 0–440–09442–9

TO
CLARE

I am grateful for the help of George Clout, Head of Readers'
Services at the Imperial War Museum, and for the advice of
General Sir Charles Harington. I am also indebted to the works
of many military historians, notably John Toland, Erich Kuby
and Hugh Trevor-Roper.

Part
ONE

Stalingrad, January 21, 1943

In his dream he could see the sun and feel its heat on his face. It was a colorful dream, something about children and animals; there was a picnic, and boats on the river. He tried to concentrate on snatching at the images but the voice on the outside kept intruding.

"Herr General . . ."

He awoke reluctantly, straining against the light. It was far better to remain where it was warm, but the voice was insistent and he could feel a hand on his shoulder gently shaking him. He grunted and coughed, his eyelids cracking open like rusty hinges. He was careful not to move too quickly. The other day a soldier had fallen asleep against a cold stone wall and when he jerked awake he had left a chunk of his cheek behind.

The face above him wore an anxious expression. "General Bergner. The car is ready."

Slowly he sat up and swung his legs over the side of the bed, pushing himself to his feet and coughing as the fetid air of the cellar stirred something in his lungs. In the far corner a young soldier was placing wood on the fire, one of the last floorboards from the upstairs room, the smoke curling back into the cellar, blackening the soldier's face and making him retch.

The old man began to stretch himself, his body feeling like a bag of twigs. There seemed to be no moisture in him. When he spoke, his voice rasped and he had to make two attempts.

"My bags?"

"They are in the car, sir."

So, it had come to this.

The aide was hovering in front of him, holding out his coat like a nervous matador before an angry bull, and the general waved him away. Slowly and painfully he moved across the cellar to the closet which for the past week had served as his bathroom. He could feel the pins and needles in his hands and feet and he silently gave thanks. He had beaten frostbite for another day and now he need no longer fear it.

The small sink was cracked and stained, the pipes long since broken. A jug of water stood in the corner and he bent to test it with his thumb. It was tepid. He shook his head in disbelief, wondering how long it had taken Rolff to raise even such a paltry amount of heat. The man's devotion was remarkable and it would not go unrewarded. If the army could not be saved, at least one man would be granted a reprieve.

He would take Rolff with him. He would not permit him to die on the streets of Stalingrad or waste away his life in some Russian camp.

Carefully he washed his hands and face, combed his hair and swilled water round his mouth, taking care not to catch his reflection in the stained mirror. The image would show an old man, older than his fifty-three years. It had been a sudden aging process and he had no desire to dwell on the sight.

He turned and walked stiffly back to his bed. The young soldier had gone and only Rolff remained, a slight stooping figure with the face of a sick child, still holding the coat and attempting a small smile. Bergner bent from the waist as he eased himself into the coat.

"Rolff, you are coming with me," he said, but the little man merely shrugged. He had seen so many things in the past two months that he no longer cared what happened to him. He was content to drift wherever the current took him. If he was to be left to die in Stalingrad, then so be it.

"Did you hear me?"

"Yes, sir, thank you." He shuffled to the door and reached for his meager coat, which had frayed at the collar and the cuffs and was little protection against the winds that swept down from the Steppes and across the frozen Volga. He stood shivering for a moment, stepped back to let Bergner pass, then followed him up the stairs.

The offices of the Barrikady gun factory had seemed a perfect setting for Divisional Headquarters, set in the center of the factory district in the north of the city with a view east across the river stretching to the horizon. They had come as conquerors in the autumn and now they were settling down to die like so many frozen rats. The building was little more than a blackened ruin, scarred by shrapnel; the floorboards had gone to be used as fuel. The windows had long since lost their panes and were stuffed now with straw and canvas.

As Bergner appeared from the cellar, a group of soldiers dragged themselves to attention but he waved at them to relax. They had not much time left and there was no need for pointless formality. It was enough that he had spent the last week with them. For a moment he thought of saying something, but there was nothing to be said. He reached into his pocket for the slip of paper, the wireless message relayed through headquarters from Rastenburg, the "Führer Order" demanding his evacuation with three other specialists to form the nucleus of command for a new Sixth Army in the east while the remnants of the old remained as a sacrifice and inspiration. Those were the words of the Führer. He looked at the men who were to inspire the others, thin men with no color in their faces, derelict shadows of a victorious army. They had lived on morsels of horseflesh for weeks and they gazed back at him silently with the eyes of the dead.

He pushed the door open and held his breath as he stepped outside, feeling the familiar sting in his nostrils and the sudden trickle of blood. He sniffed, swallowed and reached for his handkerchief. The bleeding rarely lasted more than a few moments, until the body became accustomed to the shock of the frozen winds. The temperature had remained at minus thirty degrees centigrade for a week, and although the sun rose each morning there was no heat to it, only a pale lamp giving out light, a Russian sun, a cold orb which served only as a sight aid for the enemy snipers.

One of the soldiers stepped forward and handed him a gas mask, but Bergner shook his head. It was an automatic gesture, out of a lifetime of conditioning; even at this stage he would not show anything which might be taken as weakness. It may be permissible for the ranks to use their gas masks as protection against frostbite, but a general of the Third Reich must be recognizable. He would not hide his face.

He stepped out into the packed snow, curling his toes against the cold. A group of soldiers stood by his car, one of them looking over his shoulder nervously, listening for the whine of the katyushar shells, the "Stalin organs" which arrived from nowhere, shredding men into oblivion. But for the moment there was silence.

He shook hands with his sergeant and turned to look south to the Mamaev Hill under which the Sixty-second Russian Army still sheltered, immovable since the beginning, mocking them through the winter and repelling every attack until the Volga had frozen and they could receive their supplies from the east; and now it was they who sat in comfort as their comrades closed in from the north, the south and the west, tightening their hold on the Sixth Army and waiting for it to freeze to death.

The farewells were short and virtually silent. He shook hands and patted shoulders, then turned and eased himself into the back of the big black Porsche, beckoning Rolff to sit next to him, staring straight ahead as the driver started the engine and spun the car away from the yard. An escort of soldiers on motorcycles rode alongside the car through the factory district, driving slowly through the rubble, the driver handling the big car carefully, occasionally drifting sideways on the ice, then spinning and twisting again before moving forward. Between the shattered buildings the slag heaps reared into the sky, their contours broken with shell craters and obscured by snow; the route was populated by corpses, grotesque shapes, some twisted and broken, others sprawled as if asleep and content. Bergner turned his eyes from them, thinking of the young soldier he had seen yesterday. He had fallen asleep in the snow and died peacefully while the flakes molded themselves to his face. He had remained in the one position for a day, smiling toward the east until someone had tipped him over and thrown a few shovels of slush over him.

As they made the final turn northwest toward Army Headquarters at Gumrak Airport, Bergner looked back at his command post and beyond to the east where the Russians waited, stoking up their bitterness for the final annihilation.

And still there was silence, as if they were permitting him to leave in peace; but the danger now came from within. At the factory the men had retained their discipline, but now they were on the country road and many had been living in snow holes and slit trenches. Their clothes were frozen to their bodies, and their feet and fingers were bloated with frostbite and scarred with the red welts of body lice. They watched the car, some walking, others crawling in the direction of the airport. They had survived the fifty-eight days of encirclement and had no more to lose, and so they tried to reach the car, hobbling toward the running board, aware that the Porsche was heading for safety, determined to make one last effort to escape, fighting to get past the escort to the warmth of the big car.

One man half ran, hopping on his left foot, ducking and dodging past the motorcyclists. He was only six feet from the hood when a blow from a rifle butt pitched him onto his face. Bergner looked back through the smeared window. The man was lying on his back now, one leg twitching convulsively, his left arm pointing to the sky.

"A waste," he said aloud, shaking his head and aware of the mutinous anger that was building up inside him.

They drove slowly, their route signposted by the legs of horses, the bones crookedly buried at intervals of thirty yards. Soon he became aware of the noise, the steady drone of artillery fire punctuated by the thump of the antiaircraft batteries. The sun had vanished, lost behind the smoke which rose from the airport, and now there was a concentrated mass of men making their way toward the one-story buildings and the single runway. Some dragged themselves forward, others hobbled on sticks past those who had given up, lying where they had fallen and staring blankly around them, within sight of the escape route but without the strength or the will to reach it.

A mile to the north the railway station was ablaze, blasted by bombs, and as the wind shifted, the general sniffed and was forced to swallow hard as he recognized the smell drifting beneath the black smoke. Vaguely he was aware of the driver talking to the soldier in the front seat.

"There's a stack of bodies by the station. Rejects from the hospital . . ."

He clenched his teeth, fighting to ignore the hunger and the reluctant salivation brought on by the aroma of dead men. Instead he gazed out of the window at those who clustered round the car, men in the last stages of disintegration, ill-clad, some with open wounds, staring back at him dispassionately, beyond hope or anger but retaining a hint of curiosity, wondering who this privileged passenger might be.

He found himself searching the uniforms for unit badges, anything rather than look at their faces. There were the 376th and 44th Divisions from the northwest of the encirclement, the 14th Panzer from the west which had taken the worst of the bombardment, the 16th and 24th

Panzer from the east, the 94th from the north, and even a few of his own from 79th Division; and then he noticed that they were all looking upward, listening to something. He squinted through the window and saw the aircraft banking downward from perhaps a thousand feet through orange puffballs of gunfire. It was an old transport plane, a battered Heinkel 111, coming in at an angle, its left wing dipping dangerously. When it landed after two bounces, Bergner realized that he was cheering along with the men and it had been an involuntary cry of relief, for this old plane was the escape link to the west. If it could come in, then perhaps it could get out.

The car drew up outside a squat building a mile from the runway and stiffly Bergner levered himself out, nodding to the soldier who saluted him and ushered him inside to the command headquarters of the Sixth Army.

He was led down a staircase and along a corridor to an unmarked door. The soldier knocked. "General Bergner, sir," he said, as he opened it.

Feldmarschall Friedrich von Paulus turned and smiled. "Gerhard," he said, "how are you?"

Bergner shrugged and muttered something polite. Paulus too had become an old man but he retained a certain dignity. Quietly they exchanged greetings.

Paulus looked over his shoulder, indicating the map on the wall which showed the latest positions. The Kessel, the "caldron," was diminishing hourly, the territory held by the army shrinking into a small ragged circle.

"I came in here with 208,000 men," he said wearily, "and my superiors would not permit me to leave." He looked at Bergner, searching his face for whatever feeling remained there, for condemnation or understanding or pity. "Do you appreciate that?"

Bergner nodded. He could see the torment in the man's eyes. "I know," he said quietly.

"And two-thirds are gone." Paulus shook his head and turned away, then squared his shoulders and turned back, a slight smile on his face. "Your transport is almost ready. They are refueling as quickly as possible. But first there is something I want you to see." He walked to the door and opened it, shouted for a soldier, then took Bergner's hand and smiled.

"Good-bye, Gerhard."

Bergner stood stiffly to attention, withdrew his hand and saluted: "Heil Hitler!"

But Paulus merely smiled again and closed the door behind him.

Bergner followed the soldier outside, beckoned Rolff to follow him and clambered aboard a jeep. Again they drove through crowds of men who were stumbling in all directions with no apparent aim but to remain in the vicinity of the airfield and within sight of the Heinkel.

The jeep stopped outside the stable which served as a hospital, and Bergner was led past the rows of men waiting outside. Rolff began to follow him but was turned back by a guard.

"What's happening?" he asked.

The guard shrugged. "Anyone with an appointment with the Führer is shown the hospital first," he said. "I don't know why."

Rolff went back to the jeep. For fifteen minutes he wiggled his toes and crushed his hands into his armpits, his eyes shut tight against the wind, until he felt a movement and saw that the general had returned, his face cemented into a stern mask. As the jeep moved away, Rolff was thrown to one side but Bergner did not budge. He stared straight ahead, apparently oblivious to his surroundings.

At first the evacuation of the wounded proceeded normally, the members of the headquarters' battalion forming a ten-yard corridor and allowing the medical orderlies to pass unhindered with their stretchers and up the ramp into the belly of the aircraft.

Bergner sat in a small bucket-seat behind the pilot, strapped in and waiting patiently for take-off, watching from the cockpit window as the crowd deepened around the ramp and the first sign of pushing began.

From his perch he was the first to notice the trouble. Leaning forward he tapped the pilot on the shoulder and pointed down to the spot where a soldier had slipped unnoticed behind two orderlies and was trying to make his way unobtrusively into the line of wounded, but even as the pilot rose from his seat to shout a warning the soldier was spotted by a guard and the scuffling broke out.

Briefly everyone seemed to freeze, standing as if in a tableau watching the two men fight, before, with a concerted roar, a group of soldiers rushed through the gap created by the scuffle and ran for the ramp, overturning stretchers, trampling on the wounded and grappling with the guards.

Bergner watched in horrified fascination while men were beaten over the head with rifle butts and others, bandaged and bleeding, disappeared beneath the boots of men they had once fought alongside. He heard the screams of the wounded mingle with shouts of anger, each man clawing his way toward survival, as, with mischievous timing, the Russian mortars from the west began to cough and the first bombs burst a hundred yards from the runway.

Above it all he was conscious of the sound of laughter. He turned and saw the pilot chuckle to himself as he checked his instruments. "It's always the same," he was muttering; "as if it isn't bad enough, this always happens." He shook his head, turned a key and the engines roared. Below, men were sent sprawling by the draft of the propellers. Bergner, unable merely to watch, unbuckled his seat belt and made his way back into the body of the aircraft past groups of men on stretchers and others kneeling by the portholes watching the fighting.

At the hatch, the wounded were being dragged inside as the orderlies punched and kicked out at the faces of soldiers who were trying to fight their way on board. Bergner grabbed the shoulder of one of them, who turned round snarling before he recognized him.

"How many more can we take?" Bergner asked, shouting above the din.

"None, sir. We are overloaded as it is."

Bergner nodded and clawed his way to the hatch, bellowing the one word at the top of his voice: "Attention!"

Everything stopped. Men turned toward him, gaping at him, caught instantly in a conditioned response to the voice of authority. Bergner snapped his finger at the biggest of the orderlies and nodded toward the hatch. The man sprang at the door, swung it into position and began to heave as the fighting began again. Bergner pushed a wounded soldier to one side and leaned his weight to the door, hearing it snap into place, the grind of the hatch mingling with the screams of a man who had been trapped on the outside between the door and the mob on the ramp.

Bergner stood motionless for a moment, panting, then made his way back toward his seat, staggering slightly as the aircraft began to move up the runway. As he passed one of the portholes he glanced outside and stopped again, unable at first to take in what he was seeing. Three men were clinging to the wing, lying stretched out full length, side by side facing into the wind, their knuckles white as they clutched onto the plates.

"It happens all the time," said the voice of one of the orderlies. "Every trip it's the same. They are crazy."

Bergner moved closer to the porthole, staring at the men. Their faces were squashed against the metal, their hair swept back from their foreheads, threadbare trousers flapping as the Heinkel picked up speed. The first to go fell as a wheel hit a pothole on the runway and lurched to one side, sending him slithering backward and out of sight, but the others held on. Again the aircraft shuddered as a shell exploded fifty yards to the side, spattering the fuselage with shrapnel. Bergner blinked automatically at the explosion, and when he opened his eyes there was only one man remaining; and now the aircraft was moving faster, the engines at full throttle as it careered down the runway, straining for takeoff. First the soldier lost his grip with his left hand, his arm snapping back in the slipstream. For a moment he hung on, as if by faith alone, with the fingers of his right hand. Bergner caught a glimpse of his face, a young strong face, the mouth open in a silent scream, the eyes wide and staring . . . and he was gone, swept from sight as the aircraft began to rise, heaving itself into the air. Bergner stared at the wing and thought he could see the outline of the soldier engraved on the wing by the heat of his body, until the ice formed on the metal and there was nothing.

He turned and made his way back to his seat.

He tried to sleep but the moans of the wounded kept jerking him awake. Yawning, he looked behind him and to his right where Rolff lay sleeping, his head back and his mouth open showing teeth black with decay.

He fumbled beneath his seat for his briefcase and drew out a file of papers, absentmindedly flipping through them and glancing at the orders of battle, logistical memos, intelligence reports regarding enemy strength, meteorological reports, casualty figures, ammunition requirements and, stapled together, a sheaf of radio messages which had passed between the Führer and von Paulus.

He gazed at the first signal, realizing as he read it that he knew the details by heart, even the figures of the dateline, driven into his brain as if by a brand.

"Directive of October 14, 1942," he read. "Every leader must be convinced of his sacred duty to stand fast, come what may, even if the enemy outflanks him on the right and left, even if his part of the line is cut off, encircled, overrun by tanks, enveloped in smoke, or gassed."

He flipped the page and rubbed his thumb against a faded yellow signal.

Radio message No. 1352
Top Secret
Urgent   Army Group 5
To HQ Sixth Army   21 Nov '42, 1525 hours
Führer Order

Sixth Army will hold position despite threat of temporary encirclement. Keep railroad line open as long as possible. Specific orders regarding air supply will follow.

Bergner grunted audibly, recalling the assurances from Hermann Göring that the Luftwaffe would keep the army supplied, the promise of 550 tons of supplies daily, a target which was never reached, not even by half.

Clipped to the message was a requisition list showing that the best performance in mid-January was fifty tons, and he snorted in disgust, picturing the head of the air force, the fat, posturing dandy of a man. Damn Göring, he thought. Damn them all.

He read on: Paulus's cable of November 23 requesting permission to withdraw; the reply, a highest-priority decree telling the commander to maintain a hedgehog defense: November 26, the army reduced to half rations . . . no drugs for the wounded . . . two ounces of bread a day . . . guns destroyed for lack of shells.

He leaned back into his seat and looked out into the winter sky, sorting out the details in his mind. A dreadful mistake had been made. There was no doubt about that.

Quietly, as if intoning a litany, he began to whisper the oath he had taken seven years before on that bleak day in Berlin:

"I swear by God this holy oath that I will render to Adolf Hitler, Führer of the German Reich and People, Supreme Commander of the Armed Forces, unconditional obedience, and that I am ready as a brave soldier to risk my life at any time for this oath."

Just then a small noise made him turn. Rolff was curled in his seat like a ball, still apparently asleep, his arms round his knees, his chin cupped in his left hand, the thumb of his right hand in his mouth, and he was crying softly for his mother.

Slowly Bergner packed his papers together and put them back in his briefcase. He nodded to himself and made a promise: that this time when he met the Führer he would not act like a boy cadet. He had things that needed to be said. With that resolution in mind he drifted into a peaceful sleep.

It was dark when the Heinkel landed in Rastenburg, and Bergner felt groggy as he descended the ramp. He was met by a young officer of the Leibstandarte SS, Hitler's personal guard, and the first thing Bergner noticed after the gaunt grayness of his men was his fresh skin, pink and almost translucent. He was further irritated by the greeting, which seemed just a shade overenthusiastic.

As they waited for the bags to be off-loaded, Bergner looked back at the aircraft. The men being carried off the plane were out of place here, he thought: skeletal, broken creatures. Stalingrad was only 1300 miles to the east but they looked as if they had come from another planet and another time, men who had been promised so much and who had been let down so badly, victims to the whims of a madman. Even as the word came to mind he felt guilty, but he was jolted out of his reflections by the strident questioning of the SS man, asking about the flight and making solicitous noises about the conditions he had been living under.

"When do I see the Führer?" he asked abruptly as they made their way to the car.

"He will send for you." The reply was equally abrupt, as if to add that the Führer was a very busy man.

The car drew up at a small hotel in the outskirts of the town.

At the entrance the SS man saluted again. "The Führer's instructions are that you rest and eat well," he said cheerfully. "And by the way, you will find one of your friends here."

Bergner looked inquiringly at him.

"General Heubeck from Sixteenth Panzer," he explained. "Good night, sir."

Then he was gone, leaving Bergner wondering what it was about the man's youthful enthusiasm that bothered him. He grumbled to himself as he followed the porter upstairs, watching as Rolff was led down another corridor. Perhaps it was because he had been given time to rest. He had imagined that he would have been taken directly to headquarters, the stain and the smell of battle still upon him and the anger still hot inside him.

But two hours later he had become drowsy; a bath, a steak and half a bottle of wine had softened him. He was about to prepare for bed when he heard a knock on the door. Grunting to himself he opened it.

"Heubeck," he said, standing back to let the man in. He had always liked Heubeck. The man had no pretensions. And they shared a good Prussian background. As a bonus, Heubeck was handsome, tall, silver-gray-haired with the sharp profile of an angry eagle, so very Prussian. Bergner sometimes envied him his looks. It was not fitting for an officer to be squat and lumpy. The panzer general had brought a bottle of brandy with him and the two men drew up armchairs, settled themselves down and toasted each other.

"Have you seen him?" asked Bergner.

Heubeck shook his head. "I have been here for two days. Perhaps it will be tonight after the conference."

"He still works late?"

"Till three sometimes. It's dreadful."

"Perhaps we should demand an appointment."

"It would do no good. You have to go through Bormann. He handles everything these days."

After the second brandy Bergner began to feel sleepy. He was not accustomed to it and he tried to recall the last time he had met the Führer. It was six months ago, at the Bergdof. He had been jovial that day and hospitable, clasping the hands of the generals and welcoming them. Bergner tried to remember details of his face but he could not. It was just a cartoon caricature that came to mind and he realized that he had never truly studied the man; he always looked over his shoulder or at his mouth, because the eyes were so hypnotic. It did not do to look at the eyes. Abruptly he giggled, thinking how odd it must seem to Hitler to have everyone staring over his shoulder.

"I'm sorry," he said as Heubeck nudged him. He had not been listening. He stretched for the bottle and poured himself another glass. He belched slightly and returned to the subject.

"We should have complained earlier," he said. Heubeck nodded sleepily in agreement. "We should never have allowed him to do it. It was a nonsense letting the Gestapo control soldiers who had got in trouble. We should have opposed his foreign policy in thirty-eight. We should have objected over Blomberg and von Fritsch . . . we should have resigned with Beck over Czechoslovakia."

Bergner paused. All the arguments were old ones. He had heard them all before but he had never articulated them himself. He gazed into the fire. "And above all we should have opposed him on Russia. It's a nightmare. A war on two fronts." He shook his head. "Insane," he whispered. "Quite insane."

Huebeck nodded, then rose to his feet, moving slightly unsteadily. He smiled down at Bergner. "We should have known," he said. "Let's face it. How can you trust a man who prefers rifles to machine guns?" He patted Bergner on the shoulder, still smiling, trying to draw the depression from him, but Bergner continued to stare morosely into the fire.

"This morning at the hospital I was shown the photograph of a young captain," Bergner said softly.

"Blond and handsome," said Heubeck. "And the uniform, and the jar with the heart in it."

Bergner looked up. "It's terrible. So small, just the size of a baby's, the doctor said. I never knew hunger had that effect."

Heubeck moved to the door. "Someone should tell the Führer," he said.

Bergner watched him leave and turned his back to the fire. For half an hour he sat motionless, and as he rose to go to bed he realized that what he had been thinking would land him in a Gestapo jail.

The call came early the next morning, and the two men sat in silence as they were driven through the town. Bergner felt odd, as if he had been playing some game where he was blindfolded and spun around three times so that he was not sure which way he was facing. He could barely think of Stalingrad. It seemed another life away, part of a nightmare. Here in East Prussia your nose did not bleed in the mornings. There were wooden road-signs instead of horses' legs, and pretty women smiled in their furs as they went about their business; nor was the sad face of Rolff there to remind him. He had stayed behind in the hotel, planning, he had said, to sleep until the end of the war.

As the car swept through the gates of headquarters past the gaze of the guards, Bergner lanced at Heubeck and saw that the man was sitting with his eyes closed and his fists clenched so that the knuckles showed white. What was it about an imminent audience with the

Führer that turned strong men into nervous parodies of themselves? he wondered. But then again, it was perhaps only the effects of the brandy.

They were shown into a drawing room which was tastefully and expensively furnished in pine with six green armchairs, but neither man sat down. They moved slowly, hands clasped behind their backs. Bergner was trying to concentrate on his report, but his brain seemed to have the consistency of cotton wool. And again, his throat was dry.

"General Bergner." An aide stood at the door, holding it open for him.

Bergner smiled a farewell at Heubeck, wondering why they were going in separately when they had the same story to tell. It was all very strange. He followed the aide along a corridor past the Führer's private apartment to the situation room. The door was open and Bergner walked straight in, clicked his heels and saluted, trying to focus as the bright sunlight from the French windows dazzled him.

By the map table next to the window he could see Generals Schmidt and Jodl. Across the room by a wall map of Russia he saw Marschall Keitel with Bormann at his side. He nodded to Bormann and the man smiled back at him. Some of his friends had been surprised at the warmth shown him by Bormann but the two men knew each other of old. They went a long way back.

Hitler came to him from the window, the light behind him, holding out both hands in greeting, clasping him in a hug, then leading him across to the map table, talking softly, inquiring about his health, saying he needed rest before resuming his duties; and he was talking about the war in Africa, throwing out names and places, dates, divisional strengths, saying how much he was needed and that once he had recovered he would be given responsibility equal to his talents. . . .

Bergner blinked. The man had spoken for two, maybe three minutes nonstop and there was no mention of the Sixth Army, nothing about the men left in Kessel. It was as if they had ceased to exist. The conversation concerned the future, as if the past was an irrelevance.

Bergner took a step back and cleared his throat. "But what about Stalingrad?" he said, attempting to keep his voice steady. "What are you doing about the siege?"

Hitler's eyes narrowed and he stepped forward like a boxer coming inside a jab to hook to the body. Bergner flinched but continued to stare into the man's eyes. Then Hitler turned, leaned across the map table, picked up a sheet of paper and handed it to Bergner.

"I am sending this to the Feldmarschall," he said quietly.

Bergner looked at the message. It was dated January 22. He read aloud: "Capitulation impossible. The troops will defend their positions to the last. The Sixth Army has made a historic contribution to the most gigantic war effort in German history."

He looked up. Hitler was leaning back against the table and the others were looking anywhere except at Bergner, all but Bormann, who was staring at him.

"No relief?" Bergner said, aware as he said it that he sounded foolish. It was written: defend their positions to the last.

"The Sixth Army has kept ninety enemy formations tied down on the Eastern Front," said Hitler, and his voice was toneless. There was nothing more to be said.

All the images seemed to rush into Bergner's mind at once, scrambled and jumbled, of guns being destroyed and men dying, of lice leaving a cooling body in droves to settle on another; the outline of a man's body on the wing of a plane. He tried to remember the arguments and assemble his thoughts but his mind was a logjam of fragmented memories. Hitler had turned away from him and he felt weak and helpless. Abruptly, without waiting for leave, he turned and left the room. He wanted to be away, in the fresh air, on his own. In the corridor he passed Heubeck but could not look at him.

Outside, standing on the porch, he glanced up into the gray sky and the image of the red-and-black swastika flag caught his eye. He touched the badge on his lapel, the gold party badge which had been presented to him by the Führer. His fist closed over it and he squeezed it, trying to crush it like a nutshell. It had nothing to do with him, this badge, nothing to do with the traditions of his fathers, and he knew now that it was guilt which stopped him ever looking into the eye of the madman. The pin pierced his finger but he did not notice. When he walked down the driveway he moved as if blind, unsure where he was going.

2

London, January 23, 1943

Alan Francis waited until the liftman drew breath before slipping in a question about his daughter. He was right. It was Judy and she had just sat her nursing exams: failed though; a pity but never mind; next time, maybe.

"Anyway, like I says to the warden, I says it's about time, my old son . . ." the man continued as he opened the gates and let Francis out, beaming and shouting cheerio after him. Francis was a good listener. As he sometimes said, it was a legacy from his days as a reporter. Always listen to liftmen, taxi drivers and waiters because they are the ones who know things. And always remember the kids' names. The habit had stuck.

He stood back for a moment to let a group of secretaries pass. He watched them tinkle down the corridor on their high heels, chattering like starlings. One of them looked back at him over her shoulder, a quick surreptitious glance, then turned away blushing and giggling, chewing her fingers. Francis grinned to himself. One of his girlfriends had told him that he made women curious. His curly hair and his broken nose were in contrast to the dapper conservative way he dressed. That, and the fact that he seemed interested in them, asked questions about them and never said "Really?" or "Is that so?" That's what she had said. He remembered it perfectly.

He walked quickly down the corridor, turned right and then left, then right again. The place was like a maze: Broadway Buildings, St. James's—eight floors of corridors, partitions and coffin-sized offices, painted in dull Civil Service green. The theory among the agents of the Secret Intelligence Service was that the building was designed as an elementary initiative test. Find your office and you've made the grade.

Francis had a desk in Section Five, but he was not tied to it. He had worked in Intelligence since the war began and he was responsible for liaison, collecting information from the various sections and reporting to his chief.

He was still ten yards from his office when he heard the squeals of high-pitched laughter and he groaned aloud. The donkeys were in, the three agents from Section Five who shared his office space; public-school chaps, they tended to sound like a herd of strangled ponies when they got together. But they were bright young men, intelligent and tough. Francis had a lot of time for them.

He pushed open the frosted-glass door and stood framed in the doorway, staring in astonishment at the sight of two men sprawled on the floor gazing up at a third perched on the desk. Each clutched a teacup, and on the floor lay two unlabeled bottles. The man on the desk—tall, fair-haired and pink-cheeked—turned as Francis came in and winked, but did not check the flow of his monologue.

". . . in hideous onslaught the Nazi war machine, with its clanking, heel-clicking, dandified Prussian officers, its crafty expert agents fresh from the cowing and tying down of a dozen countries. I see also the dulled, drilled, docile brutish masses of the Hun soldiery plodding on like a swarm of crawling locusts . . ."

"Bravo, Jeffries," shouted the others in unison as he came to a close, bowing low and theatrically before springing up once more and turning, smiling broadly at Francis.

"Alan, good to see you. Come along in. Have a snifter."

A cup was pulled from the filing cabinet and a large measure poured. Francis did not ask where the whiskey came from. As he had often said, there was not much value in working in Intelligence if you were not bright enough to organize a few perks.

"Made it myself," said Jeffries, as if reading his mind.

Francis took a gulp and choked. Some perk, he thought.

"Thought you Fleet Street wallahs could snift it," said a voice from the floor.

Snifter, thought Francis. And wallah. God, they were getting worse.

"To Stalingrad, I presume," he said.

"Absolutely," said Jeffries. "Marvelous news, isn't it?"

"Up the Ivans," said the others.

"Even the BBC has got the bug," said Jeffries. "They are doing *War and Peace* on the wireless tonight."

"What's the latest?" asked Francis, slightly irritated, despite himself, with their joviality.

Jeffries leaned across a desk and flipped a piece of paper at Francis, watching him intently as he read it.

"So that is it," he said when he had finished.

"A whole army gone," said Jeffries smiling. "Swept off the board. No longer a factor in the game."

"Do we know the survival figures?"

Jeffries shrugged. "Rough estimates indicate that perhaps eighty or ninety thousand surrendered."

"The Russians are still counting," said one of the others, belching slightly. "Adding up the legs and dividing by two."

Francis ignored the squeals of laughter as he reread the official Russian military reports and the additional memos from the SIS agents. There was no doubt about it. Stalingrad was the turning point.

"Oh, yes, and the boss wants to see you," said Jeffries.

Francis felt himself jump inside his skin, as he did each time Charles Robertson was mentioned unexpectedly. It was an instinctive reaction and it reminded him of his schooldays when the headmaster sent for him. Somehow he felt as if he had been found out, although there was no rational reason for such apprehension. Robertson was always the soul of charm. He simply did not suffer fools gladly, or suffer them at all. Francis always made sure to have everything on hand when he met his boss. He only hoped that there would not come a day when he slipped up somewhere. Robertson would not be interested in excuses; those who are infallible fail to understand weakness in others. But so far Francis had managed to stay ahead.

"Where?" he asked.

"In his office," said Jeffries. "I would think about . . ." he paused, "about now."

Francis left the cup on the desk, turned and made for the door, ignoring the cries of "Good luck" and "Have another snifter, old chap."

He could hear a song start up as he reached the lift. Briefly he looked up, checking the indicator. It would be quicker to walk. He forced himself not to run up the two flights. It would be silly to appear breathless in front of the boss.

Robertson's secretary waved him through without a word. He paused briefly at the door, knocked lightly and walked in. Robertson rose from his desk to greet him, smiling and holding out his hand. As always Francis was immediately aware of the man's energy, like static electricity. It was rumored that he had his own personal rechargeable batteries, fueled by a sense of duty and responsibility. He was a small man, two inches shorter than Francis, straight-backed like a regimental sergeant major; his nose was hooked, his eyes small and bright, his mouth almost lipless, his silver hair brushed back tightly against his skull. He was dressed impeccably in twills and a sharply creased cashmere sweater. When Francis had first heard that Robertson had been a Cambridge don before the war he had expected a shambling, unkempt eccentric, and when he got to know the man he had said so. Robertson had smiled politely and told him to beware of clichés.

As usual, there was the solicitous question.

"You've had a good leave?"

"Yes, thank you, sir."

"Norfolk, wasn't it?"

Francis was aware that he was being played at his own game. "That's right. A friend has a cottage there."

"Nice to get eggs from a hen for a change."

Francis smiled. There was always a short exchange of trivialities, no matter how important the meeting; and sometimes a sherry. Robertson had regularly visited Jerez before the war for the *feria* and considered himself something of an aficionado. He pronounced the word with the Andalusian lisp, and somehow it did not sound like an affectation. He said it simply because it was pronounced that way.

But today there was no sherry. Francis took a seat. The office was sparsely furnished with a desk, a filing cabinet and two chairs, the venetian blinds shredding the light behind Robertson's head so that the visitor could not see his expression.

"Well, Alan, I think we can say that the war is safely won now."

"It is certainly a major blow to the Germans," said Francis cautiously.

"More than that, I think. His gamble in the east has failed and eventually he will face an offensive on two fronts."

Francis sat in silence as Robertson spoke briefly about the Battle of

Stalingrad and what it could mean in terms of the immediate political and military future.

He was talking slowly, his eyes bright, staring above Francis's head, and Francis knew that the man was using him as a sounding board, giving his ideas some air and letting them take shape. It was something of a compliment. The other day Robertson had stopped in the middle of one of his monologues and said that it was a pity Francis had never been one of his pupils, that he had an unusually receptive mind; and Francis had basked in the warmth of his praise for days.

For a moment Robertson was silent as if lost in thought. Francis waited. At last he stood up, took Francis by the arm and led him toward the door.

"Alan, I'd like you, if you would, to prepare a report for me on Stalingrad with particular reference to those who escaped."

Francis frowned. "I thought that no one did."

"I think you will find that an order was issued for the evacuation of several top generals. I want to know who Hitler brought out of Russia."

"Yes, sir."

Robertson smiled. "Soonest," he said.

"Fine." Francis turned and left the room. Robertson occasionally used cabelese and it sounded odd coming from him. But if it was soonest he wanted, then soonest it would be.

Francis spent the day going round each of the sections in Broadway Buildings, and made telephone calls to those out of town at St. Albans and Bletchley. He collected anything of relevance and some things that were not. His various contacts in other departments answered him readily enough, the few who resented the intrusion suppressing their annoyance. If Robertson was asking for information, he would get it. Each of them knew the story which had been told at countless cocktail parties before the war; how Robertson as a student of logic had been faced with an exam question, asking him to discuss and evaluate a definition of truth. It took him ten seconds. He applied the definition to itself, found it to be untrue and left the examination room. None of his staff had ever dared ask him to confirm the story.

Francis worked all day, stopping briefly for a sandwich at his desk and clearing away the mess left by Jeffries. There had been a note: "The locusts have been and gone."

In the afternoon he checked out the files on the senior military personnel of the Sixth Army, called in his secretary and dictated a memo; that done, he selected various biographical notes, had them photocopied, stapled them to his memo and looked in at the office used by Robertson's secretary.

"You're right on time," she said without looking up from her typewriter. "He said you'd be finished by four."

Francis grinned and again tapped on Robertson's door. This time a glass of sherry was waiting for him. He sat in silence as Robertson flipped through the file.

"Thank you, Alan," he said, snapping it shut. "If anything else comes in, you will let me know."

Francis left the office feeling relieved and content. Briefly he wondered what Robertson was looking for and if he would ever be told. But it was not important. If the man wanted to tell him, he would do so. Meanwhile there was work to be done.

Charles Robertson worked through until eight that evening before locking his office and making his way to the first floor to the radio room used by G Section. An operator sat by his machine. He was half asleep and nodded a greeting as Robertson went into a booth, took out a key, slipped it into a transmitter and began tapping out a message. The operator stared sleepily at him, idly wondering what the man was sending. But the question soon slipped from his mind. It was none of his concern.

Lisbon, January 24, 1943

Ernesto Nobrega enjoyed working for the British. The pay was reasonable and he had been promised a lengthy holiday in London once the war was won; perhaps, it was hinted, he might even be offered a job. The idea appealed to him. He had been to London in 1936 and he thought it a wonderful city. Nor did he like Germans. He had relations in Spain who had suffered under Franco, and it was a reasonable rule of thumb that if you disliked Franco you disliked Germans; at least, that was the way Nobrega saw it.

When war broke out he had waited patiently for someone to approach him. As a senior clerk in the Lisbon office of the Portuguese Immigration Department he knew full well that he must be a good contact for someone in a foreign military intelligence service. Everyone else seemed to be some kind of agent, or pretending to be; they were all close-lipped about something or other. He had only hoped that the

Abwehr would be first to contact him so that he could tell them to go to hell, but the English were first on the scene and for two years he had furnished them with all manner of information, either by radio by way of a long line of operators, or by letter. He could not believe at first that something so elementary as invisible ink was being used, and he envied the German agents their microdots, those little punctuation marks which concealed whole pages of shrunken information. He wished the British would use microdots, but it was of no great importance. The main thing was that he enjoyed the subterfuge and the glamour of his job. It did not matter that he could tell no one of his double life. It was enough that he knew himself.

He received the message at six in the morning, relayed via three radio links to the small two-way machine which he kept in his wardrobe. He whistled as he worked out the code and spoke the words aloud to himself three times: "Top priority." He would get straight onto this job. He puffed out his chest as he made his coffee, and when he was ready he set out to check the hotels.

Nobrega had little difficulty tracking down his man. The German officers on rest and recuperation made no secret of their identities, and even in civilian clothes their military bearing was obvious. Normally they stayed in one of three hotels close to the promenade and spent much of their time strolling along the seafront, pottering among the shops or reading in the cafés. He had thought it would take him perhaps a day, but he was lucky. He found the name on the register of the first hotel he visited, slipped the note into the pigeonhole and settled himself into the lobby to wait. An hour later the man came downstairs, a stocky, gaunt old man with a slight limp. Nobrega watched him pick up his mail and take the lift back upstairs.

He returned to his radio happy in the knowledge that he had completed his task in record time. In London they would be pleased with him. Already he could see himself in Piccadilly Circus, riding to work on a tram and going to the Windmill Theater in the afternoon.

When Bergner read the note, just a cryptic message and a telephone number, he was reminded of the Abwehr's warning: Lisbon could be a risky city, they had said; a den of plotters; there were plenty of traps set for the unwary. So, he thought, this would be a job for them. Perhaps they could catch an agent. He reached for the phone and called the Abwehr contact.

The man said he would come straight round and they arranged to meet in the bar. Bergner ate a leisurely breakfast in his room and went downstairs, ordered a glass of mineral water and took his seat in the corner of the room, which looked out into the square below.

As soon as the agent arrived, Bergner took a dislike to him. Perhaps, he thought, it was the implied arrogance of his manner, the way he gestured to him as if to say, "Don't get up, you look exhausted." And the snap of his fingers as he ordered himself a coffee. He was another pink-and-blond young man, like the SS officer in Rastenburg, wearing that expression of complacent self-confidence known only to those who have experienced nothing of the world.

He introduced himself merely as Karl and pointed to Bergner's glass. "No, thank you," said Bergner. "This is sufficient."

"Well, then, how are you?" asked Karl when he had settled himself. He continued talking without waiting for a reply. "A monstrous experience, dreadful, absolutely appalling, yet such a sacrifice of supreme importance. . . ."

Bergner stared at him, saying nothing.

"I was listening to Goebbels this morning. You know we have a recording of his speech, and I must say that the concept of total war is the only logical . . ."

Bergner let him talk on. Perhaps the man was merely trying to be polite. Perhaps he was simply trying to create a friendly atmosphere before getting down to business. Perhaps he was actually trained to talk like this. Or perhaps he was just a born bore.

Whichever way Bergner was not interested, and when the question finally arose he heard himself answer in a steady voice, "I think I am being followed."

"I see." Karl barely managed to keep the disappointment from showing.

It took Bergner only half a minute to concoct a description of his shadower, and Karl did not seem eager to remain much longer. With a smile and a solicitous pat on the shoulder he was gone, promising to take care of everything.

When he was alone once more, Bergner wondered why he had done it. The deception had not been planned and, indeed, it was not much; hardly treasonable. But before Stalingrad such a thing would have been unthinkable; perhaps it was just the man's manner that had made him act as he had. But he knew there was something more. He decided he would take a walk and ask himself some questions.

Part
TWO

⊲ 3 ⊳

London, January 12, 1945

The Wolseley glided quietly through the blackened streets, and in the back the two men gazed out at the pedestrians trudging about their business, each one seeming to move in slow motion, clutching coats and jackets around them to fight the cold. Briefly the car came to a halt at Oxford Circus, and Jeffries peered out at the newspaper seller who squatted by his pitch, saying nothing, scarcely bothering to shout the headlines. Jeffries leaned out and offered a coin, and the man stumbled over with a copy of the *Star* and back again without a word. The city seemed to be populated by deaf mutes.

He flipped through the paper: a V-rocket attack somewhere in the South of England, a lukewarm review of the new play *Love in Idle Idleness* at the Lyric, and a feature on the popularity of swing music at the dance halls. The places were crowded out nightly, despite the threat from the buzz bombs.

He folded the paper and dropped it on the seat.

"You don't play rugger, do you, Alan?" he asked.

Francis grunted a denial.

"It's like a bleak afternoon at Richmond. You're three points ahead, it's getting dark, you're absolutely exhausted waiting for the whistle to blow and simply terrified that the other side is going to sneak away in the last few seconds and steal the game."

Francis sniffed. "They're not going to, though, are they? The other side is finished."

"Well, I wish they would hurry up and lie down."

"Yes, I know what you mean." Francis yawned. He was exhausted and if the truth be known he would have gladly skipped the party. But the invitation was more of a command. It was not often that Robertson gave sherry parties, nor did he make any attempt to cover the fact that they were special occasions. The invitations came a week or so in advance and there were always seven or eight people, including one or two of his staff, a visiting military chief and selected representatives of the government and the Civil Service. Twice the PM himself had shown up for half an hour, and chatted amiably to each of the guests before being driven back to Whitehall.

There was a house rule that shop should not be discussed, but after the first half an hour or so, when the polite small talk had dried up, the war inevitably became the center of debate, each of the guests inquiring into the opinions and special responsibilities of the others, and when the party ended, usually around nine with everyone going his own way, the guests had come to realize that they had learned a great deal about the men and the departments they worked with. Robertson in one of his more mischievous moods referred to them as "cross-fertilization" parties.

The car drew up to the curb in Baker Street and Jeffries was the first out, bowing cheekily to the policeman on the door of the block and calling back to Francis, something about the last one up to the wolf's lair was a sissy. Francis grinned and followed him, showing his pass to the security officer and wondering if Jeffries would ever stop treating the world as his own private joke.

Robertson welcomed them with a smile, inquiring about their health, telling Francis he looked tired, shaking their hands and drawing them into the company. The flat was welcoming but without the ostentation showed by some of his colleagues, who openly boasted about the way they got round the deprivations of wartime. Here there was no hint of luxury and even the sherry was handed round with a hint of apology, Robertson's eyes twinkling like those of a schoolboy dealing out stolen apples.

They were introduced to a rear admiral, a young Conservative MP and a senior FO Civil Servant, each of them nursing his glass and murmuring politely at the others. Francis felt the sherry seep into him and ease the cold from his bones. He had a headache but he tried to ignore it, and again he wondered how Robertson kept going. To his knowledge he still had not taken a holiday.

For some twenty minutes he talked to each of the guests, introducing himself, talking about the latest offerings at the cinema. He could hear Jeffries rambling on about dancing as if he were an expert. Francis wondered how the man did it, that easy manner of his with strangers; it was a gift, a legacy of his upbringing; Jeffries's charm came with his mother's milk, whereas Francis had had to work at it.

He was aware of the sherry making him drowsy, and he had to apologize to the rear admiral and ask him to repeat himself.

"Section Five, is it not?" the man said.

"That's right, sir. We're studying Communist activity throughout—"

"But don't you think it rather premature?" he interrupted. "I mean surely we should leave off worrying about the Bolsheviks until we've seen off Adolf."

"It's as well to be prepared, sir." Francis gave the standard reply. He knew from experience that the old sailor was being Blimpish on purpose, just playing games with him, and he did not feel in the mood to be drawn. He could hear the voice of Robertson to his left talking to the mandarin from the Foreign Office.

"You see," he was saying, "one of the problems about these agents in the Balkans is that their loyalty to us is inevitably going to be limited to the short term . . ." Francis maneuvered the admiral across. It was better, he thought, to let him hear it from Robertson. He would be impressed by rank.

"Our government has a historical reputation of backing what these fellows would consider to be the forces of reaction," Robertson continued. "We've always preferred kings to radicals, have we not?" The man from the FO seemed about to answer but Robertson carried on.

"It is very unlikely that these agents of ours are working for love rather than money, and once Nazism has been defeated they may well turn to the Bolsheviks for support, the more so as the Russians will have their armies on the doorstep."

"Perfidious Albion," said a cheery voice. Jeffries was smiling and holding up an empty glass, and the admiral stared at him as though he had just spat on the King. Jeffries gave a mock salute and put his arm round the admiral. "We are going to have to work at it to get back to the status quo, sir," he said. "We may need all your destroyers or else the Ivans will gobble the lot. . . ."

The man from the Foreign Office gently took Francis to one side. "Tell me," he said, "it's none of my business, of course, but do you chaps earn enough to keep alive?"

"A thousand a year. It's no secret. We start off at six hundred and go on from there. Of course, there's no problem with the Inland Revenue."

"Pointless to give with one hand and take with the other, I suppose."

"Quite." Francis wondered what the man was getting at and decided he was simply removing himself from the conversation, diplomatically allowing Robertson to continue so that he would not be forced to disagree.

"And what of our fifth column?" he was asking. "Our Communist party friends round the corner in Covent Garden?"

"No problem," said Francis. "We've had King Street wired up for some time. There's no threat for you to worry about."

"Glad to hear it," he said, smiling, then neatly changed the subject. "You were a reporter once, I believe."

Francis nodded. Something about the man irritated him. He was conscious once again of the tension which existed between the Foreign Office and the SIS. Each was perpetually trying to score points off the other. Occasionally he wondered whether or not they were on the same side. Briefly he trotted out his curriculum vitae; a foreign correspondent before the war, he had covered the Spanish Civil War and was one of the first into Abyssinia behind Mussolini's troops. The invitation to work in Intelligence had come in 1940.

"And you had no hesitation?"

"Very little." Francis decided not to elaborate. It had been a difficult choice but of little interest to an outsider. All that he wanted now was the war to end so that he could take himself back downriver to Fleet Street and return to the work for which he was trained. At least, that was what he always told himself. But sometimes he wondered; he was over forty now and maybe he could not go back. It might be hard to return to the role of observer after so long as a participant.

"And Charles?" The questions were still being relentlessly delivered. "Don't you think his fear of Bolshevism could perhaps be slightly exaggerated?"

Francis looked straight into the man's eyes. "I have never known him to be mistaken," he said quietly.

He glanced across the room. Robertson was deep in conversation with the young MP, and Francis wondered if there was any truth in the whispers that his boss was preparing to enter politics. It was being suggested that a safe Tory seat was being prepared for him; it was possible. Perhaps he too was doubting his ability to return to his old life. It was difficult to hand over the reins of power.

Francis promised himself that one day, when the time was right, he would ask him, face to face and man to man.

The phone rang and Robertson excused himself, leaving the room to take the call in his study. For a moment the conversations stuttered along until the door opened again and Robertson stood in the doorway.

"Gentlemen," he said, "I am afraid our little gathering must come to an end. I am sorry."

He moved among his guests, talking quietly to each in turn, and Francis looked hard at him. His face seemed unnaturally flushed and his voice had trembled slightly when he made his announcement. It must be the sherry, thought Francis; it was nothing, but it registered in his mind as being slightly unusual before the hubbub of conversation began again and the guests were being handed their coats and coaxed from the room. As he made for the door Robertson held up his hand, palm outward, gesturing to him to stay. When the others had gone Robertson closed the door behind them, leaned against it for a moment, then turned toward Francis.

"The Russians have started their offensive," he said slowly.

Francis whistled softly. So, he thought, it is almost over; six months at the most and there would be peace. Robertson glanced at his watch and looked at him. "A quarter to eight," he said. "I'd like you to go back to the office, find out the details and get back to me."

Francis nodded. He had been looking forward to a quiet evening, but he did not begrudge the work. It was like the old days on the paper when a big story broke; only this was better; now he was on the inside. He left the flat and ran down the stairs and was still running when he reached the pavement.

The bombardment had begun that afternoon, the heavy artillery and T-34 tank fire opening up all along the four hundred miles of Eastern Front from the Baltic to the south of Poland. The Third and Second White Russian Fronts in the north, Marshal Zhukov's First White Russian Front in the center and the First Ukrainian Front in the south mounted their offensives simultaneously, a massed army of three million picking up their weapons and looking westward, moving in trucks and tanks, in straw-filled carts and on foot, to stamp the life out of the German Reich.

Many of the soldiers had come from peasant villages, and behind them were driven pigs, goats and lambs to feed them on the march. They knew little of the modern world they were moving into, nor were they all aware of the number of their countrymen killed and maimed in three and a half years of war, but many of them had seen at firsthand the results of the German invasion, and those who had not seen had heard, and those who had not heard directly had had the words of the poet Ilya Ehrenburg branded into their minds and echoed his battle cry:

All the trenches and ravines filled with corpses of the innocents are advancing on Berlin. The boots and shoes and babies' slippers of those murdered and gassed . . . are marching on Berlin.

We have before our eyes the devastated, blood-drenched countryside. Germany, you can whirl around in circles and burn and howl in your deathly agony: the hour of revenge has struck.

There were those who had learned from their fathers that the spoils of war went to the victors. They held a slogan in their brains: *"Khleb za khleb, krov za krov"*—"Bread for bread, blood for blood."

And they knew at least two words of German:

"FRAU, KOMM . . ."

It took Alan Francis half an hour's work in his office to collect the available information. He made six phone calls and ripped sheets of wire copy from the tape machines.

As often as not the Reuters reports were quicker and more efficient than official sources, despite censorship and the fact that their information was supposed to originate from the same place.

When he had done all he could, he rang Robertson's office, knowing that Audrey would have been recalled for the evening. He counted to ten before dialing. In the early days, when she had arrived, just three months ago, he would have gone to the office, glad of any excuse to see her, but lately it had been different. Francis did not know why he was unable to sustain any passion for a woman. His interest in them lasted on average a month or six weeks after it was reciprocated, melting away like an adolescent infatuation. With Audrey the pattern had been repeated: a sudden intensity, a flourishing followed by a decline into easy friendship and sexual apathy, followed inevitably by friction when she sensed his indifference. It had always been the same and he was not sure why. But then again, it was not important; except that in Audrey's case he should possibly have resisted the initial attraction. He had made the traditional blunder of mixing business with pleasure; by becoming involved with the boss's secretary he had fouled his own nest, but he knew Robertson would not think anything of it. So long as his work was not affected it was of little consequence. If there was any problem, then Audrey would have to go.

Occasionally Francis wondered why he never felt a trace of guilt. Perhaps there was something missing in his makeup. But it was not important and eventually he accepted that he was heartless, even taking a perverse delight in the fact. One day, he realized, he might find himself on the receiving end, but for the moment there was a war to be won.

"Audrey?"

"Hello, Alan." The voice was toneless and guarded.

"How are you?"

"Fine."

"This is business, I'm afraid. I have to see Charles tonight."

"I know."

"Is it here or at the flat?"

"Neither. He wants to see you in the pub."

"Right, thanks. I expect it will take most of the evening."

"Yes, I expect so. Bye." The phone was dropped hurriedly on the cradle and Francis blew bad air from his lungs. It was a pity it always had to come to this. He reached for his coat, tucked his file into his briefcase and left the office.

Robertson was already in the bar, leaning against the counter with the three evening papers spread in front of him. He looked up as Francis came in, moved toward him and smiled.

"Let's get some air," he said. There was no offer of a drink. The pub was simply a convenient meeting place. The outdoor meetings occurred only when he was in deepest thought. Rather than meet in an office or in his flat he took his staff ambling around the streets of Mayfair. At first they had thought it was something to do with security, but eventually they realized it was simply an eccentricity, his only eccentricity.

Francis handed him the file as they turned out of Gilbert Street into Grosvenor Square, walking fast to keep up with him.

"So?" said Robertson, taking the file and looking straight ahead.

"Well," said Francis. "As one of our American friends put it on the phone, it seems that the Führer has his tail in a crack and he's swinging."

Robertson said nothing and Francis realized he had misjudged the man's mood. This was no time, apparently, for levity. He cleared his throat and continued. "The immediate military assessment has not changed in that they expect the war to last at most six months."

"I've just been to see the chief," said Robertson abruptly. "It is his view that the Russians will push straight for Berlin."

"And our plans?"

"Montgomery won't be ready to go for a couple of weeks."

They walked for a moment in silence before Robertson stopped so suddenly that Francis stumbled in surprise. He turned back to see Robertson leaning against a railing, looking seriously at him. "Alan," he said quietly, "we can't have the Russians running around the Tiergarten like so many headless chickens now, can we?"

Francis suppressed a smile. "I suppose not, sir." Although he was not quite sure why.

"They have to be slowed down somehow."

"Yes," he said doubtfully.

"Think about it and see me tomorrow, at the flat about nine."

"I will."

"And I'm organizing a special task force for a difficult job."

"Oh, yes." Francis nodded dutifully.

"Tomorrow, then." Robertson turned and strode off the way he had come.

Francis watched him go, wondering what the task force was being set up for. He knew better than to ask. If Robertson wanted him to know he would have told him. Then why did he bring it up? Why mention it at all? It was strange. And why the panic about the Russians? They had known for long enough that an offensive was planned; it was just a question of timing. He sniffed. Ours not to reason why, he thought.

As he reached Park Lane he saw a Victoria bus and sprinted for it, swung himself on to the platform and slumped into the nearest seat. He took a deep breath, feeling his heart pound at the sudden burst of unaccustomed energy, and began to wonder how in hell he could stop three million Russians reaching Berlin if they had a mind to get there.

4

London, January 14, 1945

Later, thinking back on it, the barman realized that there had been no warning. Normally he could sense trouble. He would not have survived so long in such a place without an instinctive understanding of its causes and of the type of men who started it. Sometimes it erupted noisily, brashly advertising itself so that there was a chance to make preparations. You could either soothe it away, calm it down one way or another, or if that failed, call in the friendly muscle and have it thrown out. Then again, the trouble could sit in silence, brooding and surrounded by its own menace, likely to explode unexpectedly, usually when you weren't looking.

But this time it had been different and he was honest enough to admit that he had been unprepared. There had been nothing about the man to ring any warning bells. To tell the truth, the barman could not even remember seeing him come in.

Normally he made a mental note of the customers, glancing at the door as it swung open, a smile for the regulars, a nod to the strangers. In the old days he had known everyone and a stranger was a novelty, but the war brought all kinds into the bar and he had grown wary, guarding the place with paternal care. He had been known to roar in rage if someone so much as spat on the sawdust; other men had their women to protect or some conception of their honor. Frank had his bar, and no one was permitted to take liberties with it.

Inside and out it was an anonymous place set just off the Commercial Road at the back of the Aldgate, close enough to the City to attract the occasional off-course traveler. There were no women allowed, a simple notice GENTLEMEN ONLY was screwed into the pine door; women were trouble. It was a bar for solitary drinkers and the occasional group at the tables, just the four tables set in front of the solid oak bar, sawdust on the floor, a brass rail for those who preferred to stand, a door out to the backyard lavatory. In the evenings it was a dark room lit only by gas lamps, so that there was a constant flickering of light and deep shadows.

The man had emerged from one of the shadows asking Frank if he had any whiskey. It so happened he had; it was unusual but now and again he got in the odd case or two. The man had asked for a large one and the two words were enough to note him down as a stranger.

There was no noticeable accent but the locals always made a bit of a fuss about ordering spirits. "A gold watch," they would say, or "a droppa Scotch," and if it was a big one they would ask for a double, never a large one, usually with some sort of comment about their extravagance, as if feeling the need to explain. To Frank a simple request for a large Scotch was a signal, like a jungle scout might notice a broken twig; at least, that is what he told himself.

No, he said, the man was not from around the Commercial Road, that was for sure. He was of medium build, wrapped from neck to ankle in a heavy raincoat. His hair was thick and fair, his face was just like any other, no scars, nothing like that, but small hands, not like the great hams you get on most street fighters. Frank wouldn't have picked him as one of those who staked their manhood on the cobbles, not this one. Anyway, at the time he had been more concerned with his other customers, two soldiers only, but one of them was a Scotsman and he could be trouble. All bets were off with Scotsmen. The rules did not apply. He was a small ferrety man, lean and jumpy, and for an hour he'd been grunting and barking at his mate, alternately friendly and belligerent, growling about the war and life in general.

He had looked over toward the stranger, who had glanced at him as he picked up his drink.

"Heh. What are you looking at? Yiz wantin' a photie, pal? Eh?"

"It's all right," the man said. "No problem." And made for his seat.

"Aye, all right then." The Scotsman was pacified. Somewhere in the back of his mind he had received what he considered to be an apology. He had growled at the man and the man had backed off. Fine. OK, then. That settled, he could afford to be magnanimous.

"You want a drink, pal, eh?" And to Frank. "Go on, give him a bevvy," spinning a coin onto the counter.

Frank looked toward the stranger, who nodded. "A beer, thanks." He was still on his feet, at the end of the counter.

"Away you go," said the Scotsman. "You're on the whiskey. Take a nip."

"A beer will be fine, thanks."

"Take a fuckin' nip." The Scotsman stepped forward, just one pace, his jaw thrust out. He was some five feet from the man and the reaction was so fast and unexpected that Frank stepped back into the wall, knocking over a couple of beer bottles.

Two steps forward and all four fingers were jabbed upward into the skinny throat, pushing the soldier backward and tumbling him over; the sound was horrible, a strangled gurgle and an attempt at a scream. His hands went to his Adam's apple as he rolled in the sawdust, just one turn onto his stomach before the man's heel came down on his neck. Briefly the Scotsman's legs twitched spasmodically, and then he lay still.

The man turned toward the second soldier, and for a moment there was no movement. The stranger stared at the soldier, who gazed back wide-eyed, then dropped to his knees and stared stupefied at his friend, wondering what he was doing on the floor, prone.

Frank reached for his whistle and blew it hard as the man went back to his seat and sat silently sipping his drink until the law arrived.

It was the Military Police, two of them, big men, barging sideways through the door and looking round the bar, trying to focus. The soldier looked up at them. "I think his neck's broke," he said softly.

The MPs looked at Frank, who nodded toward the table.

"Got a phone?" one of them asked, and Frank nodded again, took down the number the MP gave him and dialed for an ambulance. The two men moved across to the stranger.

"No trouble," said one.

He did not move as they approached. When they reached the table he stood up and let them maneuver him toward the door, walking slowly between them. As they passed the two soldiers, the Scotsman's friend stood up, the word "Bastard!" exploding from his lips, his right fist hooking for the man's stomach. But it did not reach. The man twisted away so that the blow thudded harmlessly into his hip, then he spun and kicked out, catching the soldier on the knee, sending him sprawling against the door before the MPs wrestled him to the ground.

Frank stood blinking, the receiver in his hand, gazing fascinated as the punches went in and the truncheon thudded against the man's skull. They kept battering and punching long after it was necessary, but Frank could not find it in himself to blame them. With such a man you had to make sure. You did not want him to wake up suddenly and break your arm with his eyelash.

Pain, he knew from experience, was red and black; a sea of it, alternating waves of red and black, going on for hours in a place where time meant nothing. He could stand the red-and-black stage, but now he was drifting up and outward and the nausea was taking hold of him so that he had to grip onto something. To vomit now would be very uncomfortable. He fought against it, trying to swallow, but there was no moisture in his throat. He counted slowly to a hundred, then attempted to open his eyes. The left one moved, very slightly. He could make out the outline of the cell and the grating on the door a few feet away. His tongue scratched and scrabbled around in the dry cavern of his mouth, testing for broken teeth. It was all right. They had not hit him in the mouth. Again he closed his eyes and started to count once more until he got back to where he wanted, in the red and the black.

When next he awoke it was sudden, straight into daylight with blood on his chin; but it was too clean: blood did not drip so quickly. It was water. Someone had thrown water over him. Opening his eyes wider he saw a face smiling at him, a blue suit and a voice drifting in and out of his consciousness, sometimes painfully loud, sometimes a whisper.

He tried to ignore it but the voice was insistent.

". . . a private in the HLI . . . a fine soldier, so we understand . . . paralyzed from the neck down . . . not good enough, Gresham . . . can't afford to lose chaps . . . bad enough when Jerry does it . . . a Catholic, apparently, with five brothers in Glasgow or somewhere and God knows how many cousins and uncles, you know how they breed . . . wouldn't do for them to know who you were or where you were, would it, Gresham? . . ."

The voice droned on and a finger was poking him in the chest, causing the pain to wash through him once more.

". . . so we are going to volunteer you . . ."

The old joke, the chestnut, the tired old military slogan; they could never resist it.

". . . we'll be in touch . . . sleep well. . . ."

And the man went, leaving Harry Gresham alone with his pain.

5

Berlin, February 3, 1945

Gerhard Bergner shivered as he climbed stiffly from the car into the drizzle. It seemed that he was always cold these days. There was no marrow in his bones. His sinuses were perpetually blocked and he was constantly troubled with headaches. Sometimes he wondered if it was possible to command an army when your nose streamed all the time. It was a problem.

The thirty-kilometer drive north from General Staff Headquarters at Zossen to Berlin had taken forty minutes and he could feel the stabbing of cramp in his calves. He was getting old, too old and dispirited for all this. Berlin was a mess, the center of the city crumbling from the bombing. He looked up at the Chancellery. The winter gardens and the banquet hall had been reduced to rubble. So much, he thought, for the promises and the vision of the future.

As he climbed the dozen steps he remembered the conferences in the past when they would wait in the great entrance hall, with its tapestries and red marble floor, then proceed through the salon into the massive living room, with its beamed ceiling, Italian fireplace and the paintings by Schinkel. Now they were directed along miserable corridors past boarded-up windows and bare, cracked walls.

In the anteroom he stood patiently while an SS man relieved him of his pistol and checked his briefcase. He nodded to his colleagues, but said nothing. He could no longer be bothered with small talk. It was too much of an effort. He would simply attend the conference, listen politely, make his recommendations and go. "Gentlemen." The voice of an aide startled him, and the door to the Führer's office was pulled open. He joined the others, filing into the conference chamber. It was like a doctor's waiting room, cold and inhospitable, dominated by the big desk at the east window where Hitler would preside over the conference. Through the windows Bergner could see the gardens; they were a mess, like the rest of the place. He took his seat and waited, checking the faces of the others: Krebs, Keitel, Jodl, Göring, Guderian, Bormann. Goebbels was absent, probably telling more lies on the radio about the wonder weapon that would win the war, but Ernst Kaltenbrunner, the Gestapo chief, was present as usual, sitting silently in a corner like a malevolent ghost.

Bergner watched them all, the firm set of their jaws, the grim expressions. No longer was there any joking or easy laughter. They all knew that the game was over. If it were up to any one of them the whole thing would have been called off and they could go home. But there was the other man to consider; the one they were waiting for.

He came in through a side door, walking slowly and stiffly, his left arm hanging motionless. As the others stood he managed a small smile before slumping into his chair. Bergner gazed at him. The magic had finally been squeezed out of him. No longer was he able to terrify his audience with a glance.

Guderian began his report. The crossing of the Oder meant that the last great obstacle into the eastern flank of the Reich had been breached. Zhukov had crossed the river with virtually no resistance being offered. The Russians were massed at Küstrin, Frankfurt and Göritz-Reitwein. If the defenses were not tightened they could be knocking on the doors of Berlin within a matter of days.

Hitler stroked his temple with the index finger of his right hand. He scarcely seemed to be listening as Guderian's voice droned on. Konev, he said, was making progress to the south. . . .

"What word of Himmler?" It was the first time Hitler had spoken and his voice was broken, a hoarse squawk like a toy bear pressed in the belly.

For a moment there was silence. Everyone knew that it had been a mistake to send the Reichsführer to the Eastern Front.

"Army Group Vistula has been bypassed," said Guderian heavily.

Hitler nodded and flapped his right hand wearily, indicating that the General should continue. He spoke for another five minutes and was followed by Göring, who huffed and puffed from his chair, grunting that the Western allies were beginning to wonder why the enemy was fighting for the Western Front to the detriment of the East.

At this Bergner grunted involuntarily and Hitler turned his gaze on him. For a moment the old fire was lit again, but Bergner held the stare. Hadn't he been saying this very thing for the past two years until one day Hitler had raged at him, accusing him of being a worn-out gramophone?

Himmler's appointment was a mistake, someone was saying, and Bergner again snorted in disgust. So, it was a mistake, there was nothing exceptional about mistakes. Hadn't there been scores of them? Ten thousand antiaircraft guns aiming westward instead of being turned against the Russian tanks; demands for armaments which could not possibly be met; the nonsense of the Ardennes offensive. Et cetera, et cetera. And still Hitler was glaring at him until he was forced to look away.

The conference turned to political considerations. The Yalta Conference was about to get under way and Stalin, Roosevelt and Churchill could be expected to agree to carve up the Reich among themselves. At the mention of Churchill's name Hitler rose unsteadily to his feet. The gray pallor turned slowly to a flush and his eyes bulged as he stared out into the center of the room. Briefly he stood at his desk, his left arm swinging slowly like a broken pendulum, then he spat out an oath and turned away, walking stiff-legged in a parody of a march toward the door. When he reached it he turned again and roared over his shoulder: "Get on with it! I have no more time for you!"

When he was gone the room remained in silence as the commanders of the Reich gazed at one another, each one thinking of the future and what it held; if indeed there was any future.

Bergner reached down for his briefcase, and when he stood to go he found himself face to face with the Deputy Party Leader.

"Gerhard"—there was a smile on Bormann's face—"may I have a word with you?"

Bergner shrugged. He did not particularly want to talk to Bormann but he had little choice. The man had become so influential that only Goebbels could match him when it came to commanding the ear of the Führer. The others called Bormann brutal, stupid and insensitive, but not to his face; nor to anyone who might report back to him.

They walked together to the anteroom and Bormann nodded to the guard, who scrabbled among a pile of hardware and handed Bergner's pistol back to him. He strapped it into its holster and followed Bormann along a corridor and down a set of steps to the garden.

"Terrible, is it not?" Bormann said as they picked their way through the rubble.

"I am in the middle of writing home at the moment," he said, taking Bergner by the arm.

"Do you miss your wife?" Bergner asked, wondering when the man would come to the point. It was unlike him to indulge in small talk.

"Of course, but this is no place for women. And Petra, how is she?"

"Safe, for the moment. I brought her out of Prussia long ago."

Bormann nodded. "Very wise. The Russians are pissing their way through East Prussia. Some of the stories coming out are dreadful."

Bergner said nothing. Bormann would never change. He might be one of the most powerful men in the country but he still talked with the vulgarity of a peasant. He recalled their first meeting in Mecklenburg all those years ago. There had been a boy, a twenty-year-old, a member of the Freikorps. He had stolen some money from one of the landowners, and Bormann, as estate manager, had sorted out the problem. He had lured the boy out into the fields and into the clutches of a gang of thugs. There had been no doubt about his guilt. The charge was murder, but Bormann had escaped with a two-year sentence. And Bergner had been partly responsible; with some others, all friends of the landowner, he had used his influence. It was all so long ago and so very sordid. When Bormann was released he was accepted immediately into the Nazi administration, and even now, reluctantly and against his nature, the man felt he owed Bergner something.

Bergner smothered a yawn, listening absentmindedly as Bormann prattled on.

"I have been forced to move into one of the secretaries' offices," he said. "It's the only place with any heat. And unbroken windows," he smiled wryly. "No proper light or power, it's a disgrace. And have you seen the latrines? The *kommandos* use them and don't even have the common decency to take a bucket of water with them." He shook his head and spat on the ground.

Bergner attempted to force whatever issue there was into the open.

"The Führer seemed distracted today," he said guardedly.

"He still has no love for the generals," said Bormann. "He eats alone, he forces himself to remain optimistic and he believes that all his military advisers are liars. It is hopeless."

"He would not listen," said Bergner, talking softly as if to himself. "He never once took any notice of anything I said."

"But you would not stop. I admired you for that."

Bergner looked away. *Admired.* The past tense. What did he mean? Did he no longer admire him? It was incredible that he should be reduced to worrying like this, fearful of the very grammar of a peasant like Bormann. But it had come to this. Everyone was looking over their shoulders and peering under rocks these days, and it was no wonder. He recalled the fate of the generals, hung on meat hooks and slowly strangled. And Heubeck; poor Heubeck, executed for what? For love of his country.

"How is Charles Robertson?"

The question thudded into Bergner's brain like an arrow. He said nothing, desperately trying to gather his scrambled thoughts together. After a pause which seemed to last forever, he shook his head.

"I don't know." At least his voice was steady and that was something.

"You have not heard from him?"

"Who?" Even as he spoke he realized he was being silly, like a schoolboy caught with stolen apples and pretending they were pebbles. Which apples? Which orchard? It was ridiculous.

"Who told you about Robertson?" he asked.

"A little Portuguese agent. We had known about him for some time. He made the mistake of crossing into Spain to see his relatives. The Gestapo picked him up." He paused. "All he knew was that there had been a meeting."

Bergner nodded. "And what have you deduced?"

"Nothing."

"And what is to be done?"

"Nothing." Bormann continued to gaze into Bergner's face, then he smiled. "If we were to talk hypothetically," he said.

"Yes. I like hypotheses."

"Then let us suggest that a top-ranking general in the Wehrmacht had initiated a contact with a leading member of enemy Intelligence. It would be assumed that he was up to no good. However, if, as our Portuguese friend suggested, the contact was initiated by the enemy, then obviously our general is, so to speak, in the clear. He could have ignored the initiative."

"But he would have been duty-bound to inform the Abwehr," said Bergner slowly.

"Well, as the Abwehr no longer exists, we can ignore that point," said Bormann. "But let us assume that contact was made, then a valuable liaison would have been forged."

Bergner had forced the initial shock from his mind and now he was becoming impatient. If there was to be some sort of inquiry, then let them get on with it. He was too tired for games. "What do you want, Martin?" he asked gruffly.

"Was there a meeting?" asked Bormann sharply.

Bergner nodded. "In Lisbon. It was very simple. The Englishman is a man of great perception. He sees beyond the present conflict and fears the imperialist ambitions of Stalin. He needed someone to try to persuade the Führer to strengthen the Eastern Front at the expense of the Western Front, to keep the Russians contained. He checked a number of people and I was the one he chose, after Stalingrad."

"I see," said Bormann, and Bergner continued, talking fast, like a criminal sharing the guilt of a crime, glad to unburden himself of his secret.

"He saw the need after the present hostilities for a strong Germany as a buffer against Stalinist ambition. He thought I would be sympathetic. He hoped I would have some influence."

"But you failed," said Bormann.

"Yes."

"And the reward for your assistance?"

"He would protect me after the war ended."

"And will he still?"

Bergner shrugged and remained silent.

"It would not do, of course, for word of this to get out," Bormann said thoughtfully. "It would be considered treason, both here and in London." He paused and smiled. "And the Russians would hardly be pleased to know that an ally was conspiring with the enemy against them."

"Quite," said Bergner. "But there is no need for anyone to know." He glanced at Bormann. "What of the Gestapo?"

Bormann shrugged. "I have had my men there for years. One of them took the Portuguese's confession."

"And the Portuguese?"

"He was not strong."

They had moved from the Chancellery into the middle of the garden, and Bormann took Bergner's arm. "I will say no more of this, except to make this point. When the war ends we will need friends. If Robertson gets in touch with you, I want to know."

"Of course." There was little else he could say.

Bormann was smiling again and leading him back toward the building. "Your car is ready to take you back to Zossen, but when you get there I want you to pack your belongings."

Bergner raised an eyebrow in surprise.

"The chief wants his top advisers near to him at this crisis hour," he explained with the hint of a smile. "We are having a room prepared for you right here . . . in the bunker."

"I see."

Bormann patted him on the shoulder. "Don't be concerned, Gerhard. The walls are the thickest in the Reich. They can survive even a direct hit."

But Bormann knew full well that Bergner was not worried about attacks from the outside. It was the insidious assault from within that was to be feared. As he left the Chancellery, Bergner could almost feel the meat hooks digging deep into his neck.

Half a mile to the east Christa Schiller awoke suddenly, sitting up abruptly so that the man beside her stirred and grunted. She blinked and tried to focus, unsure for a moment where she was, then she turned and looked down at the fat man asleep on his back, one podgy arm bent across his face. She shivered and slipped out of bed, tiptoed naked to the bidet and ran the water. This was the third time in a week that she had fallen asleep. It was unlike her, but Gerda had warned her that the pills might have a cumulative effect. As she washed she wondered whether she should take any more. Certainly they calmed her nerves and allowed her to sleep through the morning, but if they were going to have such an effect when she was working, then she could not allow herself the luxury.

The bidet was tucked away behind a wooden-framed velvet screen, and she peered through the gap at the bed. The man had stirred, wakened by the noise of the taps. He was rubbing his eyes, stretching and belching. Christa was slightly apprehensive. Her watch told her that she had delayed too long with him and it was at this stage in the proceedings that they could become awkward, wanting more, or else turning unreasonable and bad-tempered, their mouths dry from the champagne and their lust reawakened. This one was a Prussian and Prussians could be difficult; they felt guilty at having visited a brothel. They seemed to need to take it out on someone, and Christa was the nearest at hand.

Peter had once tried to explain it to her; he said it was something to do with what he called Lutheran self-disgust, an urge to purge themselves of sin by violence. Something like that. He often used strange phrases to explain things that she already understood through instinct and experience.

Quickly she slipped on her robe, put two fingers in her mouth and stretched her face into a smile, drew breath and stepped out from behind the screen.

"Good afternoon, Werner," she said sweetly. She bent down, picked up his trousers and handed them to him. The fat man grunted and snapped his tongue against the roof of his mouth. "More champagne," he said.

Christa's smile broadened. He was going to be trouble. Fat men were always the worst. Maybe it was because they had the greatest difficulty, with all that bulk between what they had and where they wanted to go. She had been forced to work hard on this one, exerting herself beneath him for what seemed like hours until she was exhausted. It must have been all that exercise and the sleeping pill which had put her out.

"Next time, Werner," she said soothingly. "Now you must leave. I'm sure you are a very busy man."

He grunted again, spat an oath. Christa leaned past him and pulled a sash on the wall as he grabbed at her, grappling with her and trying to force her onto the bed. She concentrated on counting slowly as she fought him off, ducking under the gusts of bad breath, trying to get a grip on him where it hurt, but there was too much fat. She had reached thirty-three when the door opened and from under his arm she saw Ingrid and Gerda in the doorway. They were trying to look menacing, Gerda wielding her whip. It was all she could do not to laugh as the fat man grunted something obscene, let go of her and waddled from the bed, grabbing at his clothes.

When he had gone, they sat on the bed and giggled like schoolgirls. It had been a long time since they had laughed together; not like the old days when the war was being won, when the diplomats were regular visitors and the officers arrived back from the front, when the champagne was real and the laughter unforced. All that was long ago, before things had begun to go wrong.

They spoke for a while of the past, reminiscing pleasantly, until Gerda giggled and said, "Do you know what I saw on a wall in Wilhelmstrasse?"

They shook their heads dutifully.

"It was a wreck, this building, bombed to bits, but on a bit of wall left standing, someone had chalked, 'Better a Russian on the belly than an American overhead.' "

She smiled, waiting for the reaction, but the others said nothing. The spell had been shattered. There was silence for a moment, broken at last by Ingrid.

"I heard on the wireless this morning they raped two women in East Prussia somewhere and nailed them to a barn."

Christa shivered and tried to bring the gaiety back, but it had gone. She looked round the room at the flock wallpaper and the gilt mirrors, the deep-piled carpets and the thick gray curtains. "We'll have to change the decor for the Russians," she said. "Get in some straw and take the glass out of the windows."

Ingrid smiled bitterly. "Don't tempt fate. This is one of the few buildings left with windows intact."

"The Lord takes care of his own," said Gerda.

They sat together for a few minutes longer before the two women left and Christa moved to the mirror. With any luck there might be another client before evening.

As she gazed at her reflection she tried to forget what had been said, but the image remained in her mind; the flat faces of the Mongols leered at her so that she could almost feel the bite of the nails as they were driven into her palms.

6

London, February 7, 1945

In three weeks the Russian army had pushed three hundred miles westward, and in London, Alan Francis felt as though he had personally marched every step of the way. Day and night he monitored reports, collated memos and prepared projections of possible political and military developments. Three times that week he had fallen asleep at his desk. He occasionally grumbled that this was the land of the eight-day week. But Francis could not complain, because Robertson was working even harder himself.

That afternoon he had finished a hasty lunch at the pub and was up to his elbows in paper when the internal phone buzzed and he was summoned to the boss's office. Cursing, he gathered the latest reports together and stumbled out into the corridor. He noticed his flies were undone and hastily buttoned himself up as he reached Robertson's door. It was all getting out of hand, he thought. He was falling apart, almost literally.

Robertson smiled warmly and motioned for him to sit down.

"Well?" he said, and Francis looked blankly at him. Robertson had what could be described as a grin of triumph on his face.

"Sir?"

"It seems we've been successful."

Francis waited for him to continue, allowing the man the simple pleasure of dragging out whatever good news there was.

"A call from Yalta. It looks like the Russians are digging in. They are not going for Berlin."

Francis's first reaction was one of annoyance. It was childish, he knew, but nonetheless there was just a small part of him that felt petulant. It was he, after all, who had suggested that Stalin should be fed exaggerated reports of German strength around the capital and it was he who had arranged to insinuate an SIS man in the Yalta party. It would have been nice if he had been the first to get the news, so that he could have passed it on to Robertson. But he fought to control himself. He was being silly.

"That's good news, sir," he said, smiling back, thinking that if anyone came into the room the scene would appear odd: two grown men grinning at each other like startled monkeys.

"Apparently Zhukov received a call from Stalin on Sunday telling him to consolidate. He was not very pleased. He was all set to blast his way through to Berlin."

Robertson clicked his fingers enthusiastically, shouting the word "blast" so that a speck of spittle glistened for a moment on his lip.

"But why, sir?" Francis asked. He remembered the reports he had read. Zhukov was preparing to bring three armies from the First Ukrainian Front to join the five under his own command. With such a force he could easily have taken Berlin.

"I don't suppose we shall ever know," said Robertson. "It has been suggested that Stalin was afraid of an attack from Pomerania, but I think that unlikely. For the moment let us just assume that our little ruse helped in some small way to confuse him."

Our ruse. Francis's annoyance grew in him again but he fought it.

"Certainly the Americans backed our man up," Robertson continued. "What was his name?"

"Grant, sir."

"Grant, yes. Good chap." He stood up indicating the meeting was at an end. "Anyway, tomorrow Monty begins the push for the Rhine. So we shall see. . . ."

Francis rose slowly to his feet, thinking that this might be a good time to put the question. He wanted to hear Robertson spell it out, just to make everything crystal clear.

"I suppose you think it's absolutely vital, sir, that we get to Berlin before the Russians?"

"Well, of course. It's bloody obvious." The words were spat at him dismissively and Francis blinked as he made for the door.

"By the way," Robertson said. "Is the task force ready?"

"Sir?" Francis looked puzzled, desperately trying to think back, struggling to remember . . . had he forgotten something?

But Robertson was smiling now, shaking his head apologetically. "Of course," he said. "Jeffries is handling it. Tell him to come and see me, will you?"

"Yes, sir."

Francis closed the door behind him and ambled slowly toward his office, wondering what it was that was bothering him. It was nothing, he thought, nothing to concern him. It was simply that the man had been acting out of character lately. If Francis had been asked to give evidence he would have found it impossible: a twitch of the eyebrow, perhaps, a tone of voice, a lack of humor when expected, an obsessive interest in one aspect of the job. . . . It was all a question mark adding up to nothing, a hunch, a kind of instinct, and instincts, as often as not, were faulty indicators.

Yet the man had forgotten Grant's name and he had made a mistake about Jeffries. But so what? Only, Robertson never got things wrong. Infallible people don't make mistakes.

He reached his office and flipped through the papers on his desk, trying to force Robertson from his mind. But the question remained. Why such a violent reaction to his inquiry about Berlin? It was so unexpected. He had simply wanted his theories confirmed. Robertson could have done it. He would have enjoyed doing it, listing the reasons for taking the capital before the Red army got entrenched. He could have put everything in perspective. Yet he shouted at him, swore at him.

It was all very strange.

He glanced down at the report in his hand, a memo from the U.S. War Department forecasting that the German army would crumble within a matter of days.

So it was all academic, whatever was bothering him, whatever was supposedly affecting Robertson, could be put down to overwork. If he carried on scratching the itch of suspicion it would just irritate him all the more.

"Beware forced metaphors," he said aloud. He yawned. Jeffries had been angling for a beer for days. He would have a few that evening, and there was that young Wren officer he had promised himself. He reached for the phone and resolved to cease scratching. He was going to relax for an evening. He would forget about the war if it killed him.

Jeffries was standing pointing at the wall when Francis got to the pub. He squinted and read the notice.

AS MUCH ALE AS POSSIBLE IS BEING SENT TO OUR FIGHTING MEN AT THE FRONT. YOU MAY THEREFORE BE DISAPPOINTED AT NOT GETTING YOUR SUPPLIES.

Jeffries shook his head. "Never end the damned war if the bloody army is legless all the time," he grumbled. "Don't know what the world's coming to."

Francis let him grumble for a while and sat in a corner drinking the beer he had been bought. He was tired and only half listening as Jeffries rambled on, and merely grunted a reply to keep him going, until something he said made him sit up.

"What makes you think that?" he asked.

"Don't know. The old boy seems a bit jumpy, that's all."

Francis nodded. "He got me confused with you today. About the special patrol."

"Oh, that," said Jeffries gloomily. "Bloody thing."

"What stage is it at?" Francis asked.

Jeffries shrugged. "We've got a few chaps together out in Gloucestershire somewhere. A real coven of villains."

"Must have been hard to recruit at this stage in the war."

"Well," he sniffed, "I talked to AG2 in the War Office and told them it was a do-or-die thing. At first they were a bit huffy. They wanted to know what we were up to. They didn't like it when I couldn't tell them. But eventually they produced a few names."

"How?"

"An appeal to patriotism in some cases, a chance to slit gullets in others. A few were glad to get out of jail. Mind you, it's not for everyone. They need to have had special weapons training, explosives, unarmed combat, all that. So, if I can recall, we have a couple of patriots, a trio of crazies, and a few out-and-out villains."

"To do what?"

Jeffries shrugged his shoulders. "Who knows? Only the boss, and he's not talking. But as our old commander used to say, I don't know if they scare the enemy but, by God . . ."

He let his voice trail off into the distance as the girl came in. She was prettier than Francis remembered and she was looking round the bar for him.

"There she is," said Francis getting to his feet, "young Julie." He waved and the girl made her way over to their table and Jeffries stood up. He had been about to tell Francis that there was one other stipulation, that the members of the unit had to be fluent in German. Maybe he would mention it later, and maybe not. He probably would not be interested anyway.

At dawn the next morning the first four assault battalions of British and Canadian soldiers left the Dutch town of Nijmegen, heading southeast eight miles toward Cleve, moving slowly under the cover of shellfire and supported by air power of 769 bombers. Operation Veritable had begun on time, the battalions taking their first tentative steps toward the heartland of the Reich. As they set off, the rain began to fall and by ten thirty the tanks had slowed and were becoming bogged down in mud, while behind them the army of two hundred thousand stamped their boots and waited to go.

Sixty miles to the south, General William Simpson, commander of the U.S. Ninth Army, watched the downpour and checked regularly on the level of the Roer River. His task was to cross the river so that the German reserve troops would be forced to defend their rear, allowing the main thrust to go ahead. But word was coming through that the Roer dams had been sabotaged, and as the level of the river rose, Simpson made the decision to postpone his attack. In the north, Veritable had been bogged down. By the weekend it had become obvious that the Allies were going nowhere fast.

Gloucestershire, February 8, 1945

"There's something about you that irritates me, son." The voice was hoarse, a South London accent. "Seems to me you're sort of sneering at me, like, behind my back, 'cos you got a toffee accent. Well, let me tell you, I don't like it one bit, not one little bit. . . ."

Harry Gresham yawned behind his hand as he watched the big CSM jut out his jaw and poke his thumb into the soldier's breastbone, where it hurt. God, he thought, how much longer? As an induction test it was transparent in its simplicity, but Brewster obviously thought he was being subtle; push them as hard as possible and if they crack, if they react, then they are not good enough, not secure enough in themselves to be of any use. Brewster was acting the part well, strutting his six-foot frame round the barn, taunting and teasing, but Gresham had come to the conclusion, days earlier, that he wanted one of them to lash out so that he could indulge in a spot of physical correction.

Gresham had watched the charade for three days, and so far none of the fifteen men had succumbed. He was beginning to wish that one of them would. It would serve the big man right.

". . . I expect you think you've seen a bit, do you?" Brewster was saying, indicating the small trestle table where the folder lay containing the man's service record. "You were in the para game, were you not? I expect you think that jumping out of airplanes gives you some kind of . . ."

The soldier had been staring at a point somewhere above Brewster's shoulder across the barn into the mid distance, and now he turned to Gresham and gazed at him. Gresham shrugged his shoulders, just a twitch, scarcely noticeable, but it was enough. The soldier yawned, stepped back two paces and squatted on a bale of straw.

Brewster was halted in midflow. His face flushed and he glared down at him.

"Get up, soldier." The word "up" exploded from him like a mortar bomb.

Gresham sighed. Brewster was becoming a pain in the neck. It was time for him to go.

"All right, CSM, that will do," he said softly.

Brewster turned and stared in surprise, then his face cracked open into a lopsided grin. He had been astonished at Gresham's attitude ever since he had come to the farm. The man had such a terrible record of insubordination that Brewster had failed to understand how he could be so passive. But now at last he was conforming to type. Harry Gresham looked as though he was about to fail the Brewster test.

"What-did-you-say-soldier?" Each word was given the same heavy emphasis, the big jaw thrust out once more, but Gresham ignored him. He got to his feet and lazily walked past the sergeant major as if he were invisible.

"Oi!"—a nasal cough. "Stop where you are!"

Gresham stood by the door, then slowly turned round. He sighed and moved forward two paces until he was standing three feet from the big man.

"I didn't give you permission . . ." Brewster snarled.

Gresham was bored. He decided to give the man what he wanted and dropped his left shoulder slightly, so that Brewster leaned away then kicked hard for Gresham's groin. Gresham stepped one pace back, neatly caught the toe of the boot in both hands, twisted and pushed so that Brewster staggered backward, toppling over in an awkward heap into a collection of hoes, rakes and scythes.

Gresham turned and walked to the door as Brewster threshed among the straw, fighting to get to his feet. He pushed open the door, stood back to let the soldier pass, then closed it behind him, slipping the beam across the latch. As the two men made their way toward the farmhouse, they heard Brewster roar and in the distance the answering bellow of a milk cow.

He had sat for an hour on the bed in the main bedroom, studying the files. He put them down and gazed round the room. It was a cheerless place of peeling wallpaper and dull gingham curtains, the bed and a dresser the only furniture. He would be glad to be gone. It was just a question of making the right choice.

He looked at his watch, leaned across to the door and pulled it open, yelled a number and sat back on the bed.

The first man was of medium height, dark with a livid complexion; he moved easily into the room and stood in front of Gresham, looking down at him.

Gresham kicked the door shut. "*Guten tag,* Roth."

"*Shalom.*"

Gresham grinned and glanced at the man's file. He had decided to conduct the interviews in German. From experience he did not trust army records.

"Why did you volunteer?"

Roth glanced at the report. "It's all in there," he said.

"You tell me." Gresham was mildly irritated at the man's desire to fence with him.

In reply he tapped the side of his nose.

"We may be fighting on your Sabbath," said Gresham.

Roth smiled, just the hint of a grin. "I'm not Orthodox."

Gresham looked at him for a moment in silence. "I don't want someone knotted up with revenge."

Roth shrugged. "It's my last chance," he said.

"You've had relatives killed?"

"And missing."

"You will obey orders?"

Roth nodded. "From what I've heard about you, Gresham, if I don't you'll kill me. Correct?"

Gresham shrugged.

"And if I'm dead I can't kill Nazis." He waited for a reaction but there was none. "My old Jewish grandfather always told me to play the percentages."

Gresham smiled. "All right. Once the object of the exercise is over I'll leave you behind with the spare ammunition."

"Good," said Roth.

"You can personally mop up the remains of the Third Reich."

"It will be a pleasure."

For a moment the two men watched each other in silence.

"You're German Jewish," said Gresham.

Roth nodded. "Berlin. The family left when I was ten."

Gresham leaned across the bed and picked up his file. "You can go," he said.

Roth left the room, Gresham placed a tick against his name and shouted another number.

An hour and six interviews later Gresham was no further forward. He picked up the next folder and flipped through it.

The name on the flap was John Patterson, and he frowned. He had not seen this man. He was one of the latecomers. He sniffed: "Patterson, alias Necklace."

Why Necklace? he wondered. He yelled the number and the man came in. They had got it wrong again at Records. The spelling was wrong.

Patterson was an inch or two over six feet, with a small head and massive shoulders. He came into the room sideways and turned to face the bed, the little eyes blinking. There seemed to be no neck. Gresham was reminded of a giant bullfrog.

"Where did you learn your German, Patterson?" he asked.

"At home." The voice was surprisingly light. "I've got an aunt from Hamburg. I grew up with both languages."

"You didn't volunteer for this job?"

"No."

"You have trouble taking orders, do you?"

Patterson blushed and put his hand to his face. His head seemed to vanish as he rubbed his hand against his skull. "Sometimes I get annoyed," he said softly. "Sometimes officers annoy me."

Gresham glanced at the file. "You have another six years to do."

"Yes."

"And how do I know you wouldn't get annoyed if I gave you orders?"

"You don't," he said, leaning back against the door and staring round the room. "But I don't like jail. And they promised me this job would clear my sentence."

Gresham nodded.

"It's behind the lines, isn't it?" asked Patterson.

Gresham said nothing and the big man continued. "Behind the lines," he said again.

"So, how do I know you won't take off as soon as we leave England?"

"No guarantee," said Patterson, "but it wouldn't make much sense, not with my sentence quashed. I wouldn't be all that bright to wander around Europe on my own." He gazed at his shoes. "It's not as if I merge into the background . . ." And he laughed to himself, his body shaking with mirth.

Gresham put a tick against his name.

Malcolm Driscoll had the gangling posture of someone not long out of adolescence. He was a small-boned, light-framed man who, if left to develop naturally, would have scarcely reached ten stone. But he had obviously worked on himself. His sleeves were rolled up and Gresham saw that the slim arms were like wire cables, the veins standing out like strands of barbed wire. His face was lean, the blue eyes clear. It seemed as though you could strike matches all over him.

He stood almost at attention as Gresham glanced at his file.

"Wellington, Sandhurst, then you buggered it up."

"That's right, sir."

"There's no rank here, Driscoll."

"Sorry."

"Army family?" he asked.

"Yes, sir. My father was a colonel in the Blues."

"Are you Scottish?"

"Yes."

"And you could not live up to your father's expectations?" Gresham looked up, but Driscoll stared over his shoulder and said nothing.

"So, you cracked up," said Gresham.

"They called it a nervous breakdown."

"Yes," said Gresham quietly. "They would, wouldn't they?" He sniffed and stood up, walking round the young man as he had seen Brewster do earlier. "And now you're a training officer in the commandos."

"Correct."

"With the rank of lieutenant."

Driscoll nodded.

"A reasonable enough achievement," said Gresham.

"Not if one is born to be a general," said Driscoll.

"And your father? What does he think about you buggering it up?"

"The family have been very understanding." Driscoll continued to stare ahead, focusing on nothing.

"But underneath you detect a basic disappointment. Am I correct?" He looked at Gresham for the first time. "I am a textbook case. I believe the psychiatrists have a word for it."

"No doubt," said Gresham. He sat down again and sighed. "I assume that success in this little operation would mean you had redeemed yourself to a certain degree."

Driscoll shrugged. "I was told it was hazardous enough to warrant a decoration . . . if it succeeded."

Gresham nodded. "We can't promise a VC, but I would think the colonel might just feel obliged to pat your shoulder."

A movement at the window distracted them. Driscoll looked out and saw Brewster ducking into a jeep. He watched as it bucked away along the farm track toward the road.

"What I don't understand," Driscoll said, "is why you bother with the CSM if you are basically in charge."

Gresham flipped the file on to the bed and closed the curtains. "Simply because we are still in the army and we need the goodwill of the brass. I think the new phrase is public relations or something. It does no harm, and it costs nothing."

Driscoll looked inquiringly at him. "You must have protection from the top," he said.

Gresham did not answer, simply held the door open and watched Driscoll leave. He marched out of the room, almost as if he were on parade.

When he had gone, Gresham looked down at his pad. Three out of twelve. The mixture was just right. They would do. He had anticipated a four-man unit. Anymore would be cumbersome, any less could be fatal. He had his components but a drop of oil would do no harm. He reached for the telephone on the dresser, lifted the receiver and dialed a London number.

"They say it happened two years ago. The unit was billeted in a village called Eaton Bray in Bedfordshire, a mile or two from a unit of Canadians. They got on all right, the British and the Canadians, used the same pubs, played football. Maybe there was the odd scuffle, but nothing much.

"The girl was seventeen and not particularly pretty, but soft and shy. They say her eyes were the best thing about her. She blushed easily, if you know what I mean, didn't know anything about soldiers and looked away when they whistled at her. She met Gresham one day, just like in the pictures, staggering home with the groceries, and he helped her. After that he took her for walks and they could often be seen on the Downs, sitting and talking.

"One night she came to the pub and left crying. No one knew what was said, but it seemed that she wanted more from Gresham than he could give her. He was like an uncle to her and she did not want that.

"It was what they call puppy love, I suppose. So, Gresham took her away from the pub and walked her home, leaving her about a hundred yards from the house. He came back and got a bit drunk, and that was that as far as he was concerned. Maybe there were some who thought he was daft not to take advantage of her, but if they did they would not have said so, not to Gresham, and I suppose most of them respected him for it.

"She was almost home when she met the Canadians. It was dark by then. To give them the benefit of the doubt, they were probably only teasing her. At least, that's what she said later when she was eventually persuaded to talk about it. It seems that they saw the tears and asked what was wrong, but she made the mistake of running away and when they caught her and tumbled her over into the grass they were probably only having a bit of fun.

"They reckon that only one of them got carried away at first, but once it had started they couldn't stop. She was raped by each one in turn, and when it was over, instead of being sorry, they hit her and broke her jaw and left her unconscious in the ditch. Her young brother found her in the morning.

"Three nights later someone broke into the dorm of the school where the Canadians were billeted and opened up with a Bren. No one saw who it was, whether it was one man or more, and no one knows the casualties. It's not the sort of thing that gets put in the records. The unit was moved on that very night before dawn, and no one heard of Harry Gresham for a year."

When Roth had finished his story, there was a moment's silence before Patterson shrugged and sniffed. "So that was what made him crazy?" he said.

"No," said Roth. "It seems he's always been like that."

* * *

The next morning the three men awoke to find the others busily packing. They lay on their bunks in silence and nodded good-bye as the other men left. Silently they washed and shaved, pulled on their boots and made their way out into the frosty air and across the yard to the farmhouse. In the kitchen Harry Gresham stood by the oven, cracking eggs into a frying pan. The table was set for four.

"Welcome," he said as they trooped in.

They sat at the table and waited in silence. Eventually he turned and put down the pan.

"You have been selected," he said simply. "For the moment you will not be told the nature of the operation. We can't have you talking in your sleep. Just content yourself with the knowledge that it should be straightforward enough and that when you return you will find a cash bonus credited to you." He paused. "Five hundred pounds, just as an additional incentive."

Roth whistled, but it was Driscoll who asked the question. "Can you tell us where we are going?"

"Berlin," said Gresham.

Again Roth whistled. "And I suppose it's too late to back out now," he said.

In reply Gresham handed him a plate of bacon and eggs. "You know the phrase, gentlemen . . . a hearty breakfast. Enjoy it."

For an hour he watched as the three men lobbed grenades through rubber tires and tested the Bren guns, firing bursts from the hip while running at a sprint, then letting go a single round with the gun set at automatic. He showed them a small arsenal of German weapons and watched as they studied the attached instructions. That done, they weighed them up, testing for balance. When they were ready, they fired them at chalk targets on the stone walls set at ranges of thirty to a hundred yards, until each one of them pronounced himself happy with both the Mauser Karabiner 98K and the big Sturmgewehr 44 assault rifle. He took them to the barn, pulled away a tarpaulin to reveal an MG42 machine gun and stood back as they prowled round it, like dogs sniffing a bait before crouching beside it and stripping it down.

In the barn they went through an unarmed combat drill, throwing each other around in the straw until they ached. Gresham noted with satisfaction that Driscoll possessed a strength far in excess of his weight, and he was surprised to see how nimble the big man was.

That done he took them on an exercise, he and Roth going forward to attack a position while the others covered them; and within a few minutes he found out what he needed to know. At each point, when he turned, Driscoll and Patterson were in exactly the right positions.

By the end of the day he was satisfied, made his call to London and nodded as the voice told him to stay where he was for the moment. An officer was on his way to see them. Gresham replaced the receiver and groaned aloud, hoping that they would soon be gone and the play-acting would be over.

The major arrived early the next afternoon, in a jeep with a driver and a corporal.

When Gresham appeared at the farmhouse door he saluted sharply. "Johnston," he said. "With a *t.*"

Gresham looked at the mustache, the flared nostrils and the highly polished boots, then over his shoulder at Patterson. This would be the type from whom the big man would not like taking orders.

"Right, chaps," said Johnston, once the introductions had been made. "Let's see what you can do."

For two days the four men struggled across fields carrying forty-pound packs. They attacked selected positions, struggled across streams, threw each other over their shoulders and slept rough, with Johnston and his corporal watching from a distance through field binoculars and issuing instructions over a shortwave radio. Whatever he asked for they did, silently and uncomplaining. Gresham had asked them to cooperate. It did no harm and relieved the boredom; and it cost nothing.

On the second evening as they trudged back toward the farmhouse, Johnston drove up, stepped from the jeep and slapped Gresham on the shoulder.

"Most impressed," he said. "Splendid squad."

"Have you seen enough?" asked Gresham.

"Absolutely. I'll be off in the morning. Tonight we'll have a few beers. On me."

"Fine." Gresham watched him step smartly back to the jeep and thought that perhaps he might have judged the man too harshly.

The Harrow was a small pub set back from the road. The bar was cramped, low-ceilinged, with heavy, blackened beams spiked with horse brasses, and as soon as they entered Gresham stiffened, his body tensing and his fists clenching involuntarily as he glanced at the four large soldiers leaning against the counter.

Johnston had easily elbowed his way past them, shouting questions over his shoulder about drinks, but Gresham had seen the surreptitious contact, a scarcely perceptible nod between Johnston and one of the soldiers.

Gresham held back, standing by the door with the others as Johnston returned with the beer, and as he took his glass he saw the biggest of the soldiers eyeing Driscoll and pushing himself away from the bar toward them, an insult welling in his throat.

Gresham put his glass on the window ledge and turned toward the door, motioning the others to follow him, leaving the soldiers stranded and Johnston spluttering, his hands full of beer glasses.

At the jeep he caught up with them, shouting at them to come back.

Gresham waited until the others had climbed into the jeep before turning on Johnston. He stepped forward and looked hard into his face.

"Let me see if I have this right," he said. "You set your biggest ape on the smallest of our lot to see if we allow him to be insulted? Correct so far?"

Johnston opened his mouth to speak but Gresham carried on, talking slowly. "You wanted to see how good they were against live opposition. Right?"

Johnston had recovered his composure. "Needed to find out how tough your chaps were," he said huffily.

"Yes," said Gresham. He turned away and vaulted into the driver's seat, then bent low and nodded. "They're tough enough not to have to prove anything," he said. "Not to you, or to them"—he jerked his thumb toward the bar—"or even to themselves anymore."

He started the engine, kicked it into gear and spun the jeep out of the yard, leaving Johnston alone and staring openmouthed after them.

8

London, February 23, 1945

Alan Francis had retained enough sense of wonder to feel just slightly awestruck on the few occasions he was called upon to attend Cabinet briefings. As he stepped out of the car in Whitehall and made his way behind Robertson into the Cabinet Office, he thought back to the old days when he went into such buildings with a certain detachment and the slight air of arrogance common to the observer. It had all seemed so simple then, to listen, ask questions and later come to leisured conclusions. He nodded to the policeman at the door and followed Robertson through the hall, up two flights of stairs and along the corridor to Room 10, where the briefing was scheduled to take place.

The table was already laid, with small cardboard folders next to a place-name for each man. He exchanged smiles of greetings with the others and took his seat, slipping open the file and glancing at the memoranda. The meeting quickly came to order and he followed the reports on the relevant memos, each Civil Servant being careful to follow the text almost to the letter.

The military situation was progressing satisfactorily. The Russians were consolidating in the east, but had made no major push for the capital. The Allied bombings were proving to be hugely successful and meeting little resistance. Francis ran his finger down the list, pursing his lips at the extent of the estimated casualty figures. Berlin was being bombed daily and Dresden had been virtually reduced to ashes. Operation Grenade, he noted, had got under way that day, while Veritable made steady advances in the north.

The PM was preparing his address to the House on the decisions reached at Yalta and was planning a visit to the front.

Francis looked up as his name was mentioned, and a clerk leaned across the table to hand him a report of special interest to Section Five. He flipped through the pages: there was fighting in Rumania, with the Rudescu regime under attack from Communists who were demanding the dissolution of his government. Flicking the top off his pen he underlined two sentences: "In reality the country is being run by the Soviet High Command and the government is applying through the Allied Control Commission for a meeting to study the situation. So far the Soviet chairman has not called the meeting."

In Bulgaria the Communists were in control of the coalition government, but in Yugoslavia the partisan leader, Tito, was continuing to stand up to Stalin, refusing to allow the Soviet army any power in administration.

"In a nutshell, gentlemen," said the Foreign Office representative, "the PM's recent meeting with Stalin should result in the following: that the Russian sphere of influence become apparent in Rumania and Bulgaria while we maintain our interest in Greece and negotiate equal terms over Yugoslavia and Hungary."

Francis felt the need to say something, as much out of a desire to enter into the proceedings as to elicit information. He already knew the answer to his question. "I thought," he said forcefully, "that it was implicit in the terms of Yalta that no Communist-dominated government should be forced upon the various Balkan states, but it is apparent from these reports that such a situation has already developed. . . ."

He flinched slightly as a well-known voice broke into his carefully modulated speech.

"We are faced here with a reality that is unappealing to say the least," Robertson snapped. Francis turned, but Robertson was directing his statement to the chairman and Francis felt his heart begin to pound. He hoped that it was not he who was coming under attack. "The reality," Robertson continued, "is that we cannot trust the Soviet government as far as we can throw it, and this applies, particularly, to Stalin himself. His word is meaningless."

The others looked away, murmuring to themselves. Such strong language was not often forthcoming at such briefings. They were normally gentlemanly affairs, concerned with information rather than opinion. Yet there was a passion to Robertson that was unusual and certainly out of place. Francis began to itch again, but said nothing more until the meeting broke up.

They left together as they had arrived, sitting side by side in the back of the Daimler. Francis gazed out at the crowds as the car eased its way along Whitehall. He had the feeling that Robertson was studying him, and flinched slightly as the man leaned and spoke softly to him.

"So you think there will be trouble in the Balkans?"

Francis turned. Robertson was peering at him, waiting for an answer.

"It seems that way, sir," he replied.

"And does it worry you?"

Francis shrugged. "From what I can gather we could be in for protracted periods of difficulty if the Russians extend their sphere of influence." He took a breath, aware that he sounded more than a little pompous, but Robertson had settled back in his seat and was nodding in agreement.

For a moment there was silence.

"What are your plans after this is all over?" The question was sharp and unexpected.

"Back to Fleet Street I suppose, sir," said Francis quickly.

"You only suppose?"

"It seems logical."

Again there was a silence while Francis chased ideas around in his mind, wondering what Robertson was leading to. He was about to ask, when again Robertson put a quick question to him.

"What are your politics, Alan? A bit Leftish, aren't you?"

"I'm not committed either way," he replied. "Emotional Socialist if anything, I suppose."

"And does this emotion influence you at the ballot box?"

Francis smiled. "Not really. I've been too long an observer. A bit cynical, sir, about politicians in general."

"You're from the northeast originally?"

"Sunderland, sir."

"Hardly Tory country."

Again Francis smiled. "They're not exactly thick on the ground up there." He waited for a moment, but Robertson was silent and so he decided to take a chance. "Why do you ask, sir?"

Robertson smiled enigmatically. "Just thinking aloud." He gazed out of the window as if to close the subject, then turned back toward Francis.

"Did you know that the PM has instructed Montgomery to keep German weapons intact in case they are required against the Russians?"

Francis shook his head.

"Of course," Robertson continued, "there will be no record of such an order."

"Well, quite." Francis nodded in agreement, wondering why Robertson had told him. It was unlike him to toss out scraps of unsolicited information. Francis wondered briefly if he was being tested, if his boss was running something up the flag to see if he saluted it, but Robertson had lapsed again into silence, gazing once more out into the traffic. The silence was awkward and Francis found himself searching for something to say in order to fill the vacuum.

"What happened to your special unit, sir?"

"They're not my unit," said Robertson so sharply that Francis blinked. It was a strange disjointed conversation, as if two strangers were searching for some subject they had in common and succeeding only in irritating each other. But somehow he felt compelled to continue.

"Well, anyway, what has happened to them?"

"They're about to embark for Holland," said Robertson gruffly, his tone implying that the interrogation was at an end.

"I see," said Francis.

"Got to get the V-2 rocket plans before the Russians, do you see?"

"Good Lord," Francis breathed. Now, that was something. Robertson had turned toward him and was glaring at him, his eyes bright again as if he had just snapped out of some distant reverie. "This goes no further, of course," he said.

"Of course not, sir."

"Right. Here we are again. Back to business." He smiled as he watched the car draw up to Broadway Buildings, and he gestured Francis to get out first. As they stepped into the lift, he began talking about cricket and the days when there would be peace once more and an Englishman could happily play his native game on the village green without distractions. And the image of the commandos disappeared from Francis's mind.

"You know I'm going out of town this evening for a day," he said as Robertson moved away down the corridor, but if he had heard he paid no heed. Francis shrugged and watched him go. There had been a time when the man would have asked where he was going, just out of everyday politeness.

As the train left the city behind, Francis leaned back into the seat and gazed out into the fields at the thin layer of snow flowing luminous in the dusk. The sky was heavy and dead-looking, except for the occasional crow wheeling among the trees seeking shelter. Francis thought back to the early days of the war, and of the dogfights in the skies when the air was a busy and dangerous thoroughfare, but now there were only memories and the hope of a better future.

Looking out, he began to lose the feeling of being involved in the insanity of warfare. Everything seemed so peaceful. He closed his eyes and attempted to relax, but his brain refused to slow down. Despite his attempts to think of nothing, his mind still found problems for itself to solve; papers and memos floated before his eyes like ghosts. Trying to relax was like attempting to sleep without dreaming. He gave up and scrabbled in his briefcase for a newspaper.

He skipped through the news of the battles, old news he had read on the tapes and in dispatches earlier. He gazed wearily at a photograph of soldiers moving east, Canadians and British front-line troops, it said. They looked bored and he could not blame them. They wanted it to end quickly. To die in wartime was dreadful enough; to die right at the end was madness.

He scanned the film reviews and the comment items until a small news story at the foot of an inside page caught his eye:

ROBERTSON CANDIDATE FOR S.E. TORY SEAT

So, it was out in the open. He glanced at the sparse biography.

"Mr. Robertson was a Cambridge don before the outbreak of hostilities, teaching modern languages, and since 1940 he has been working in an advisory capacity with the Foreign Office."

He smiled to himself, thinking back to their conversation that afternoon. Maybe Robertson had something planned for him. It was only logical; otherwise, why all the questions?

He glanced again at the paragraph in the newspaper. "Advisory capacity," he said aloud. What a multitude of achievements were contained in such an anemic phrase. It was a pity that people did not know, or could not know, the extent of the man's contributions to the success of the war, that his work would never be appreciated. Francis began to list the operations that Robertson had been involved with: there was the code-breaking of enemy signals, the false information which led to Hitler abandoning the invasion, the tactics in North Africa which kept enemy armies tied up unnecessarily in the Balkans, the strategy of deception which made the Normandy landings possible, not to mention the recruitment of agents throughout Europe.

As Francis ticked off Robertson's achievements on his fingers, an idea gradually took shape. Here was a hero who deserved his place in history; his was the heroism of the intellect, every bit as admirable as that of those who fought with the gun and the grenade. He wondered why he had not thought of it sooner. He had always had a vague idea that one day he would write a book; all reporters wanted to write books, it was one of the clichés of Fleet Street, and here was the obvious opportunity. He would write about Charles Robertson and the SIS.

He nodded to himself. He would take his time about it. There was no hurry. The Official Secrets Act would see to it that the work would not be published for years. Robertson would be long dead by the time it came out and so might the author . . . but it would be a fitting epitaph for the man, and for himself. It was so obvious, such a natural thing to do. And here he was going to Cambridge for a day, the very place Robertson once worked. It was an omen. Like many of his kind, Francis had a healthy respect for the power of omens. It was only the inexperienced types who derided such things, like young coppers who laughed at the idea of coincidence; the old hands didn't; they'd seen it often enough. They believed in chains of events and fates and destiny.

In addition, he would learn more about Robertson and his background. If he was going to work for the man, he should know everything about him. Indeed, Robertson would expect it of him. He closed his eyes, dreaming of book covers, and fell into such a deep sleep that he had to be shaken awake by a ticket inspector as the train pulled into Cambridge.

Julie was waiting for him on the platform, leaning against the barrier talking to the ticket collector. She winked at him as he bent to kiss her.

"How long has it been?" he asked.

"Too long," she said as she took his hand and led him out into the yard. He groaned when he saw the two bicycles. "I thought you were joking on the phone," he said. "How do I cope with this?"—waving his bag at her.

"Ride one-handed," she said, and so he did, wobbling slightly and swerving across the road. But the ride cleared his head and he was enjoying himself by the time he reached her house. It never occurred to him to ask how she managed to get two bicycles to the station.

There were two others at the house, the woman who shared with Julie and her boyfriend, a young RAF officer. At first Francis was aware of the slight air of superiority about the flier, the guarded but noticeable contempt of the uniformed fighting man for the deskbound noncombatant, but Francis soon joked him out of it. He had long since cast off any guilt about not fighting physically for his country. He had crossed that particular bridge years ago, and soon they were laughing together, the four of them, as if they had known each other for years.

In the morning he asked to be shown round the colleges. Julie sighed and pouted.

"Just like every tourist," she said. "Still, I suppose you must. It's like London, I expect, with everyone demanding to see Madame Tussaud's."

"I've never known anyone who wanted to see Tussaud's," said Francis.

"Snob," she said.

They cycled around the town for an hour and strolled arm in arm by the river, chattering about nothing. When he mentioned the college where Robertson had taught she took him along without question, making no attempt to ask him what it was that particularly interested him. If he wanted to tell her, he would tell her.

They strolled through the grounds, left their bicycles by the archway leading into the main hall and wandered around the place. It was almost empty and Francis was surprised. He had expected the place to be thronged with students.

"On a Saturday morning in wartime?" said Julie. "Hardly the busiest time."

"I suppose not." Francis shrugged. He crossed the quadrangle to a small cubicle where a porter sat idly reading the morning newspaper. On an impulse Francis tapped on the glass panel and the old man flinched, startled, then slid back the glass.

"Excuse me," said Francis, "but I wonder if you can help me?"

"Could be," said the porter.

"Do you remember Charles Robertson, by any chance?"

He grinned broadly. "Course I do. He was always good to me."

"And presumably he gave classes here?" Francis searched for the word "Tutorials?"

"He did, sir, right over there," and he pointed across the quadrangle to a room on the top floor.

Francis felt the need to give some sort of explanation. "I work with him in London, you see."

"Oh, yes." The smile widened. "He's something to do with the government now, isn't he?"

"That's right."

"And will he be coming back, afterward?"

"I really don't know, but as I'm here perhaps I could take a look at his study?" The porter looked doubtful. "Just so that I could tell him. I'm sure he'd be interested to know who is taking care of it while he is away."

"Well, I don't see why not." The old man heaved himself off his stool and led them across the quad, chattering about Robertson, what a learned man he was and how his students liked him, how he always had a good word for him, the porter.

The oak door had no name or number. "Mr. Dawson," whispered the porter confidentially as he knocked.

Dawson opened the door a couple of inches and peered out at them over the rim of a pair of spectacles, a thin young man with sandy hair and a pallor which suggested that he rarely escaped outdoors.

Again Francis went through his story, half expecting Dawson to object. He would not have pressed the matter. It was not important, merely idle curiosity. He was not exactly sure why he was bothering. He could always come back if and when the book was commissioned, but Dawson was standing back and opening the door in a mute gesture of invitation.

It was much as he had imagined: a small, wood-paneled study with a leaded window overlooking the quad, a desk and three chairs, a mass of books piled high and low, and papers everywhere.

Nice work if you can get it, he thought with a reluctant twinge of envy. He had not gone to university. His parents had needed his wage. He fought back the resentment; after all, he had done well enough without its benefits. He tried to imagine Robertson at his desk with his students grouped around him. It would not be like this, he thought. There would be no mess. Robertson would have kept the place tidy.

Julie was talking to Dawson as Francis snooped around, not sure what he was looking for, just getting a fresh idea of the man, perhaps picking up little clues to his personality, getting the feel of him as he was, in the sheltered surroundings of his past before everything was turned upside down. But there was no clue. Dawson had made his anonymous presence felt. There were no pictures or photographs, no concession to any personal taste, only a small wall-plaque, some eighteen inches long. Francis peered at it, squinting to make out the list of names and dates and the Latin inscription at the top, all in gold leaf. He looked back inquiringly at Dawson.

"Those who got double first under the old don," Dawson said dismissively.

Francis nodded and made a mental note of the names. They would be worth looking up sometime; surely these men would be able to furnish a few anecdotes of the old days.

When they got back to the house he asked Julie for a piece of paper and he wrote down the names he remembered. There was Grenville Jones in 1930. Thomas Smyth in '31, somebody Learmonth in '32 and Harry somebody in '33; Harry Gresham, that was the name. But he could go no further. It was too bad. His memory was not what it was.

9

Berlin, February 27, 1945

With the arrival of the refugees from the east, the shivers of apprehension in Berlin had become trembles of alarm. Each rumor was
hardened into a fact and every fact exaggerated into fresh rumor, the
process constantly feeding upon itself until the men of the Red army
had evolved in the public imagination into monsters. The image was
boosted by the outpourings of the propaganda machine over the wireless, and Goebbels added to the effect with his own horror stories
from the front.

A black market for cars and petrol developed as police were seen
in the streets wearing tin helmets and carrying rifles and each bridge
and railway station was manned by armed guards. Coffee and spirits
became hard currency, and anyone who knew anyone in authority
began to solicit for travel papers. The city was being bombed daily,
and every evening those who lived in the center shuffled down into
the cellars to sit out the bombing.

They called themselves "cellar tribes" and each night, as the city
crumbled above them, they sat in silence and brooded. There were
some among them whose fear was tinged for the first time with a kind
of guilt, a realization that perhaps the hordes of unwashed barbarians

were going to exact a terrible vengeance that in some ways might be deserved. One or two of them articulated this feeling but most were nagged by it, deep in their subconscious, so that they became sullen and irritable. In London too the crowds had come back to the tube stations in fear of the V-rockets, but there at least there were stories and jokes and occasionally a song. In Berlin there was only silence.

Christa Schiller was one of the few who still attempted to inject some sort of levity into the black gloom that settled like soot over the cellar tribe. Three times in the past week she had been forced to abandon the salon in the process of entertaining a client, and each time she had said that the shuddering of the earth beneath was due to the man's passion. But inevitably the joke fell on deaf ears. That night she scuttled gloomily downward to the cellar of the big apartment block, a building which had once belonged to a single family and once had the best wine cellar in town. The racks were still set up but they were empty now, and dust poured through the cracks in the ceiling like a series of egg timers as the earth shook, covering everyone in a fine layer of silt.

Christa found herself a spot next to Gerda, the redhead, and they shrugged their shoulders at each other in a mutual gesture of discomfort. She felt absurd, crouching in the dirt, an old coat pulled over her silk slip and the heat of sex still within her.

She was accustomed to absurdity, having often been forced into ludicrous poses for the gratification of her clients, but sitting in a Paris negligee and an army coat waiting for the roof to collapse on her was the most ridiculous situation of all. Opposite she could see the man who had shared her bed only moments earlier. He stood shivering, clad in a coat and slippers, flanked by two large hausfraus who talked to each other over the top of his head. Christa could not resist it. She winked hugely at him, a lecherous wink, and he turned away, his lips moving in a silent oath, while the two women looked down at him and scowled. Beside her, Gerda giggled, but a heavy thump above and to their left sent them scrambling to the floor as the dust filtered through and someone screamed.

Christa felt her arm being tugged, and she turned to take the towel which Gerda was offering. Silently she folded it once, wrapped it round her mouth, covering her nose, and knotted it behind her head. That done, she bent forward, still squatting, pressing her hands into her stomach. The word had gone round that such an exercise prevented the lungs tearing in the event of an explosion. A movement to her left caused her to glance up. Gerda was shifting position, leaning against the wall, staring straight ahead of her. Gerda did not care whether her lungs tore or not. If they were going to tear, they would tear; she was something of a fatalist. But not Christa. She would try anything that might save her; all she wanted was to survive this dreadful period, to get out and away before the Russians came. But she knew no one. None of those she had entertained were of any value. They had either gone or else they paid her no attention when she tried to contact them. As far as they were concerned, their commitment to her ended with the money they left at the salon door, and she could not bring herself to blame them. Only Peter had ever promised her anything, and he had not been seen for eighteen months. He had promised her so much and then vanished. Poor Peter, he must have been killed or else he would have come for her. She hoped that he had died quickly and that there had been no pain.

A second heavy concussion caused her to shudder, and she heard herself whimper. If the bomb was to come, she prayed it would happen fast so that there would be simply a blackness; more than anything else, she dreaded being maimed and helpless under the rubble. Consciously she forced the image from her mind, but another fought its way in. She saw Russians, squat men with flat faces, leering at her. She could almost smell them as they reached out for her. It was said that they raped children and grandmothers alike, that they bit into breasts so that they could see the marks made by their teeth. It was some sort of gruesome signature, a personal autograph; they cut off fingers to get at rings, and for some reason they were obsessed by watches and clocks; they rode around on bicycles, Goebbels said, and wore top hats, slept on straw like beasts; when they took over a house they put the rations in the lavatory bowl, and somewhere in Prussia they had killed a family because one of the children had flushed away their food by mistake.

It was all too horrifying to imagine. The only escape, so they said, was to hide in an upstairs room because, being peasants, they were scared of tall buildings and would not venture more than one floor from street level. Maybe that was nonsense. Who knows? Anyway, you could not live upstairs forever; you had to come down sometime, and they would be there with their flat faces and their hammers and nails.

She shuddered at the thought, but now Gerda was shaking her and smiling. They could hear the muffled blast of the all clear in the streets. It was over for another night.

Stiffly she stood up, took the towel from her face and followed the crowd out of the cellar and up into the gloom of the street. She coughed as the dust swirled into her throat. She could see the black clouds rising over Friedrichstrasse. It had been close this time. About thirty yards away an apartment block had been gutted, and she could feel the draft and the heat of the flames on her cheeks. Silently she pushed her way into the street, clutching Gerda's hand and looking up. The salon had been unharmed, a stubborn sentinel to lust, the old madam had called it, defying the bombs. There had been too much laughter inside it and perhaps it would survive. Christa was superstitious enough to believe that perhaps the building had a charmed life. If not, she would be forced to work from home and that would be difficult. Perhaps she might be forced to get in touch with her cousin; but not yet. Angela's puritanical glare of disapproval was almost as frightening as the thought of the Russians. Almost, but not quite.

One kilometer to the west in the bunker beneath the new Chancellery, Gerhard Bergner grunted as a guard shook his shoulder and told him that the bombing had ceased. He rose to his feet, rubbing his hands on his thighs. His palms were damp and he looked at them disapprovingly, then wiped them again on his jacket, feeling the beat of his heart. It seemed to be pounding noisily. He glanced at the others, who were smartening themselves up, pulling at collars and cuffs. It would not do for them to hear his heart pound like a scared chicken. He held his hand over it, pressing it back to keep it quiet. They would talk if they heard his heartbeat, they would say he was getting old. He was not that old, not really old; it was just the effect of the siege, not being able to break out and fight properly, always stuck under some damned little building waiting for others to decide one's destiny.

"I'm sick of all this," he said to himself, and looked up quickly as an SS man turned and stared at him. He had not realized that he had spoken aloud. He would need to be careful in future. As he climbed the stairs he wondered if the Englishman would soon send his emissaries; perhaps they would come soon. He only hoped that they would be competent.

John Patterson awoke slowly, twitching and coughing and rubbing his eyes. The gloom through the stained window showed a rubbish tip of beer cans scattered around the bed. He raised himself onto one elbow and blearily surveyed the scene. In one corner of the room under the sink, two plates had come to rest on the linoleum, one lying broken, the other tilted against a bottle, showing traces of the meal of the night before. Squinting, Patterson could see the remains of a dried egg. Someone had stubbed out a cigarette in it; that would have been the Irishman, he thought. He lay back. The pillow smelled of the cheap scent of the woman, a sweet smell like old honey. Automatically he reached for his trousers under the bed, his fingers scrabbling for his back pocket. He nodded to himself. The money was still there. That was something. He swung himself out of the bed and stumbled across to the sink, scratching and yawning. He washed his face, reached into the wardrobe and pulled out underwear, a shirt and a jacket. His kit bag lay on the top of the wardrobe, already packed.

When he was ready, he glanced quickly round the room. It seemed as if a bomb had exploded. Patterson shook his head and swore under his breath as he closed the door, but immediately he reached the street he felt better. It was good to get away, back to somewhere where things were cleaner and simpler. He whistled as he made his way toward the bus station.

Malcolm Driscoll sat silently in the passenger seat, scarcely listening as his brother chattered to him; something about his latest girlfriend. Young Bernie was happy, glad to be able to talk now that the family was out of the way. It had been a bit of a strain, the previous evening at dinner. His father had been garrulous, discussing the war as if it were already over, comparing it to the carnage of the Great War. Today, he had said, there were merely skirmishes compared to the old days, and so he had rambled on until his wife gently admonished him.

They had sat up till midnight, but there was no mention of the mission. Driscoll had said only that he was going away for a few days. There was nothing more to add, nothing to say, and he did not want to worry his mother unduly.

At the station he shook hands with Bernie, and stood for a moment watching as the youngster reversed the car in a semicircle and backed away up the hill. As he bought his single ticket for Dover, he permitted himself a small luxury, picturing the look on his father's face on the day he returned.

In Stepney, Cyril Roth dragged himself away from his mother's embrace and made his way down the street toward the tram stop. He took a deep breath. It was a relief to be gone. The last two days had been suffocating as he plowed through the deep furrows of his family's affection. He reached the corner, turned and waved. It had been only a forty-yard walk but he had turned and waved every ten yards. To have waved back only three times would have been taken as some kind of rebellion against his mother's name. He smiled to himself as he turned the corner, clutching his brown-paper bag of bagels and gefilte fish. How she had got them he did not know, but somehow she had done it. He waited until he was three streets away before handing over the parcel to a small boy. On the tram he met an old school friend, and they chattered together all the way west to Liverpool Street. He had the feeling that he would not see his mother again. But this was nothing new. Each time he left he thought it would be for the last time. But he always came back.

In Dover, Harry Gresham waited until he had seen the three of them arrive before making his way to the public phone box. He dialed a London number, waited, nodded, put the receiver down and waited again for five minutes, smiling at the queue which formed and ignoring their grumbles and the way they tapped their watches. Eventually the phone rang once more and he took down two names and an address. That done, he made his way back to the harbor.

They had been sitting in the stern of the boat in silence for fifteen minutes, each man alone with his thoughts as they watched the Dover cliffs recede in the dusk behind them. It was Patterson who finally broke the silence.

"How long till we get there?"

Gresham shrugged. "About two hours."

Patterson reached deep into his throat, coughed and spat over the side.

"*Gesundheit,*" said Roth, grinning like a monkey. Patterson took a backhanded swipe at him, and they sparred with each other playfully without getting to their feet. Gresham looked from one to the other. They were a good unit. At first neither one of them had given away anything of himself, each one wary of the other like young stags, but gradually the self-imposed barriers had been taken down. They respected one another as soldiers and that was the beginning; then the first few jokes, mostly by Roth, followed by the inevitable card games which Driscoll always won. In Civvy Street they would pass each other without a word, as all they had in common was their training and their single-mindedness. It looked as though the mix would be just right. He certainly hoped so. He glanced at his watch and nodded toward the bows.

"You can change now, whenever you want," he said. They stood up as one and moved toward the cabin of the MTB, each one looking incongruous in his civvies, Patterson in his big jacket and flapping flannels, Roth in his tight checked suit, and Driscoll with his twills and Harris Tweed sports coat, more out of place than any, like a young squire caught unexpectedly among thieves.

Within a few minutes they were back in the stern, identically dressed in their serge battle dress and canvas-soled shoes, their berets stuffed into their webbing belts. And now they sprawled on the benches round the gunwale, comfortable and self-assured, the awkwardness gone, and it was Gresham who felt like an intruder in his suit. He got up and moved past them toward the cabin.

The bucking of the boat indicated a change in current and caused Driscoll to glance up at the clouds and sniff the spray like a dog. He remembered the last time he had made this crossing, farther down the coast, heading for Normandy with the biggest armada the world had ever seen. They had all been scared that day, crushed together in the landing craft as it bucked toward the coast, some of them making jokes about sardines in a tin can but most of them silent.

He remembered the faces clearly enough, as if they were sitting beside him, but he could not put many names to them; except young Graham, who had squatted next to him and kept talking all the time, saying he was glad there was a crowd because you don't die in a crowd, it was safer with a crowd around you. Driscoll did not tell him; no one answered him; no one explained that the safest place was on your own. Crowds hamper your movement. You can't get yourself out. There are obstructions, too many people to collide with.

Crowds tended to get bombed and strafed and sprayed with lead. No, Driscoll could do without crowds. Two was one too many for him and eventually he told the kid to shut up.

Everyone expected Graham to be the first to fall. They knew it in their bones, the way he kept turning his head round like a sparrow and gabbing incessantly. He would be the one. But at the end of the day he was still there, saying I-told-you-so, except that by then he had a smaller audience.

Driscoll squinted at the coastline ahead. This was much better; a small boat, a small unit you could trust, a job which would be quick and straightforward. It would do. Right at that moment he was a contented man.

Gresham took his time changing, folding his suit carefully and laying it on his case. The others had packed neatly and methodically, as soldiers always did; they had snapped their cases shut and chalked them with a number so that they could be picked up at Dover when they returned. He nodded to himself, glad that they had done exactly as he had asked, without question. In another corner of the cabin lay the four packs. He slipped his tunic on, feeling the rough serge scratch his skin, bringing up gooseflesh and resurrecting all kinds of memories, jumbled images that he would rather forget. He touched the three cloth captain's pips on his shoulder, reached into his pack, fumbled for a moment, then drew out a long, slim leather scabbard. He looked at it briefly before drawing the blade out and laying it gently across the calloused skin of his palm, feeling the blade slice gently through the outer layer.

He applied a little more pressure and felt the sting of it as it drew a thin trickle of blood. He balanced the knife on his palm and gazed at it. They called it the killing knife; eight inches of burnished Sheffield steel, the blade triangular so that a wound would not heal. He remembered the big soldier who had tapped a piece of meat with it, a tough chunk of fresh ration, just a touch with the point and the blade had gone through the meat and sliced through his hand.

Gently he caressed himself again before moving to the sink. He cleaned the blade, replaced it in the scabbard and ran the water on his hand until the sliver of blood congealed. Only then did he make his way back to the deck.

The others were playing cards and he watched them for a moment, listening to the abuse and the good-natured curses. They were becoming friendly; they would be showing one another pictures of their girls next. He only hoped they would not have long to wait. He would not like to be around when they became impatient.

By the time they reached Ostend the rain was coming down hard, but they seemed oblivious to it as they stood waiting for clearance at the harbor. As they disembarked, Gresham shook the captain's hand and trotted up the steps, the others behind him, grouping round him at the quay, clutching their packs by the straps. Silently they stood waiting, saying nothing. Groups of soldiers passed them, glancing across at them curiously, mostly old soldiers, given a cushy billet guarding the port from an attack that would never come.

A young lieutenant glanced at Gresham's papers and sniffed. "I'm going to have to check this," he said, looking at Patterson with an expression of distaste as if he had just encountered the enemy.

"I think you know about us," said Gresham.

"Can't say I do, but if you wait a moment . . ."

They stood in the rain, content to let the man play his game. If he needed to prove something, it was his problem. After ten minutes he returned, clutching a piece of paper. "Must have got lost," he said. "You know how it is."

Gresham walked past him toward the harbor office. "Find us a lorry," he said over his shoulder. "Unless you've lost that too."

Half an hour later they were on the move, squatting under the canvas roof of a three-tonner heading northeast. Briefly Roth wondered where they would be billeted and what the job was. He wondered when Gresham would get around to telling them. For a moment he thought of asking but decided against it. Maybe it would be as well not to know.

Part
THREE

10

Berlin, March 21, 1945

The voice from the wireless was flat and emotionless, a dull monotone without inflection, as if it were a machine and not a woman that was telling the story.

"They came unexpectedly at four o'clock, about twelve of them driving half-tracks. They were wearing white uniforms and big fur boots and some of them were drunk. The first vehicle came up the main street fast and swerved toward a little girl who was standing on the pavement watching. They missed her and crashed into a shop window. The little girl ran away and I think she was all right although I never saw her again.

"They got out of the vehicle, one of them reeling around a bit because his head was cut, and they waved to the others. I was watching from the window . . . no, I wasn't scared then. I thought they would just round up the men as prisoners or something. They split up into groups of twos and threes and began going into houses and shops, shouting all the time. They have such strange accents, all nasal as if they had pegs over their noses or they had catarrh or something.

"Then I saw the Bürgermeister being dragged from his house. He had been a fool. He should have taken the flag down from his window, and then maybe they wouldn't have known. But he couldn't have realized how they would treat him. He kept looking over his shoulder back into the house, and then his wife was brought out. She was naked. It was strange. My first thought was how fat she was. I had always thought she was quite a trim woman, but maybe she always wore corsets.

"There were only six of them in the street, the four soldiers and Herr Lang and his wife, but I could hear screams from other houses. I think that was the first time I began to feel frightened, but I didn't stop watching. They made the Bürgermeister kneel and two soldiers started doing things to Frau Lang. She struggled a lot, but it was hopeless. They were doing things to her right there in the street, in the snow. I kept wondering why they had brought her outside when it would have been warmer inside. I still don't understand that bit. One held her while the other did it, all with his clothes on, and she writhed around for a while, but when the second one did it she never moved. All this time they were holding Herr Lang, and he just knelt there staring and not moving, as if he were a statue.

"Then when they had finished with her, one of them raised his pistol and shot Herr Lang in the head. He rolled around for a moment and then lay still, just sort of twitching until one of the half-tracks came along and ran over him, forward and back, I don't know how many times, until he was flattened like a frog in the middle of the road. They let Frau Lang crawl away after that and I don't know what happened to her. I never saw her again.

"When they came into my house I tried to hide, but there was nowhere. I went under the bed, but it's a small bed and my body pushed it up so that the legs were off the ground. They would have had to be blind not to see me. I could feel the bed wobble as I lay there. I don't know how long I stayed there but I was getting very stiff and could scarcely breathe, so that it was almost a relief when they came in. They were drunk, I think, three of them, two with flat faces and a tall one with steel teeth."

"What's that?" the voice of the interviewer broke in.

"False teeth, made of tin, I think."

"I see."

The woman hesitated, the momentum of her narrative gone.

"And what happened next?" coaxed the interviewer.

"I was very frightened and I couldn't speak. They kept saying '*Uri, uri.*' "

"Watches?"

"Yes, they seemed to be very keen on clocks and watches. I gave them mine, the one my husband gave me, and the two with flat faces held it to their ears and laughed and started to fight over it. I thought I might get away then, but the one with the tin teeth shouted at them and they stopped. Then they pushed me onto the bed and did it to me."

There was a silence for a moment and then she continued. "It was very painful. I don't know how long it went on for. They smelled very bad. Then one of the flat-faced ones hit me with his pistol. I saw it coming down at me and it seemed to take a long time to reach my head. Then nothing, like a dream. No pain or anything, not till I woke up and then there was pain."

"They left you for dead?"

"I don't know. I don't know if they meant to kill me or not. A lot of the others were killed, I think. I went out and crawled down the street. I kept losing consciousness. There was a truck with some people in it. The men lifted me inside and we went west. I think we traveled for two days."

"But you didn't encounter any more Russians?"

"No. They had been a patrol, I think. The main body of the army had not caught up. We didn't have to go through their lines or anything."

"And how do you feel now?"

"Ashamed."

"May I ask your age?"

"Sixty-one."

Christa stabbed at the button and the radio faded away, the woman's voice drifting into the distance until there was silence. She shivered and drew her coat tightly round her body, wondering why she had to listen. It was like the old woman had said: "I didn't stop watching." She had to hear it even though it was always terrible, but she wouldn't wait for the propaganda that came afterward, telling them to fight for every street and explaining the Führer's plan for a counterattack. She did not bother with such nonsense.

Shivering slightly she stood up and looked round the flat, wondering if there was anything more she could do to brighten it up. The little lamps gave off a dull yellow glow onto the hessian on the walls. It all looked quite reasonable, but it was hardly what might be called erotic, although she had tried. They would not pay the salon rates for this, and she could not blame them. It was just as well that she had put away some money during the good times. She need not starve for a while. She could survive quite comfortably until she got out.

Again she glanced at the message from the salon, a shiver of hope running through her. Just the address and the one name: Claud.

It had been over a year, and in normal circumstances she would not have felt any emotion at the mention of his name. As a lover he was mechanical and uninspiring. Like other Swiss she had met he seemed to have no sense of humor, except that one time when she had teased him.

"I thought all Red Cross workers were supposed to be saints," she had said, and he had replied that saints had to learn about sin in order to fight it; it had been a joke, or at least she had assumed as much, because his mouth had twitched slightly in what might have been a smile.

But now she would do her best for him, plead with him if she must. He was an escape route. He could get her out with the Red Cross team, she was sure of that. The Swiss could fix anything.

She selected a silk blouse and black skirt, spat on her shoes and polished them till they gleamed. From what she could remember, he liked her to act the whore. He liked caricature. She made herself up extravagantly and winked at the image in the mirror. She would play the whore for him. It would be a command performance and afterward she would ask for special payment.

She walked the half-mile to the Adlon Hotel, where the Red Cross delegation had taken rooms. It was still possible to get warm baths there, and decent food, or so she had been told. She waited until the doorman was distracted by a party of guests, and slipped surreptitiously through the door. With such makeup it was obvious what she was doing there.

Quickly she moved past the desk and up the stairs, checking the room numbers at each landing. She took a deep breath when she reached the door, then knocked sharply. The door was opened almost at once.

She smiled and squeezed past him, looking at him with what she hoped was a seductive expression. As always she felt slightly ridiculous as she worked herself into the role. But she got on with it, playing up to him, and when it was over he could hardly speak; he lay panting, his eyes closed.

"Christa," he said at last, "you were superb."

She wondered if the time was ripe or if she should wait until he came round a little more. She had rehearsed a speech and various poses. Maybe she should try now, play on whatever emotions he had, if he had any. But even as she was thinking he rose on one elbow and gazed at her.

"Berlin is in a pretty bad state," he said.

"Awful."

"And no place for a woman."

This was too good to be true. She pouted. "I know. And it will be worse when the Russians arrive."

"I wouldn't believe all you hear," he said.

"Perhaps, but even if only a fraction is true . . ."

He smiled at her. "I expect you would like to leave."

She nodded dumbly.

"You have connections in the Chancellery, have you not?"

She looked at him in astonishment. How did he know? She had never told anyone, except perhaps Peter, and he would not have said anything. Anyway, Peter had nothing to do with the Red Cross. She wondered what was happening, her mind racing to try to answer questions that sprang from nowhere.

"My cousin is secretary to one of Reichsleiter Bormann's aides," she said. There was nothing to be gained by deception.

"Quite. And I would like you to get in touch with her so that you might meet a certain Gerhard Bergner, a general in the High Command."

"What?" She blinked, covering herself with a sheet, moving her hands around as if they had a life of their own.

"You are to tell him to expect friends. And you are to mention the word Lisbon." He smiled at the look on her face. "I know. It all sounds very dramatic. And of course you are to say nothing about me. I am merely passing on a message, a favor to a friend."

"Peter?" she said hopefully, but the look of incomprehension told her she was wrong. She shook her head, wondering what it was all about. "And what about me?" she said, hoping she did not sound too desperate.

"I am told that you will be given safe passage out of Berlin, if you so desire."

"To the West?"

"Yes." He smiled again and tickled her under the chin. "So, my dear, your little performance was not necessary after all." He rose to leave. "But it was appreciated nonetheless."

She left the hotel in a daze, hardly able to take in what she had been told, and it was not until she was back in the flat that she found the money in her bag, a large wad of notes; enough, as Gerda was fond of saying, to choke a horse. There was more than she could have expected, far more than the rate for the job.

She sat on the bed and stared blankly at it for a moment, then lay back, kicked her legs in the air and whooped like a child, giggling and shaking until she began to cough.

Everything was going to be all right.

With one part of his brain Bergner knew that what he was doing was pointless, yet still he carried on, almost to the point of obsession, sitting in the small room hour after hour without a break, surrounded by maps and daily reports of the military situation, plotting and planning until he knew exactly what had to be done. It infuriated him that there would be no result from his labors, that he was doing it all for nothing.

For the third time in an hour a soldier rapped on the door and handed him a message torn from a teletype machine. He looked at it, thanked the soldier and read the message aloud: "Enemy action in the Danzig-Götenhafen sector, mostly repulsed. Braunsberg taken by the Russians so that the front runs east between Braunsberg and Heiligenbeil. . . ."

He moved round the small trestle table to the wall, which was dominated by a five-foot-square map of Europe with smaller detailed maps pinned beneath. They were covered with colored flags and pins indicating the military situation on both fronts. Bergner stretched upward and moved three pins, stood back and surveyed the scene, then moved back to his desk and made notes on a pad.

He had made himself the most informed member of the High Command, and had committed every detail to memory. He could juggle battalions and divisions around in his head with ease, and he was proud of himself although he looked upon what he was doing, preparing the defense of Berlin, as little more than an intellectual exercise, like chess or bridge, and at that moment just as irrelevant.

It was no more than a game because Adolf Hitler would pay no attention to whatever conclusions he reached. The Führer got on with his own plans, moving battalions along both fronts, defending positions with divisions that no longer existed and rushing companies into attack without artillery support, and often without transport. On Bergner's wall the pins told the reality of the situation, but it was in Hitler's befuddled mind that the plans were made.

Bergner continued scribbling. He knew that he was being given this exercise merely to keep him out of harm's way. His command had been taken from him and they were treating him like a child, keeping him occupied. He might as well have been making Plasticine tanks for all the good it would do. Yet still he kept going, working out of mindless loyalty, obeying orders like a dog because he had been well trained all his life.

So intent was he on his work that he did not hear the woman come in. When she touched him on the shoulder he shuddered and turned quickly. He vaguely recognized her from the conferences, but he did not know her name; just that she always looked as though she had stepped in something nasty.

"Yes?" he said.

"My name is Frau Müller, Angela Müller."

"Yes?"

"You know I have a cousin who is a whore?"

The absurdity of the question staggered him. He raised his eyebrows and laughed. It was the most ridiculous way of putting things. If she had said she was going to fly to the moon that evening he would have been less surprised. But she was staring at him, her lips pursed, waiting for an answer.

"I did not know, Frau Müller," he said, trying to force the smile from his face. "You have my sympathies."

"You surprise me, sir," she said with the trace of a sneer.

"Good gracious, why?" What was the woman getting at?

"She seems to know you." Now she was accusing him, and the tone of her voice annoyed him.

"Look, woman, I have told you I do not know your whoring cousin. Now, say whatever it is you have came to say." God, he thought, it had come to this, a general of the High Command being insulted by a mere typist; and about prostitutes at that.

"She wants to see you. Says it's important," she sniffed. "She said to mention Lisbon to you."

He frowned and saw that she was watching him, then he shrugged. He did not know quite what to say and was glad when she took the initiative, reaching into her pocket and handing him a slip of paper.

"This is the address," she said. "She is at home right now."

Bergner took it. "I will give her your regards," he said.

"There's no need for that, Herr General." She turned smartly and left the room, and he thought he could almost smell a scent of self-righteous contempt which she had left behind.

Slowly he stood up and reached for his greatcoat, trying not to think about what he was doing. Somewhere inside him his conscience was trying to claim his attention, but he ignored it. He would deal with it later, when he was out of this tomb.

As he made his way along the corridor he tried to imagine what she would look like. He had never consorted with prostitutes. It had always been something for others, but now he felt a curious sense of titillation. He was quite jaunty as he climbed the steps into the main building and saluted sharply as the SS guard came to attention.

"I shan't be needing an escort this evening," he said.

"But I have my orders, Herr General." The voice was firm.

"Don't be ridiculous," said Bergner, moving forward, but the guard stepped back and into his path and as he did so the truth came to Bergner quite abruptly. He had always assumed that the guards had accompanied him on his walks for his protection. It had never occurred to him to think otherwise. Even now, as he looked at the man, the idea would not take firm root in his mind. It was too appalling to consider.

"I said I did not need you," he snapped.

"I am sorry, Herr General."

He was about to ask on whose orders the man was acting, but he choked back the words. He would not demean himself. It had to be a Führer order. He turned and walked back downstairs. He would have to speak to Bormann. Bormann would sort it out.

An hour later, Angela Müller left Bormann's office, collected her coat, made her way out of the Chancellery, crossed Wilhelmstrasse and headed east. She was still nervous. It was the first time she had been alone with the Reichsleiter, and she had had to force herself to be calm in front of him. As she walked, she tried to banish the curiosity and the small nub of resentment from her mind. She did not understand what was going on, and she grumbled to herself that she was not paid to be a messenger. But Herr Bormann had said it was urgent. He had said he was relying on her and she clung to that phrase. At least she was not being forced to act as some kind of sexual go-between as she had first thought. She could not have borne such a thing. It was urgent and he was relying on her. She repeated the words and began to feel quite important.

At the sound of the knock Christa switched off the wireless and rose from her chair. Automatically she patted her hair into place, the professional smile already set as she opened the door, just two inches on a chain. The smile remained, fixed and mirthless, as she slipped the catch and pulled the door open.

"Angela, how nice." She stood back in an exaggerated gesture of welcome, but her cousin did not come in.

"I have a message," she said. "Your friend the general cannot come. But he asks you to keep in regular touch."

"How?" Christa frowned.

"Through me. I am to check with you daily."

"Why?"

"I don't know."

Christa shrugged, trying to keep the bewilderment from her face.

"Well, anyway, Angela, thank you for—"

"No thanks are required," she said coldly. "I am acting under the Reichsleiter's orders. I have no choice." She stepped back, ready to leave. "And you are to say nothing."

"What's to be said?" asked Christa.

"Quite." Angela turned and walked smartly to the landing, and Christa slammed the door behind her. Again she snapped the wireless on, but she could not concentrate. She was disappointed. She had been looking forward to meeting a general.

11

Wesel, Holland, March 22, 1945

"They say you can kill a condemned man by postponing the execution."

"Oh, yes," said Patterson, yawning. Frankly he was getting irritated by Roth and his ideas. Whenever there was a silence, Roth had to fill it with some half-baked theory or other. The others had become accustomed to nodding and grunting at the right moments so that he wouldn't get offended.

The two men were sitting on a bench in a small wooden hut in a field to the west of the Dutch town of Wesel, at the rear of Divisional Headquarters. The rain was spattering on the tin roof and dripping through the joists.

Patterson watched as a raindrop clung to the end of the beam, briefly reflecting the light before dropping onto Roth's thigh, but the man appeared not to notice. He was far away in a condemned cell somewhere, inside the mind of a man waiting for the hangman. Patterson had no idea how he had suddenly got onto the idea of executions. His mind seemed to be forever wandering. Driscoll said once that he had a butterfly brain, and it was a good image; he was always flitting from one thought to the next, never settling for any length of time.

"What's the word for that glandular stuff that clots the blood?" he was asking, tapping Patterson on the knee.

"Don't know," said Patterson.

"Adrenaline. That's it. You see, what happens is that the bloke in the cell is all ready to go. You with me?"

Patterson nodded.

"His heartbeat is up, his pulse is racing and there's all this adrenaline flooding through his system, clotting his blood up. Now, tell him it's all off, he collapses like a burst bag. The adrenaline has got nowhere to go, so it builds up. Do it often enough and . . ."

Patterson yawned. "And that's what's happening to us?" he said, glad that he had finally cottoned onto Roth's point. Maybe he would stop now.

"Exactly. Every day we're ready, but we don't get the word."

"Ah, well, never mind." He did not worry. It seemed quite sensible to wait. There was no point trying to trickle their way through hundreds of miles of Germans when the army could do it for them. Anyway, his heart was OK, his pulse wasn't racing. Roth was crazy. It was as simple as that.

He got up and peered out through the door of the hut. The rain was easing and he moved outside away from the noise of the little man's voice. He ambled through the bivouac area to the edge of the field and gazed over the mud to the east. Just a few miles through the trees lay the Rhine; the last great barrier, they called it. Once over the river they could strike straight for the heart of Germany. He glanced at the soldiers as they moved among their bivouacs. There was an air of tension about them. They were so near and yet so far; all they wanted was to get it over with so that they could go home and tell lies to their wives. For three weeks he had watched from the rear as they fought their way eastward, and occasionally he felt guilty, a camp follower with nothing to do, but the mood soon passed. Now and again they would grumble at him and he could see the questions on their faces, wondering what these four men were doing riding on the back of the army like a tick on a bull. Sometimes he could sense their hostility. But there was nothing he could do and nothing he could tell them, so he simply kept out of their way.

He wandered to the main road. It was peaceful. There were no Germans left on this side of the river. They would be massing on the other side, waiting like a homesteader in a Western, ready with his gun for the Indians to attack. It was a nice idea. He often had ideas like that, even as a kid, but he had soon learned to keep them to himself. If he ever mentioned them he was laughed at; especially by the girls, always sniggering about his size. So he had kept his thoughts to himself.

But the idea of the homesteader appealed to him; alone and friendless with the enemy at the front and the back, and running out of ammunition, his family looking for a miracle that wasn't going to happen. All he could do was fight to the last bullet, and maybe set fire to the place and perish rather than fall into the hands of the Indians.

Patterson nodded to himself; maybe Gresham would like the idea. He had told him about the tick on the bull's back and he hadn't yawned or called him a fool. He had simply nodded and said "Yes." That was all, but it was enough; just the one word and Patterson would follow him into hell because of it.

He tensed his shoulders and threw a few punches at the air, feeling healthy and fit; boredom did not bother him as it did the others. He watched the soldiers cleaning their rifles, scraping at their webbing and growling at one another. Up front they were taping out the route to be taken to the river, and in the woods the sappers were working on the camouflaged pontoons. They would have made an excellent target for the Luftwaffe, if only there had been any Luftwaffe. But it was a dead weight now; everyone knew that. Göring had let them all down. So all there was left was to cross the river and finish the job.

He turned and saw Driscoll in the field behind the mess tent. He was doing press-ups in the mud. Patterson counted as he watched; twenty-five, then ten with a clap of the hands in midair, then stop. Fifteen one-hand push-ups, then a rest, and fifteen with the other hand. It seemed that he could go on all day.

He remembered the big soldier who had laughed at Driscoll. The little man had not taken the bait. He had just kept going, harder and harder, until the soldier stopped laughing and merely gazed in wonder. He had never seen anyone so fit; it was unnatural. Driscoll had put on a display for him. It was his method of answering the laughter, the best way, and they left him alone after that, didn't even make fun of his toffee voice, at least not in his hearing. They just accepted that here was some kind of little superman and good luck to him.

Patterson turned fast as he heard someone come up behind him. A young soldier stood still, holding up his hands in mock surrender.

"You're wanted back at your bivvy," he said.

Patterson nodded his thanks and moved back toward the tents, walking fast.

"Maybe you're going to war," shouted the soldier, but he ignored him. Maybe, though; maybe it was time.

He reached the hut just behind Driscoll. Gresham and Roth were standing waiting for him. When they were seated Gresham spoke.

"We are to join the Americans."

The three men looked at one another and Gresham continued: "I've been informed that Patton is going to cross first."

"But that's not the plan," said Driscoll.

"Maybe, but that's what London thinks." He glanced to the corner where the kit bags lay. "So, pack up your troubles. We're leaving immediately."

They got to their feet, and were waiting by the truck within a couple of minutes. As they climbed aboard the soldier looked at them curiously, but said nothing.

Slowly the truck rumbled along the west bank of the Rhine past Düsseldorf, Cologne, Bonn and the bridge at Remagen and on to the Moselle. Most of the time the men slept, occasionally wakening to gaze through the canvas flaps and exchange a few words, but for the most part they sat in silence, each one thinking about the Americans and wondering what it would be like to follow them into battle. They had all met Americans. They were, in general, an open, inquisitive people. Americans wanted to know what was going on. It was to be hoped that they would take their silence in good spirit.

South of Coblenz they came across the first patrol of the Third Army. The truck was waved to a halt, and a young captain glanced at Gresham's papers before waving them on, smiling and wishing them good luck. They sat quietly for the rest of the trip, to Bingen, eastward to Mainz and south again to Oppenheim. It was dark when they reached the town, passing through convoys of trucks and armored personnel carriers. In the distance they could hear the thump of artillery fire.

From the beginning there was tension. The major who took Gresham's papers mutter something about having no time for all this.

Gresham looked down at him from the truck, reached forward and pointed to the priority signal at the top left-hand corner.

The major grunted and sniffed. "We have no accommodation, gentlemen," he said, "but I guess you can sleep in the truck."

Gresham nodded and watched as a GI was sent to the driver with directions.

"Report to the bridgehead in the morning," said the major.

Again Gresham nodded and stretched out for his papers. As the officer turned and strode away, Gresham thought he heard him mutter something about there being a war on, something about playing housemaid. But it was not important. So long as they cooperated, everything would be all right.

The truck was parked in the yard of a garage and they remained inside, ate their rations and settled down for the night, sleeping soundly as the first of Patton's men crossed the Rhine.

In the morning Gresham sought out the Divisional Signals Office, sent his message and was issued a jeep, picked up the others and headed for the river. The Americans paid them little heed. They were jubilant, chattering noisily to one another and gazing east where the pontoons were being maneuvered into position, the landing craft chugging backward and forward across the water like holiday ferries. The Rhine had been crossed with surprising ease and the loss of only twenty-eight men; all that was needed now was consolidation before the final push east.

Again they waited until late in the afternoon, when they were given permission to join the traffic jam waiting to cross the river. Driscoll sat in the driving seat, with Gresham beside him and the others in the back. Finally they moved, bumping onto the pontoon, the jeep swaying as the tires hit the steel struts; on the other side they could hear the grind of wheels and the squeal of tank tracks.

They were fifty yards across when Driscoll suddenly cursed and kicked at the brake pedal as the truck in front came to an unexpected halt. Patterson and Roth were thrown forward, and Gresham held on to the windshield frame for support as his head snapped forward and back.

"Sorry," Driscoll grunted.

"It's all right," said Gresham. "Not your fault."

They peered to their right to see what had happened. A group of GIs was jumping from the truck and balancing precariously on the bridge, laughing and whooping. The first to jump unbuttoned his trousers and sent a stream into the river, followed by the others, fumbling with their buttons, pushing and jostling, one of them pointing to the sky and arching his water toward the east bank.

"Children," muttered Driscoll disdainfully.

One of the men heard him and turned, grinning, twisting round from the hips so that Driscoll had to duck beneath the dashboard to avoid the spray. When he looked up again his face was white with anger, his hands clenched tightly round the steering wheel so that his nails dug into his palms.

"Easy," whispered Gresham, but Driscoll continued to stare at the soldier until the man had buttoned himself up and hopped back into the truck.

From behind, Patterson made an attempt to ease the tension. "Hard to tell who's the enemy," he said.

And Roth joined in. "If you're Jewish everybody's an enemy," he said.

Driscoll smiled, the color returning to his face. The mood had passed, for the moment.

That afternoon Gresham made his customary search for the Signals Office. He found it by the river, a makeshift construction, a tarpaulin stretched between two lorries. He joined a line of three soldiers and waited silently for his turn. He handed his message to the operator and stood to one side until he received the acknowledgment. As he turned to go, the operator called him back and handed him a slip of paper.

"Came in half an hour ago," he said.

Gresham thanked him, walked quickly to the jeep, perched on the driving seat and began decoding the message.

For a moment he sat stock-still, then stood up and jumped from the jeep, looking for the others. It took him five minutes to find them sitting silently together by a lorry, their hands cupped round mugs of tea, with no one around them, each one cocooned in his own thoughts; nobody had approached them. They sat as if contaminated.

Patterson looked up as Gresham approached. He was always the first to notice things, as if he were equipped with antennae. Patterson was not a man to creep up to in the dark.

They gazed at him expectantly as he approached.

"We're off," he said.

For a moment they sat motionless, then Roth grinned, stood up and began to run, sprinting between two lorries toward the jeep.

Patterson set off after him, moving fast, his elbows pumping, looking like a huge schoolboy let loose for the holidays. Driscoll smiled at Gresham, feeling the tension oozing from his pores; it was good to be going, just the four of them, getting on with the job with no one else to worry about, and at first he was not quite sure what the big GI had said as Roth skidded to a halt like a character from a cartoon film, the mud spraying from his boots.

"IS THAT THE WAY YOU RAN AT DUNKIRK?!"

Roth reached him first, walking smartly up to the soldier, who grinned at him then doubled up as Roth's kick caught him on the kneecap. As he groveled, Roth grabbed him by the ears and brought his knee up under his throat, then stood back and watched without expression as the man writhed in the mud. For a moment none of the Americans moved and Patterson had time to reach Roth's side, waiting in a crouch until the GIs reacted, rushing them, the first falling under a kick from Patterson, two others grappling with Roth, so that by the time Gresham and Driscoll had covered the twenty yards there was a scrum of bodies. Gresham roared for order, pulling at legs and arms until he was tripped and fell into the mud. . . .

It took the American Lieutenant only a minute to reach the scene, and briefly he stood staring in disbelief at the sight of four men back to back astride three soldiers lying motionless while a semicircle of GIs stood off, five yards away, four of them with their rifles at their shoulders, like a firing squad. The lieutenant had to choke back an impulse to yell "Fire!"—get it over with quickly and ask questions afterward—but instead he shouted for order, and as the GIs lowered their rifles three of the group charged them, kicking and punching, while the fourth stood with his hands on hips, shaking his head so that, at first, the lieutenant was not sure whether he was laughing or crying.

12

London, March 28, 1945

When Audrey Stevens received the invitation to Francis's flat for the evening, she accepted without hesitation. Perhaps she might despise herself afterward, but she doubted it. Long ago she had come to the conclusion that pride was basically masculine; it was always the men who were taking care not to do anything that might ruffle their feathers. If a woman was in love she would do whatever needed to be done. Alan had called. He wanted to see her. That was enough, but if she was to go back to him it would have to be on her terms.

Thinking it over she made her way through the darkened streets of Victoria, past groups of people who seemed to shuffle in the shadows. Something of their conversations reached her, complaints about the new ration on meat, rumors about a return to the blackout, mutterings in the gutter. People were tired. It seemed that the war would never end and the lights would never shine again. Soon it would be six years, and a generation had grown old before its time.

She wondered if he might have changed the flat around and if there would be any traces of another woman's presence, but what did it matter? It had been a short-lived affair. People had short-lived affairs all the time, especially in wartime. It was nothing to get upset about and she had wasted too many tears already.

"Darling."

He was the personification of charm, guiding her into the flat, taking her coat, asking how she had been and apologizing for being so busy, but you know what it's like. . . . There was tea and a plate of sandwiches. The flat seemed the same, clean as ever, but then Alan was known for his tidiness. Every morning he would polish his desk with a duster and rearrange his papers. She knew that it drove some of his colleagues to distraction, and she had seen Mr. Robertson grit his teeth in annoyance. But everyone had his or her idiosyncrasies.

He was bending over her asking about saccharin, yet he knew she didn't take saccharin. Maybe the new woman did and he was getting confused. She smiled at him and listened. No, she hadn't seen *Henry V* and yes, she thought Olivier was a marvelous actor. She looked at him. Maybe it was the way he held his cup or the almost feminine manner in which he nibbled his sandwich, but something about him irritated her.

"What do you want, Alan?" Her voice was steady.

"Just to see you." But he was struggling, a silly smile on his face.

"Do you want to take me to bed?" She would have preferred to have been coarser, but she never could say the word sex without blushing.

"If that's what you want." It was a feeble reply and she treated it with the contempt it deserved, staring at him in silence until at last he gave in.

"I wanted to ask you about Charles."

"Ah," she said. So that was it. She thought of getting up and leaving, but her feet ached. She sat where she was.

"I mean, is there anything unusual . . . ?"

She shrugged. She would let him work for whatever it was he wanted; not that she cared why he was interested in Charles Robertson. She did not care what he was interested in. It didn't matter.

"I was simply wondering," he struggled, "whether you noticed if he was under a strain."

"It's been a long war."

"Yes, but lately. What has particularly interested him?"

"Berlin," she said. "He thinks Eisenhower has lost interest in the city."

She gazed into the fireplace. Vaguely she was aware of him rising to his feet. She could hear his voice asking questions, but she did not answer. She simply sat still, clutching her teacup and wondering what she was doing in his flat. There were better places to be and better things to do. He was beginning to annoy her; the sound of his voice, the way he paced around the flat . . . the very smell of him sickened her.

Abruptly she stood up, placed her cup on the chair and moved toward the door, but still the questions were being thrown at her.

"What?" she said irritably.

"I just want to know if there's anything . . ."

The pleading sound of his voice satisfied her. She would throw him a crumb of comfort, the first thing that came into her mind.

"He's been in regular touch with the OSS," she said, "ever since the patrol went missing."

"They're missing?" he said incredulously.

She nodded triumphantly and opened the door. "There's been no word from Gresham for days," she said.

Briefly she glimpsed the astonishment on his face before she slammed the door, ignoring his shouts to come back. As she ran down the stairs she felt bloated with a sense of triumph. She had not debased herself at all, and it was not until she reached the street that the tears came and she cursed him, using words she scarcely knew.

Viv Jeffries was pleasantly surprised to see Francis. It was not often that someone turned up at his rooms unexpectedly and suggested a beer or two. Certainly not Francis, who was always such a predictable chap; he rarely turned up out of the blue and so it was especially welcome, and good to get away from the paperwork for a while.

They chatted amiably as they walked to the pub on the corner, and retold old stories for half an hour in the Snug until there was a gap in the conversation and Francis could slip in his question.

In reply Jeffries giggled and looked over his shoulder like some conspirator. "Walls have ears," he said, leading Francis into the corner and whispering. "Right cock-up, old chap," he said. "It transpires that our cutthroat band acted a little hasty, sort of premature as it were." He gulped from his glass and continued. "Bit of a scrap with some of Patton's brigade."

"Patton?" said Francis.

Jeffries nodded. "They went across with Patton for some reason or other, got in a bit of bother and haven't been heard of since."

"What do you think has happened?"

"Disposed of, I shouldn't wonder. Drowned in Coca-Cola or something. Two of their chaps were pretty badly hurt and they wouldn't take kindly to that, us being allies. . . ."

Francis whistled through his teeth. "So the mission is postponed."

"Don't know, but old Robby has been hopping around trying to find them. He's even been seen with the OSS." He nodded triumphantly as Francis raised his eyebrows.

"What, personally?"

"That's right. Imagine. After all the bother we've had with them."

Francis could see that Jeffries was enjoying himself. The man was an inveterate gossip, although only within the service. Francis took further advantage.

"You were involved in the recruitment, weren't you?"

Jeffries nodded happily.

"Was one of them named Gresham?"

And now it was Jeffries's turn to whistle in surprise. "Top of the class, old chap. How did . . ."

"Harry Gresham?"

"Ten out of ten. Have you been snooping in my files?"

Francis shook his head and tapped his nose. "Intelligence," he said.

"Well, I'll be buggered."

There was a standard response to such a line, but Francis did not make it. His mind was racing in all directions; he was adding up two and two and making eight.

Charles Robertson got little sleep that night. He thought perhaps he might have dozed for a couple of hours, but then next morning his brain was still working overtime, chasing problems into corners but finding no solutions. He perched on a bench in Green Park, his eyes half closed against the warm spring sunshine. At last the weather had improved and with it the spirits of the Londoners, strolling with their children and gazing at the daffodils and crocuses as if they had doubted that the sun would ever shine again.

Two children toddled up toward Robertson and chattered at him, but he paid them no attention. It was as if he did not see them. His lips moved soundlessly and eventually the children left him in peace, looking back at him and nudging one another.

Eventually he blinked and shuddered slightly, as if he had awakened from a deep sleep. He stood up and began to move south toward Constitution Hill, and from fifty yards he recognized McLean. He was standing staring at a dormant flower-bed, conspicuous in his white coat and close-cropped haircut. He had the jaundiced look of someone accustomed to sunshine who had just spent a winter in England.

McLean nodded as Robertson approached and moved into step alongside him. He was taller by some four inches, and he stooped slightly to hear what Robertson was saying.

"Any word yet?"

"I'm afraid not, Charles. The man I want always seems to be somewhere else."

"So where are they? Are they still at the front?" The questions were spat out at the big man.

"I told you. I don't know."

Robertson glanced up at him. "Why are you dragging your feet?" It was a calculated insult but it did not work.

"I'm afraid there's a war on, Charles," McLean said calmly. "And it does not help when your fellows join in on the other side."

Robertson grunted in anger. "Look, we've been through all this already. I thought I made it clear how important—"

"I'm doing my best," McLean said quickly, interrupting him.

"And I will have an answer as soon as possible, but you must understand that the military will extract its pound of flesh. They are turning a blind eye out there and letting your chaps rot for a while." He paused. "And I for one am not inclined to blame them."

Robertson said nothing for a moment, then smiled. "Well, then," he said, "what do you think about our Supreme Commander?"

"I suppose it's predictable; Ike was never all that keen on going for Berlin. You've seen the cable he composed?"

"Yes."

"Officially it makes sense," McLean continued, glad to change the subject. "Our spearheads are still hundreds of miles from Berlin, while the Russians are practically on the doorstep. It seems reasonable to surround the Ruhr and move south, and have Montgomery go for Lübeck to cut off the Germans in Scandinavia. . . ."

"I am aware of the military excuses," said Robertson, and the scorn was back in his voice. "The reason, however, is that he wants to suck up to Stalin. Neither Ike nor your President shares our distrust of the man, and neither of them foresees the obvious political problems over Berlin."

McLean was silent. Basically he agreed with the Englishman, but there was nothing he could do. His department had made its assessment. If the men in command chose to go the other way, there was nothing to be done. Anyway, everyone knew that Robertson had this particular bee buzzing in his bonnet. McLean glanced at him. His face was expressionless. He looked exhausted.

"I hear that the British Chiefs of Staff are condemning Ike's decision," he said.

Robertson nodded. "Yes. And yours?" he asked.

"They will back him," said McLean.

"God!" The word exploded from Robertson, like a dog barking angrily. "Well," he said, "this makes it even more imperative to find out what has happened to our men."

"Maybe it would help if you told me what they were up to."

Robertson stopped and looked up at McLean. "I would if I could," he said.

"You don't know?"

Robertson shook his head.

"You mean, it has come from the top?"

Robertson went through a little charade, puffing at an imaginary cigar, making a victory sign with his right hand. Then be began pacing again, almost bumping into a group of women pushing prams. McLean only half listened as Robertson muttered; something about the common herd: what did they know about decision-making or real problems? What worries did they have? They had the privilege of grumbling about those in charge; they could always blame someone; they could always shift the responsibility for their existence onto others; endlessly complacent, repeating their tired jokes and stale slogans. The dumb herd.

"What?" said McLean. What was he rambling about?

But now Robertson was smiling again, forcing the charm to wash through him. "I'm sorry, Jim," he said. "Just taking a mental crap, as you fellows would say." He held out his hand. "Do your best for me, won't you?" And he turned and walked away, moving fast.

McLean watched him go. It was unusual to see the man so exposed. He had never heard him grumble before, or use gutter language, even in fun. So the mission had been authorized from the top. Robertson did not know its objective. He wasn't sure if he believed it, but he would act as if he did; if there was any chance of a postmortem over this, then Jim McLean did not want to be on the slab. He always covered his exits and he was not about to change now. He resolved to do what he could for the Englishman.

He only hoped that the GIs hadn't kicked the shit out of the four Limeys.

13

Oppenheim, Germany, April 13, 1945

The door opened suddenly and the light zipped into the room, catching Harry Gresham in a crouch. His first reaction was to raise his arm across his eyes, but he resisted it; he simply sat and stared, the white glare seeming to light up the back of his skull like a flamethrower. He could feel his eyes begin to water and he wanted to curl up in a ball away from the brightness, like some dying animal, but he continued to stare defiantly ahead. How long had it been without light? Two, three days? He was not sure, even though he had been counting the changing of the guard; they might have switched routines just to confuse him.

"On your feet, boy." It was a Southern accent.

He remained where he was, crouched on the bench, pressing his toes hard against the floorboards, waiting for the blow and trying to guess where it would come from, behind the beam of the torch. He guessed wrongly and ducked into the fist as it bunched into his cheek, but as he spun to the side he grabbed out with both hands and got a grip of a leg, just enough to keep his balance as his knee clattered against the floor.

He was still falling as he struck upward flat-handed, aiming between the legs. He heard the familiar gasp, the sucking of breath, as he hit the spot, but as he struggled to his feet, reaching for the man's throat, he was grabbed from behind. Two long arms were clamped round his chest and his feet kicked away so that he stumbled. It seemed like he was always on the floor these days. He waited for the kick to the head or the neck, but it did not come. Instead the guard turned, still clutching himself in the groin, spat in Gresham's face and rubbed the spittle into his eyes with his thumb, cursing and grunting obscenities.

They dragged him backward into the corridor, and he squinted back at the tiny square cell where he had lived for—what was it?—seven, eight days. It seemed like forever, as if he had been born in the place; a box without light or heat, just a bench and a bowl and occasionally a meal thrown at him to keep him half alive.

There was no feeling in his legs as he tried to walk. He had slept badly and they would not respond. He was a sack of meat, and bad meat at that.

The big sergeant was looking down at him and smiling. Gresham remembered him. He was the sadistic one. Back home he would have been a sheriff from Alabama, kicking niggers all over the place. He would have loved that. He had tried to imagine them all back home. It was a game he had played in the darkness of his cell.

"We're moving up, English," he said cheerfully, his hands on his hips, a stub of a cheroot between his teeth. "We're going to war. Pity you're not coming with us. Coulda shot you, trying to escape." He guffawed and winked at the two men who were holding Gresham, and they grinned back dutifully.

"Seems, though, we have to send you back west somewhere. They're going to court-martial you. Maybe they got a firing squad for you." And he laughed again till he started coughing.

Gresham tried to speak, but there was no moisture in his mouth. He swallowed and coughed, the words coming out as a croak. The sergeant leaned toward him, his head on one side. "What's that you say, English?"

"Where are the others?"

"He wants to know where his friends are," the sergeant bellowed. "Probably wants to do a little kissing and cuddling with them. Is that right?" He tickled Gresham's chin. "You all are faggots, isn't that right? All Limeys is faggots...."

"Where?" said Gresham again.

"No idea, boy." The smile faded and he turned away, watching as they dragged Gresham outside. "If I had my way I'd send you back with the Kraut prisoners. I'd tell them you was a Jew. You'd be a pretty sight when you got to Belgium."

Gresham heard him laugh as they dragged him toward a truck. He was still laughing as they lifted him and threw him in the back and slammed the steel doors shut.

Again he was in darkness, blind and stiff. He peered at the crack in the door but he could see nothing, and as the engine jerked into life he was sent sprawling. He crawled to the side of the truck and tried to work out where he was going. The driver made two turns and the motion became smooth, as if they were on a big main road with few turns, probably an autobahn.

He ran his hand along the spine of the door, feeling for the nut that secured the handle. Perhaps when they came to get him he might have a chance to escape, but he doubted it. Anyway, there would be little reason. He discounted the idea that he was going to a court-martial; that would have been far too public. It was more likely that he was being taken back to British lines, where he would be able to get in touch with London. He was glad now that he had not attempted to escape from the Americans. He had given it serious thought and he was convinced that he might have got away. But what then? It would have been virtually impossible to have contacted London, and he did not know where the others were. Maybe he would have made it to Berlin alone, but he doubted it. He would have needed too much luck. Any operation needed its share of luck, but this would have demanded too much. No betting man would have backed him and Gresham always played along with the odds. Only fools went on suicide missions.

He decided to do nothing, just to wait and see what transpired. As he tried to find a comfortable spot, the driver dropped through the gears and came to a sudden stop, so that he was thrown onto his back again. He began to feel like a bean in a tin can, and every part of his body ached.

The door was flung open and he blinked again as two GIs reached for him, helping him out into the sunshine. He looked around. They had arrived at a deserted crossroads, and it occurred to him that perhaps he was going to be shot. It did not make any sense, but he had the feeling nonetheless. He looked to his left and his right and there was nothing but bare fields. No houses or barns anywhere, the only other object being a similar truck parked alongside.

He began to struggle, but the soldiers had a firm grip of him. They were dragging him toward the second truck, and when they reached the back of it he saw a group of six soldiers in a semicircle, holding their rifles to their shoulders and aiming them into the tailgate. For a moment Gresham wondered what was inside to justify such a show of force; perhaps a truckload of alligators. They're going to throw me to the alligators, he thought, and shook his head at the idea. He had been too long in solitary, he told himself. His mind was failing.

The soldiers pushed him forward, lifted him and threw him hard into the back of the truck so that he pitched onto his face, his nose smacking into a man's leg. The boot was enormous. He looked up into the grinning features of John Patterson and past him at Roth and Driscoll. They looked terrible, white-faced and blotchy, but he had time only to gain a quick impression before the door clanged shut and he was in darkness once more.

But now the odds had changed. Now, if need be, he could organize an escape. They should never have put them together. That was a big mistake.

"Hello, Harry." Driscoll's voice was hoarse, like his own, sandpaper on wood.

"Gentlemen," said Gresham. "Nice to see you."

They began talking at once, each with a story to tell, each one testing out his vocal chords. It was like a starving man with a food hamper. They could not stop, chattering aimlessly, gibberish, no one listening. They sounded like a pond of frogs. And they were still talking all at once when the truck slowed and stopped. They fell silent and listened as it reversed, made a right-angle turn, moved forward and turned once more, going back the way they had come.

Gresham frowned. What in God's name was going on?

The answer arrived immediately when the grille in the front of the truck snapped back to reveal the face of the driver.

"Good afternoon, boys," said a pleasant voice. "Bill Rodgers, Sixty-fourth Division, Intelligence Corps, taking you to war."

Gresham crawled to the grille and pressed his face against it.

"What's happening?" he asked.

"Sorry about all this toing and froing, but the men would have got a little uppity if they thought you were getting off scot-free. Got to let them think you're being taken west."

"You've been in touch with London?"

"They've been in touch with us," said Rodgers. "You guys have certainly got protection. Have a good trip." And the grille was snapped shut once more.

Gresham sat back and relaxed for the first time in three weeks.

They were all asleep when the truck finally arrived at its destination. It was dark and they had no idea how far they had traveled. The door was pulled open and they had their first look at Rodgers, a small man with a crooked grin and a battered face.

Gresham hopped down, stretched his arms and bent down to rub his legs. "Took a chance," he said, "coming solo."

Rodgers's grin widened. "That's why I told you early. Didn't want you plotting evil back there."

Gresham looked around him. They were in a yard of what seemed to be a small farm, just a whitewashed house and one barn, apparently deserted.

"Twelfth Army is pushing for Magdeburg," said Rodgers. "Should be there by the weekend, and then it's just a kick in the ass away from Berlin."

"And where are we?" asked Gresham.

Rodgers hopped back into the cab and returned with a map. He pointed out the location to Gresham. "A day and a half from Berlin," he said. "You're to stay here till you get fit. Me, I'm the nursemaid."

"How did you get this job?" asked Gresham.

"I guess somebody doesn't like me." But the grin on his face showed that he didn't care. It seemed to Gresham that Rodgers was the kind of soldier who didn't care too much about anything.

"You'll find plenty of food and drink inside," he said. "And you shouldn't be bothered. This place is pretty isolated."

"And if anyone turns up?"

"You still have your papers?"

Gresham patted the pocket of his tunic and Rodgers nodded. "I'll look in each day," he said. "You're to be ready to go anytime." He squinted at Gresham, looking at the bruises under his eyes. "How long before you guys are fit?"

"Five minutes," said Gresham.

"Care to tell me what you're up to?"

"No."

"Thought not." He climbed back into the cab, kicked the gearstick and spun the wheel. As the truck lurched away he waved back at them.

"Nice chap," said Driscoll.

"For a Yank," said Roth trudging off toward the house. It was only then that they saw the limp. They would have to ask him about that.

They scoured the place like scavengers, looting the cupboards and squealing like children at a party, ripping the legs from the chickens, stabbing at the ham and screwing the tops from the bottles of beer. They ate standing up, saying nothing, the only sound the noise of jaws and the slapping of tongues. When the first ravages of hunger had left him, Gresham wandered to the window of the kitchen and stared out over the fields. After they had gorged themselves he waved them upstairs, saying that he would take the first watch. The others looked at him, wondering if such a precaution was needed, but he said it was. He did not want to be caught napping.

They nodded sleepily and moved upstairs. As he stared out into the dusk, his stomach full and his mind half asleep, he felt at peace and he thanked God for the Americans. They had added an extra ingredient to the team. They had made them angry and welded them together. It was a sobering thought.

The soldier lay on his bunk, his arms behind his head. He was dozing and contentedly waiting for his dinner. He had thought everything out and had come to the conclusion that things could have been a lot worse. The shame of being taken prisoner was offset by the fact that the war was lost anyway, and if he'd had to make the choice he would have picked the Americans as his captors.

Rather the Americans than the Russians. He had seen enough of the Russians since the early days of the Winter War and the six months of the '42 campaign. He could do without Russians. They were barbarians. Hadn't he personally accounted for three of them at close range, and God knows how many more when he was in charge of the howitzers?

No, the Americans were all right. He was lucky. Others had not made it. The action which led to his capture had been fierce, a mortar bomb exploding far too close killing two of his men and wounding another. Eventually when it became apparent that they had no chance, he had been relieved to discover that his commanding officer had made the obvious decision to surrender, having conveniently forgotten the Führer's decree that they fight to the last bullet. Some of the ranks had been reluctant to give in; the fools, they were the sheep, the idiots who believed everything they were told, mindless creatures who, even now, would cheer if the Führer were to walk into the room. They even believed Goebbels's nonsense about some new wonder weapon. They would lap up everything they were given, but not he, not Gunnar Grashof.

As for the future, he had nothing to fear. When the war was over he would go back to Hamburg and a new life. From what he had heard, the Americans were planning to pour massive aid into Germany. They could not afford to let it collapse into one big potato field as someone had suggested; they would build up the economy as a buffer against the Russians. It was obvious; and he would be a part of the new Germany, of that he was certain. There would be construction instead of destruction and plenty to sing about.

He smiled to himself and drifted into a gentle slumber, the chatter of the other soldiers washing round him. At first he did not notice the guard at his side or hear his name, and he grunted angrily when the man shook him roughly by the shoulder. He opened his eyes and swore. He was not accustomed to being treated like this.

The GI was grinning at him and pointing with his thumb to the door. Slowly Grashof rose from the bed, smoothed down his tunic and marched out of the barracks, his chin held high. They were probably going to transfer him to officers' quarters, he thought, away from the rabble. Silently he cursed the GI, who was prodding him between the shoulder blades. The oaf. What right had he to treat him in such a manner?

He was taken across the compound to a hut which served as the barracks headquarters. Maybe he was to be interrogated. Well, he would welcome the chance to say nothing, to stand to attention and give only his name, rank and number while they tried all they knew to get him to talk. He would show them how silent he could be.

There were two men in the hut, standing by a desk. Gunnar Grashof heard the door close behind him and he looked around; just the two men, a small American, grinning at him, an arrogant type. The other gazed at him without expression. For the first time Grashof felt an involuntary shudder run up his spine, and he coughed to make sure they had not noticed.

He knew enough English to understand that they were talking about him, his height and his weight. They were looking him up and down like undertakers. He stiffened as the American mentioned his name to the fair-haired man.

He decided to take the initiative.

"What is happening?" he asked in his best accent.

"Be quiet!" said the American.

He glared at them, hoping that they had noted his displeasure.

At first when he heard the command he did not believe it. It could not be. He blinked as the fair-haired man stepped up to him, stared him in the face and repeated it. And now the apprehension grew in him. Briefly he thought of refusing, but there was no life in the man's eyes. He would think nothing of striking him, Grashof was sure of that.

"In there," said the American, gesturing toward a door at the back of the room.

He moved to it with as much dignity as he could muster, and opened the door. It was a tiny room, the air fetid like a stable, and three men stared up at him, two frightened-looking men and a giant, all staring up at him like oxen and wearing only blankets.

Slowly he unbuttoned his jacket and handed it to the American. He paused for a moment, then felt a finger poking at the base of his spine. He slipped out of his trousers and took off his shirt, standing shivering in his underwear.

"And the rest," said the American.

He swallowed nervously and undressed, standing naked and cold.

"Sit," said the American as though he were addressing a dog.

He moved next to the giant, holding his hands over his groin, and squatted on the bench. As the door was shut on him he began to wonder if Goebbels had been right and that Americans took delight in torturing and killing their prisoners.

One of the men was muttering something, and Grashof bent to hear him. It was Kesselring's decree to the troops: "Who does not live in honor will die in shame."

Grashof shivered, shook uncontrollably and fought to hold back the tears.

14

London, April 15, 1945

The Cabinet Office briefing room was stuffy that afternoon, the spring sun slanting through the venetian blinds and slicing through layers of cigarette and cigar smoke so that the stenographer was forced to shake his head every few minutes and rub his eyes. He had never known such a meeting. It seemed as though it would go on forever. There were representatives from the Foreign Office and the various military departments, men from the U.S. army and its intelligence service, all with something to say, each one gazing in rapt attention as the dapper little man from SIS rose to speak.

Like the others, Charles Robertson wore a black armband, having come direct from a memorial service for Franklin Roosevelt, who was being mourned in Britain as if he had been Prime Minister.

He took off his spectacles, folded the legs and placed them precisely in front of him, the lenses upward. He paused for a moment before speaking.

"Gentlemen, I have spoken at these briefings many times and given you statements and assessments based on intelligence gathered from our agents throughout Europe. I have done this in my capacity as an adviser, and in many cases I have been gratified to see that you have acted on that advice. For that I praise you. On the occasions you have chosen to reject my advice, I forgive you."

A murmur of laughter trickled through the room but came to a premature halt. There was no trace of humor on Robertson's face. He was being deadly serious. He held up one hand before continuing.

"Today I come not to advise, but to beseech you to use your combined influence toward one end." He paused and placed a sheet of paper on the table in front of him.

"Exhibit one, if I may so call it," he said, "dated March twenty-nine, a message from President Roosevelt to Marshal Stalin, and I quote: 'I cannot conceal from you the concern with which I view the developments of events of mutual interest since our fruitful meeting in Yalta. So far there has been a discouraging lack of progress made in the carrying out, which the world expects, of the political decisions which we reached at the conference. I am frankly puzzled as to why this should be and must tell you that I do not fully understand in many respects the apparent indifferent attitude of your government.' "

He looked around the faces, noting the various reactions before continuing. "March thirty, gentlemen. A radio message from General Eisenhower to Field Marshal Montgomery." A second slip of paper fluttered onto the desk. " 'That place,' meaning Berlin, 'has become, so far as I am concerned, nothing but a geographical location and I have never been interested in these.' General Eisenhower, as you are aware, believes that the decision to leave Berlin to the Russians means no change in basic military strategy, and he argues that by pushing to the south, the city will fall more quickly."

There was an unmistakable sneer in his voice and some of the listeners glanced across at Jim McLean of OSS, but the man remained impassive. If he was annoyed by Robertson's jibe, he gave no sign.

Robertson spoke again. "The following day, Churchill to Roosevelt: 'If we deliberately leave Berlin to them,' meaning the Russians, 'this may strengthen their conviction, already apparent, that they have done everything. Further, I do not consider that Berlin has yet lost its military, and certainly not its political, significance. While Berlin remains under the German flag it cannot in my opinion fail to be the most decisive point in Germany. Therefore I should greatly prefer persistence with the plan in which we crossed the Rhine, namely that the Ninth U.S. Army should march with the Twenty-first Army Group to the Elbe and beyond to Berlin.'

"Then again, on April one, Churchill to Roosevelt: 'The Russian armies will no doubt overrun all Austria and enter Vienna. If they also take Berlin, will not their impression that they have been the overwhelming contributor to our common victory be unduly imprinted on their minds and may not this lead them into a mood which will raise grave and formidable difficulties in the future?' "

Robertson tapped the table with his knuckles. "Remember, gentlemen, that this cable was dated April one, known popularly as April Fools' Day. I leave you to judge who is the fool."

This time McLean made no attempt to hide his anger. Robertson had intended to insult him. He had come out into the open.

Now the papers were falling on the desk like autumn leaves.

"Stalin to General Deane: 'Berlin has lost its former strategic importance. The Soviet High Command therefore plans to allot secondary forces in the direction of Berlin.' And, gentlemen, if you believe that, you believe anything. This was followed by Churchill again cabling Roosevelt, urging once more that the Allies go for the capital. He was not so easily fooled."

He stared round the room, stopping to linger on the face of each man individually. "Which brings us to the present," he said slowly. "I understand from my colleagues in the U.S. military department that General Patton recently urged Eisenhower to let him take the capital, pointing out that it could be done in forty-eight hours. I would add that German troops have been falling back in confusion, one general even going so far as to inform Montgomery of the existence of a cache of gas bombs. The intelligent ones in the Wehrmacht have long been aware that the war is lost to them. I would also point out that General Simpson's Second Armored and Eighty-third Infantry divisions could attack down the autobahn and be in the city in two days, there being only isolated enemy units in their path."

He gazed at McLean. "Am I not correct, Mr. McLean?"

McLean nodded. "This is our information," he said steadily.

Robertson cleared his throat. "What I am saying, gentlemen, is that the U.S. and Russian armies are virtually equidistant from Berlin at this moment, and I am suggesting that a joint communique be sent to Eisenhower within the hour informing him of our combined advice to go for the city immediately. The importance of this cannot be over-emphasized."

He gathered his papers together like a courtroom lawyer and turned away toward the door. "An hour, gentlemen," he said and left the room.

For a moment there was silence and then everyone seemèd to be talking at once, murmuring to one another, stretching, lighting pipes, like an audience at the end of a play.

Alan Francis did not move. To his right he could hear the words of two Foreign Office Civil Servants.

"What was that all about, do you think?"

"For the benefit of the record, I shouldn't wonder. The chap's got his eye on the House. He was getting in some practice, I expect."

"So that he could say 'I told you so' in the future."

"Quite."

Francis pushed back his seat and left the room, wondering what would happen in an hour when they had refused to act on Robertson's advice. What would he do? What *could* he do?

He left the building and saw Robertson marching along Whitehall. He had ignored the car, preferring to walk. Francis followed him, noting the jaunty manner of his stride. But he knew it was an illusion of good health. Audrey had said that occasionally he took sleeping pills. He was under some strain; there was no doubt about it, but only rarely did it show through. And only those who knew him intimately could detect the signs.

He had installed a teletype machine in his flat and pinned a campaign map on the wall. Rarely was there any sherry or talk of the weather, or the little rituals of polite behavior. He had dispensed with the trivialities so as to concentrate completely on the job in hand.

Again, as he stepped up the pace to keep his boss in view, Francis asked himself why he had never simply come out with a question about Harry Gresham, why he did not confront him with it. Not that there was anything sinister in the connection; it was just that something stopped him, told him to hold back: the itch again, the hunch. And the other day when he had gone to the flat and asked about Nordhausen. He remembered the conversation syllable by syllable.

"Quite a discovery, sir," he had said.

"Oh, yes," Robertson replied abstractedly.

"Quite something to come across all that V-2 hardware."

"Yes."

"And the blueprints."

"Mmmm."

And that was all; no mention of the man in Berlin with the rocket secrets, no connection whatsoever. In itself it was nothing, but Francis had filed it away for future reference. And now this strange virtuoso performance. It was all very odd.

It took Robertson twelve minutes to walk back to the office, and for three-quarters of an hour he sat motionless at his desk. His instructions to his secretary were explicit, that only one call was to be put through to him.

At four thirty he picked up the phone, dialed a number and waited. The answer to his question was a single-syllable reply. Robertson said "I see," gently replaced the receiver, smoothed back his hair, picked up his coat and left the office. He took the lift three floors down, looking straight ahead all the way so that he did not see Alan Francis moving behind him, watching as he went inside.

Francis felt slightly foolish, like a second-rate private detective, but nonetheless he waited by the radio room, nervously smoking a cigarette. Robertson was inside for three minutes, and when he re-appeared he marched straight down the corridor and downstairs and out of the building. Francis waited for a moment, then opened the door, nodding to Ron the operator. He moved among the wire machines, glancing idly at the copy as it flowed onto the desks. He was waiting for Ron to say something, knowing that the man was an obsessive chatter merchant who couldn't stand a silence.

"Just had your boss in here," he said at last.

"Oh, yes."

"Clever man, Mr. Robertson."

"Brilliant."

He allowed a few moments to pass so that he would not appear too eager. "Was it the military report he was looking for?"

"No. Transmitting," said Ron.

"Oh."

He waited, knowing that the man would offer more.

"Comes in regular, uses the machine in the booth." He nodded toward the back of the room to a small cubicle like a telephone box.

Again Francis let some time pass before moving over. There was a radio in the booth, a teleprinter and a shelf stacked with files.

He turned with a start as Ron came up behind him. "That's his file," Ron said, reaching past him and picking out a slim folder.

Francis thanked him and glanced at it. There were a dozen radio reports, each with a geographical position, and a time slug and a set of numbers. The latest was dated and timed just five minutes earlier.

"Seems he's been talking to the front," Francis ventured.

Ron peered over his shoulder. "Wiesbaden," he said.

"And the message?"

"Code," Ron sniffed. "All in code. Could be anything."

"Maybe he has a woman in Wiesbaden," Francis said, grinning foolishly.

"Shouldn't think so."

Francis had forgotten. The man had no sense of humor. Carefully Ron took the file back and slipped it gently into place. Francis wished him good afternoon and made his way back to the office. He was none the wiser, but the itch in his brain continued to nag at him. He would have to do something about it.

The signal took ten minutes to reach Bill Rodgers. The radio operator ran to his tent with the message. Seeing the priority heading, Rodgers sprinted to the truck, hoisted himself aboard, fired the motor and spun away toward the farmhouse.

Gresham was asleep when he arrived and at first Patterson was reluctant to waken him, until Rodgers insisted.

He wakened fast, took the message to the table he was using as a desk, flipped through a paperback book until he found the page he wanted, counted down the lines and across, then mouthed the one word: "Scuttle." Then he turned to Patterson who was looking blankly at him.

"We're off," he said. "Berlin."

"Eric Ruhland, private."

"Present, Herr Leutnant," said Patterson.

"Werner Schlem, corporal."

"Here," said Driscoll.

"Holger Sturm, private."

"Here, already," shouted Roth, and Patterson grinned at him. Roth had kept up the banter nonstop as they changed into the uniforms, jokes about the only Jewish Nazi, complaints about the smell of German sweat, jokes about the goosestep. He had even strutted around the yard singing the "Horst Wessel Song," until Driscoll had told him to shut up.

They stood in the yard, tugging at their sleeves and stamping their feet to get accustomed to the boots. Patterson ran his finger round the collar of his tunic. "This is too big," he said.

"What?" Roth squealed at him.

"How did they capture this bloke?" said Patterson, muttering to himself. "Must have been as big as a bear."

Gresham leaned into the truck, dragged out the weapons and handed them out—the Mausers, the Sturmgewehrs and the Walther pistols—watching as the men checked them out; Driscoll swore softly as he dropped the pistol in the mud. "Damned things," he grunted. "No good for anything."

"They're all right for throwing at somebody," said Roth. "As a last resort."

Driscoll swore again. He'd never met a soldier yet who had a good word to say about pistols. On this operation they were being carried for decoration. Nothing more.

Roth was fumbling in his pack, checking that he had his killing knife. He would not move without it. At first there had been an argument. Gresham did not want him to take it, he was worried that a British-issue weapon might cause problems, but Roth had argued that he could have taken it from a dead British soldier, or a prisoner. And the others backed him up. They all had their knives and they felt better for it.

"Ready?" asked Gresham. They nodded.

Rodgers whistled as he saw them, grinning as the three men climbed into the back of the truck and Gresham pulled himself into the passenger seat.

They drove for twenty minutes toward Stendal, and turned off the road onto a farm track.

"Want to see the map?" he asked, but Gresham shook his head. He knew the area blindfolded. The map was burned into his memory.

"Two miles to the autobahn," said Rodgers. "You shouldn't have any problems. The Ninth Army is in a state of total confusion and the local civilians are said to be helping deserters."

Gresham nodded. "And did you manage to get the papers?" he asked.

Rodgers delved into his jacket and pulled out an envelope. "Movement orders, compliments of U.S. Intelligence. They will see you through to Berlin. You're supposed to be joining Steiner."

Gresham flipped the envelope open and glanced at the papers.

"They're not perfect," said Rodgers, "but they should convince any Kraut NCO who asks to see them."

"Thanks," said Gresham, slipping them into his tunic.

Briefly they shook hands, and Rodgers watched as Gresham climbed out of the truck and made his way up the track, followed by the others in single file.

"Good luck," he said, talking to himself, "whatever it is you're doing." He watched them until they vanished into the dusk, then reversed the truck back into the road.

Half an hour later he was back at his billet to find the communications tent a surge of excitement, men rushing to and fro like ants, with messages and bulletins.

He grabbed at one of them. "What's up?" he asked.

"The Russians," the man said. "They've restarted their offensive. Millions of the bastards heading for Berlin."

Gresham waited until the sound of the truck had died away before holding up his hand and ushering the three men into the side of the road. It was already dark and the lane was deserted. They stood in a semicircle round him, and he looked from one to the other before speaking.

"You probably realize that I had to wait until now before spelling out the details of the operation," he said slowly. "I had my orders. We did not want the possibility of a slip of the tongue, however innocent." He paused.

The others waited for him to continue, saying nothing.

"It will be a fast job, into Berlin and straight out again with a German general in tow."

Roth whistled and opened his mouth to speak, but Gresham silenced him. "It is simpler than it sounds," he said. "The man wants to come. He knows we are on our way."

"Why?" said Patterson.

Gresham shrugged. "All I know is that he has been offered some deal. We are to get to him before the Russians."

"And do we have a contact in the city?" asked Driscoll.

Gresham nodded. "A woman," he said. "One of our agents used her for eighteen months until he was killed."

"Used her?" Roth repeated, frowning.

"She is a whore," said Gresham.

The three men looked at him with added interest.

"Our man found her in a brothel in the early days. She was quite valuable, I understand, unwittingly, of course. Pillow talk, diplomats and majors. She thinks he is still alive."

For a moment there was silence, then Roth chuckled. "The general and the prostitute," he said. "Sounds like fun."

"A piece of cake," said Patterson. "Nothing could be simpler."

"Questions?" said Gresham.

"When do we start?" said Roth grinning, his teeth flashing in the dusk.

Gresham again looked from one to the other before getting to his feet and moving down the track, the others scrambling to catch up.

It took them an hour to reach the autobahn. Gresham stepped straight onto the shoulder of the road and continued walking without a pause. They moved silently through the night, seeing no one, slipping through the gap of no-man's-land between the two armies, stopping every hour for a ten-minute pause.

Just before dawn, Gresham began hunting for somewhere they could rest. They left the autobahn, walked a kilometer up a farm track to a small copse and stretched out for four hours, each man taking an hour's watch. Again they set out, until Gresham had calculated that they were twenty-five miles from the city and close to the German lines. They began to move parallel to the autobahn until they came in sight of a village. They stopped and Gresham dipped into his pack, pulled out his binoculars and gazed ahead. There was no movement in the place, but he could see two gray military vehicles parked by the road.

Nodding to the others he stepped out into the middle of the road and marched toward the village, his rifle held by his side, waiting for the challenge that would soon come.

When the voice shouted "Halt!" he waved his arms in the air and smiled, looking for all the world as if he was glad to be home.

15

Berlin, April 18, 1945

The monster which was born to live for a thousand years was thrashing around in its death agony, its heart rotten, its skull smashed into rubble, its brain barely functioning forty feet underground, a diseased, blind brain sending out messages along withered nerves to limbs which had long since been amputated. The beast was insane, and waited in a trap of its own design for its inevitable end. . . .

"Time for your walk, Herr General."

Bergner struggled awake, trying to free his mind from nightmares of dying monsters, grunting as he shook himself.

"Four o'clock, Herr General." The voice had the wheedling tone of a hospital orderly clucking at an old infirm patient. Time for walkies. Like a man talking to a dog.

Slowly Bergner raised himself from the narrow bed and reached for his jacket. He ignored the SS guard and made his way to the washstand, splashing some cold water onto his face and coming instantly awake.

"I have work to do," he said, speaking into the bowl. He would not deign to turn round and face his captor.

"But it is four o'clock. We always take our walk at this time."

"Well, we are not taking our walk today," he snapped.

"Very well, Herr General." The man moved away, smiling, waiting for Bergner to follow him. After a few moments Bergner turned and allowed himself to be escorted out of the room. Had he not gone, he would have been forced to remain alone for another seven hours until the next exercise period; not even Bormann could help him now, such was the anger of the Führer, crazy in his belief that all his generals were conspiring against him. It was better not to provoke him, Bormann had said; the man was quite capable of ordering his execution. It was no empty threat; it had happened to others. And so Bergner had accepted the situation knowing it would be temporary. The Russians would soon be here.

The guard stood back to let him pass, and Bergner tried to ignore the surly grin on the man's face. He climbed the stairs to the Chancellery garden, feeling a stiffness behind his knees that had not been apparent before. He was cracking up, there was no doubt about it, his body rebelling against the conditions in which he was living.

And now he could smell the dust and feel the smoke in his lungs. You could hide in the ground like a rabbit for only so long, he thought, but eventually you had to come up for air and face reality. He wondered whether the Führer could ever face it again or whether he would remain with his illusions, whether he would ever come up to face his new masters or stay where he was forever, in his burrow.

He coughed as the dust swirled into his throat, and grimaced at the constant whine of the ventilator that blew bad air round the bunker, adding to the lethargy and the bad temper of the occupants.

The usual guard was waiting for him, four men with their rifles held loosely, standing at ease. When he appeared at the top of the stairs they came to attention; at least they still did that. He was still permitted a facade of respect.

The air was warm and damp, but there was no sign of spring. Those trees which had been left standing were stripped of their leaves, dead in the mild sunshine. Slowly he wandered out into the street and across to the Wilhelmplatz. Briefly he had a childish desire to run away, just to see what would happen, but he fought it and walked slowly eastward. A group of soldiers marched past and saluted him. He returned the salute and wondered what would happen if he ordered them to find him a jeep and take him away. But it would have been merely an embarrassment for everyone. The SS would have forbidden it; they were the rulers of what was left of Berlin.

The city was a crumbling slum now and Bergner picked his way over the rubble, vaguely taking in the images in front of him but scarcely conscious of detail. To his right, a boy in Hitler Youth uniform with a bandage round his head was digging a tank trap and giving orders to little children. He looked about fourteen years old. Fifty yards farther on, a line of women in coats and boots, their hair tied in scarves, were leaning against a wall, clumsily trying to aim their anti-tank bazookas across the street while a sergeant bellowed instructions at them.

Bergner shook his head. "Women and children," he muttered.

The guards looked at one another as he spoke, thinking at first that he was talking to them, but it became obvious that this was a private conversation.

"So it has come to this," he was saying. "Housewives and school-children . . . small bodies, small hearts . . ."

He walked for two kilometers, turning left and right, passing through squares and up alleyways littered with debris. There was no pattern to his movement. He simply turned when he felt like it, doubling back, passing between the guards and seemingly unaware of their presence. It all looked the same to him now, just a mass of destruction.

He stopped so abruptly that one of the guards stumbled against him, and they were asking him what was wrong, why had he gone so pale, before following his gaze up the alley to the lamppost where the soldier hung, his neck broken, revolving gently. As they watched, the bloated face swung into view, the tongue black and protruding and the message scrawled in ink on a placard on his chest:

I am a traitor to my Führer.

It was nothing new, the guard was thinking as he looked back into Bergner's face. Such fat fruit hung all over the city. They deserved their fate. But Bergner was transfixed as though he had never seen a corpse before.

"You are sick, Herr General?"

Bergner said nothing. He stood silently, his lips moving as if in a silent prayer, thinking of the soldier on the wing of the Heinkel, and now here was another, hanging out to dry like so much washing. Maybe they were brothers, he and the man on the wing; certainly they had something in common, for neither had been killed by the enemy.

"Herr General."

Bergner turned sharply, pulling away from the hand at his elbow. He walked fast now, heading back toward the Chancellery, looking around him to get his bearings. He wanted to get back underground, to seek the burrow. Grumbling to himself, he pushed his way through a column of civilians trudging home from work, their faces grimy and pinched. He felt no compassion for them. It was they who had brought this madman to power and who had allowed him to keep that power while men died on airplanes or choked on lampposts. They had cheered him at Nuremberg, blindly signed their oaths of allegiance and gone into battle with songs on their lips.

Again he stopped. Thirty yards across the Charlottenburger Chaussee a group of men crouched on the pavement, busily working on something; beside them lay a strange, brown, inanimate mass. Slowly Bergner moved toward them, narrowing his eyes to focus better. The first object he recognized was the head, lying two yards away from the body and grinning into the sky, the bit still in its mouth and the reins trailing away into the gutter.

As he approached, one of the men glanced over his shoulder and gazed at him sullenly for a moment before returning to his task. In a canvas bag by his left hand lay the hunks of roughly cut meat, and still they scrabbled inside the horse, hacking and scrabbling, oblivious to anything but the butchering.

Bergner turned away and began to run, his legs moving stiffly, and the SS men had to move quickly to keep him in sight. They were not sure if they heard what he was saying. Later they put it together, the scraps of words and meaningless phrases, something about snow and horses' legs and a heart the size of a baby's . . . and something about a siege and that soon it would snow and cover everything up. But they knew it never snowed in April. Not even a general could make it snow in April, especially this general. . . .

Christa Schiller hurried home, clutching the bread under her jacket and moving fast, staring straight ahead. She had queued for an hour for this loaf and it would take only a few seconds for some fat hausfrau to wrestle it away from her, so she kept to the outside of the pavement away from the shop fronts and the doors of the lobbies.

Two soldiers passed close to her, but they ignored her. None of the men looked twice at her now and she could not blame them. Under the shapeless jacket and the tin hat she might have been somebody's grandmother scuttling homeward, rather than an object of desire. The thought amused her. It was another life. Now she lived from day to day, thinking only of survival. At night she sheltered with the others in cellars, and during the day she scrabbled for food. Sometimes there was no warning of the Mosquito raids: families died in their beds and later their friends searched for them, questioning neighbors and counting heads in the shelters. As often as not they were met with a shrug. The dead were dead, the missing were missing, and those who were alive had little time for them.

As she turned a corner she felt her hat slip to one side and she grabbed at it, noticing a small boy grin at her. It was ludicrous, one of the city's most highly paid prostitutes clutching a loaf and wearing a tin hat. Around her waist she carried a water bottle to fill up at the standpipe. That would be another queue. Everything was a queue these days. You queued to survive. But it would not be long before even that basic law would cease to apply and people would fight like animals.

The old would be the first to suffer, but soon the weakness would affect everyone. Already Christa was aware of the lethargy brought on by bad diet. She would fall asleep at odd times and she needed two or three naps to get through the day.

She crossed Friedrichstrasse and turned into her street, clawing her way over a pile of bricks into the alleyway to the front door of the apartment building. The entrance was scrawled with chalk messages and phone numbers. Occasionally strangers would arrive and copy down the numbers. It was all they could do, with the telephones useless and the post nonexistent. They were like tribesmen leaving messages for each other on trees. Soon, she thought, it would be smoke signals. She glanced at the door. There was a new message. Frau Haag had gone, leaving an address for her son to find her. Christa was glad. The old woman was a busybody, forever poking her nose into other people's business. No one would miss her.

Automatically she glanced up the lobby before entering, then sprinted for the stairs so that she was panting by the time she reached her landing, the key already in her hand.

She quickly let herself in, leaned back against the door and gazed at the biggest soldier she had ever seen. Beside him stood three others. Her mind searched for explanations. And then the smell hit her. The apartment was like a cowshed. By the look of these men they had not washed for days. She blinked as one of the men got up from his seat and moved toward her, his hand held up palm outward in a gesture which seemed to say that there was nothing to worry about.

He spoke with a slight Bavarian accent, and as she listened she felt the tears well in her eyes. It was going to be all right. They had arrived. It was just like the cinema. Rescue. In the nick of time.

The introductions having been made, Gresham led Christa into the kitchen and closed the door.

"You are even prettier than they told me."

The compliment sounded forced and mannered, but so what? thought Christa. It was nice. Compliments were always welcome, even if they were paid for a reason.

"Have you been here long?" he asked.

"Three months."

"Visitors?"

"The occasional soldier."

"Gestapo?"

"No." She wondered what he was getting at; first the compliment, then the interrogation.

"SS?"

"No."

She decided to take the initiative.

"How's Peter?" she asked quickly.

"Very well. He sends you his . . . regards." There was just the correct length of pause, as if he was slightly embarrassed.

She closed her eyes and sighed. It was perfect. Peter was alive.

"Where is he?"

"In London."

"And will I be permitted to see him?"

"Of course."

She smiled. It was too good to believe. In her imagination she saw Peter in London, standing in front of Buckingham Palace. He would take her to all those places she had seen in the newsreels, the Tower, Big Ben . . . they would walk through Regent's Park and take tea in the Ritz, like young lovers . . . but she permitted herself only a moment of daydreaming. She knew the danger of dreams; far better, as she had learned years ago, to expect the worst so that anything good turned up as a bonus. The soldier was speaking to her again, more urgently this time.

"You have been in touch with the general?"

"Yes."

"Can we meet him tonight?"

She shook her head. Of course, he would not know. "I have never actually met the man."

Gresham frowned. "What do you mean?" He seemed confused, his original brusqueness gone. To Christa he looked like a small boy who had been told it was not his birthday after all.

"He's been held in the Chancellery bunker," she said, and his frown deepened. "Virtually a prisoner."

Gresham shook his head, like a boxer who has taken a surprise punch, and for the first time Christa felt a shiver of apprehension. Surely it did not matter. They would find a way. "It seems that the Führer no longer trusts him," she continued, wishing that he would say something and not just stare like that, into space. "He is allowed out, though, twice a day."

Gresham looked up. "Where does he go?"

"It depends. He just wanders around."

"But he is alone?"

"No. There is always a number of SS with him."

Gresham spat out a word which Christa had not heard before, a sharp English curse, probably obscene and certainly expressive. He walked around the small kitchen, clenching and unclenching his hands while Christa tried to find something to say that might help.

"I see my cousin each day," she offered.

He turned and looked at her. "Ah, yes, Frau Müller," he said.

Christa nodded. How did he know Angela's name? She was tempted to ask, but again he was firing a question at her.

"When do you see her?"

"She comes every afternoon, usually around two."

Gresham glanced at his watch. "I'd like to meet her," he said.

"Of course."

"And may we stay here until we've made contact?"

"By all means. And if you need to remain overnight, there's a flat downstairs which might be empty."

"Good. Would you show me it, please?"

She led him out into the living room, where the others sat motionless and silent.

Gresham snapped his fingers, and Driscoll and Patterson got to their feet. He told Roth to stay where he was and followed Christa out of the flat and downstairs, the others behind him.

Frau Haag's flat was locked, but Patterson bent low, took a pin from his collar and began working the lock. For a moment he stopped as an old woman passed them on her way downstairs, but the interruption did not last long and soon the door clicked open and they went inside. It was a large flat, barely furnished, with nothing to show anyone had lived there.

"You stay here," said Gresham. "Get some sleep, and a wash."

They nodded. Christa and Gresham returned upstairs.

"Right. I'm going to sleep," he said. "Would you be good enough to wake me when your cousin arrives?"

"Of course." She watched as he stretched out on the single bed. The other man, the small one, was already asleep. For a moment she stood gazing at them, then turned and made her way into the living room.

Angela arrived on time, knocked once and entered without waiting to be admitted. She stood in the hallway sniffing as if she had entered a farmyard. Christa greeted her.

"I have someone who wants to meet you," she said coyly, leading her by the hand and ignoring her questions. She tapped on the bedroom door and a moment later Gresham appeared, his hair tousled, his eyes puffy with sleep.

Christa introduced them and Gresham led Angela into the room. They were alone for fifteen minutes. Christa could hear his voice, muffled and insistent. When Angela reappeared she was nodding in agreement at something he had said. Christa looked at Gresham with new admiration. If he could get through to Angela, she thought, he could do anything. She watched as Angela left the flat, then turned to the kitchen to make some coffee.

At three forty-five Gresham and Driscoll left the flat, clattered down the stairs and stepped into the street. They felt confident. They had their papers in their pockets and they knew they would not be challenged. Even if an officer chanced upon them, he would pay them no attention. The army was acting out a farce and every soldier knew it.

Christa's flat, in a street to the east of Friedrichstrasse, was a ten-minute walk from the Chancellery and the two men strolled twice past the building before turning into Wilhelmplatz. There they stood together, talking about nothing, just two soldiers of the Reich waiting for the final battle, waiting with the rest to defend the streets of the city to the last bullet as the Führer had ordered.

Gresham looked at his watch and glanced across at the Chancellery gates. He tapped Driscoll on the arm and they made their way across to Wilhelmstrasse as the group emerged through the shattered entrance archway and turned north. The man looked older than the photograph Gresham had seen, and they passed close enough to him to see the frown on his face and the movement of his lips.

They let the group pass and walk fifty yards ahead before they turned and followed them; even from a distance they could see Bergner stop at random, shaking his head on occasions.

"He's crazy," said Driscoll quietly.

Gresham nodded in agreement.

"So?" asked Driscoll.

"It changes nothing," said Gresham. "Just makes it more difficult."

"What was it Patterson said?" Driscoll muttered. "A piece of cake."

"Not anymore," said Gresham. "Think of it as a challenge."

Driscoll glanced across at him to see if the man was attempting to be jocular. But there was no mirth in him. He was deadly serious.

Later that day Angela found Bergner alone in his room, and passed on the envelope Gresham had given her. He said nothing, merely nodded, and did not appear to take any interest in the letter. She shrugged as she closed the door. It was none of her business. She did not really understand what it was all about. She did not know either why the fair-haired soldier was so interested in Herr Bormann. Perhaps it was just natural curiosity on his part. Anyway, as she told herself again, it was no concern of hers. She had done what he had asked and now she could get on with her work.

◀ **16** ▶

Berlin, April 18, 1945 (evening)

It had been such a long time since she had done anything like it, and she felt foolish as she strolled through the streets. She could not remember how long it had been; years, many, many years. She felt like an adolescent again, in the days before she was properly organized. It had come full circle and she was back again to the days of mincing through the darkened streets, painted like a clown. But if this was to help get her out of the city, then so be it. She had no choice.

The first soldier who approached her was unsuitable and she moved away fast, leaving the man flabbergasted. It must have been the first time he had ever been turned down by a whore. She smiled to herself; the poor man would probably never get over it.

She stood now in a doorway off the Friedrichstrasse, her shoulders pressed against the tiles of the lobby, shrinking back as the soldiers came past. Again they were unsuitable; too big, too small, too many.

Eventually, after almost an hour, she saw him, on his own, muscular and broad, about middle height. She glanced along the street.

It was almost deserted.

"Hello, soldier." Even as she said it she had to fight to keep the chuckle from her voice. It sounded so ridiculous.

At first he looked startled, and then he understood and began to smile.

"Are you in a hurry, soldier?" My God, she thought, it's all clichés, but her words had their desired effect. He was posing now, chewing and squinting at her, looking, he thought, tough and world-weary. To Christa it appeared only that he had something in his eye.

"How much?"

At least he was direct. She gave him a price and he nodded. She led the way down the street and turned into the alleyway leading to the flat, feeling that familiar shiver of apprehension. She would not want to be caught with him here. There was no one around, just the high wall and the backs of tenement buildings, rotted dead buildings with bricks scattered in heaps and wire struts protruding.

He was at her elbow now and it was almost as if he had read her mind.

"This will do. Here," he said, dragging her by the waist into a gap in the wall, a ragged cavern which had once been a lobby.

She struggled, trying to bite back the scream, telling him that the flat was just round the corner and it would be much more comfortable, but he seemed to want to get it over with, as if the very squalor of the place excited him.

She struggled and fought him, and he was grunting in her ear, obscenities and endearments mixed together. He could not understand why she was resisting him, and his fingers were reaching for her—stubby, calloused hands under her skirt, pinching at the softness of her flesh. She tried to get her knee round to thrust at him, but he knew too much to let himself be caught. Not here, she kept saying in a hoarse whisper, the flat, it's just round the corner. Bring him back to the house, the fair-haired soldier had said, and we'll do the rest. She began to scratch at his face and neck, but he did not seem to mind that. She pulled her head back as he bit into her neck. As she swallowed, trying to scream, his head jerked backward and she could see behind him in the shadows a large outline.

"Look away," said a voice, and she recognized the high-pitched tones of the big man from the flat. He must have been watching all the time, she thought, in case of trouble. She shrank backward as the soldier let her go. He was standing rigid now, his tongue protruding, his eyes bulging in terror, and she could see the big man's thumbs on his throat.

"Look away." It was a command. She closed her eyes briefly. There was a movement but no sound. When she looked again the German was slumped against the wall, and his neck was twisted so that he stared over his shoulder, seeing nothing.

Christa bent double and retched, over and over, shuddering with horror; the sickness seemed to last forever. When she looked up the body was squatting grotesquely in its underclothes, and Patterson was folding the uniform neatly and laying it on the ground.

She watched reluctantly as he dragged the body by its feet toward the rear of the building. He was looking up, searching for something, and she could hear him grunt as he placed the soldier on his back, the feet sticking out into the back court. That done, he leaned against a girder, pushing hard with both hands, his head seeming to vanish into the great folds of his shoulders. Her mind went back to her church days and the story of Samson pushing down the pillars. Instinctively she pressed closer against the wall as she heard the rumble from above, and saw Patterson move quickly back along the passage as the rubble crashed down. Briefly she saw the corpse kick out as the first of the bricks bit into the flesh, but it was only a reaction and then there was only dust.

As Patterson led her away she looked back at the bricks and gasped. The corpse's left hand was stretching out toward the sky as if alive. She pointed, but Patterson merely shrugged. "It's not important," he said, "there's many like that all over the city."

"Please," she whispered, not knowing why it mattered, but the man's saliva was still wet on her neck and she did not want to leave him like that.

Patterson looked around, moved across the alley and returned with a broken bucket. He ambled up the passage and placed it gently over the dead hand.

"Dust to dust," he said as he took her arm again, and she let him lead her back to the flat, her legs shaking so that she was forced to hold onto him for support.

Gresham took one look at the uniform and cursed quietly. "This is a damned private."

Patterson shrugged. "If we pull his helmet over his ears, no one will notice."

Gresham looked up at him, then moved quickly past him across the room to where Christa was swaying, her eyes glazed. He took her by the arm and led her to the sofa, cradling her head in his arm, and laid her down gently.

"I'm sorry," she said quietly. "It's just that I've never seen . . ."

But he placed his hand on her lips and told her to get some rest, then beckoned Driscoll to follow him downstairs, and shut the door gently behind him.

They worked on the map, the four of them, till late into the evening. It had to be done to perfection because there was no quick exit, no thrilling escape with squealing tires and smart driving. The streets of the city were clogged with debris and stalled, abandoned vehicles. It was a job which required stealth. At ten thirty Christa knocked on the door with mugs of coffee, apologizing, saying she did not know what it was made of these days, ersatz on ersatz. Silently they drank, and when it was finished Gresham nodded at Driscoll and Patterson.

"Get some sleep now," he said simply.

Christa watched as they left the table, muttered a good night and moved into the big bedroom. She saw them stretch out like robots. They were asleep before their heads hit the pillows. She glanced at Gresham. Sleep, he told them, and they slept. Could he get them to do anything? Perhaps, she thought; perhaps he could.

Roth could not sleep. There was too much activity in him; he was wound up like a rubber band, waiting for the dawn. He lay staring up at the ceiling. It must have been a child's room, a nursery in the old days; there were little ducks chasing one another across the walls and spiders grinning from the center of silver webs, beckoning to bluebottles. Roth grinned. No wonder children grew up crazy with things such as this on their walls to give them nightmares. He stretched and he could hear through the wall the movement of the woman. He waited, counting to a hundred, counting backward from fifty, but it was no good. He glanced across to the other bed, where Gresham lay on his back, his arms folded across his chest as if he were lying in state, his face peaceful in repose.

He sniffed. It had all seemed so simple the other day when the job was explained; just in and out, an escort job, anyone could have done it. But he had thought even then that there would be some sort of a snag; there always was. No matter how it was planned and how meticulously the job was prepared, there was always something unforeseen. It was bad luck this time, though; double bad luck. How were they to know that their man was being held prisoner, and crazy with it?

It was a pity. Had he only been sane and reliable there would have been no problem getting out of the city. No one would dare question a general. He could requisition any vehicle he wanted. It would have been so easy. All that was left now was to make the best of it and pray.

Still he could not sleep. He turned over onto his stomach and clutched at the pillow, but that only made matters worse. An idea crept uninvited into his mind and he began to feed it. She was a professional, after all. He had nothing against German women. No harm could be done, and when it was over he could get a full night's sleep. Even as he worked out the angles, Roth knew what he was doing. Whenever he had a choice to make, he picked what he wanted to do, then justified it later with reasons. He lay still for a moment, then swung himself out of bed, tiptoed from the room and looked back. Gresham had not stirred.

He closed the door gently and moved up the passage, naked but for a sheet wrapped around his middle. Christa's door was open. Slowly he moved toward it and peered inside.

"Hello." She was awake, as he thought she would be. If he had been asked to make bets he would have given odds on it. Christa was the kind whose door was always open. Smiling, he gripped the sheet round him and made his way purposefully into the room.

The sound of pain percolated through the dream into Gresham's mind, a low moaning as if the wound were deep and dreadful. He sat up sharply, listening. It was a regular sound, punctuated by sharper, higher-pitched cries. It took him only a few seconds to run from the room up the passage and grab at Roth, pulling and twisting, his arm round his throat, dragging him away and sending him hard to the floor. It was only because Roth reacted almost as quickly that Gresham's heel did not find his face as he stumbled backward, knocking over a table. Again Gresham was onto him, leaping forward and smothering him, Roth still warm and damp, musky with sex. As they thrashed together in the corner, a jumble of arms and legs, Christa scampered from the bed. She grabbed Gresham's wrist as he was about to lunge at Roth's face, the force of him twisting her over so that she landed on her back, her legs kicking air. She squealed with fright and Gresham stepped back, brushing his hand across his face as if he were trying to get rid of a fly, looking confused and disheveled. For a moment there was silence, and then he looked down at Christa. "I'm sorry," he said quietly, "I thought you were being hurt."

She shook her head and watched Gresham leave the room. Roth stood up, rubbing his neck. She looked at him, searching for an answer, but he simply shrugged and led her back to the bed, tucking her in like a father with his daughter. He winked at her, turned and followed Gresham down the passage. As he reached the door to their room, the story of the village girl and the Canadians came back to his mind. He shivered involuntarily and vowed not to go too close to Christa again. Nothing was worth risking Gresham's anger. Maybe someday the man would get round to explaining himself, over a few beers perhaps, but somehow Roth doubted it. Meanwhile there was a job to be done. He resolved to forget about women till he got back home, where things were not so complicated and there were no interruptions.

17

Berlin, April 19, 1945

It took them twenty minutes to inspect the alley. It was perfect, just thirty yards long, some fifteen yards wide, the apartment blocks empty. Patterson and Driscoll had checked the east, Gresham and Roth the west. They had found no one. The place was derelict. A fire had raged down both sides of the alley, leaving charred walls. Some of the floorboards remained, black and crumbling, but all the windows had gone. Not even the refugees would use the place, certainly not during the day.

Gresham looked at his watch; nine forty-five. He should be arriving in half an hour. If he took the correct route and played along with the initial charade, then all should be well. If not, they would have to use force, but with luck there would be no need.

He looked down the street from the end of the alley. It was half empty; a few civilians wandered past him, but there were no soldiers to be seen. If any trouble started, the civilians would freeze. It was standard practice. They stood like statues, locked in a tableau until their minds registered panic, then they would react, the wise ones running for cover, the fools acting the hero; except that on this occasion there would be no time. They would do the job and be gone in a matter of seconds and there would be no noise, if everything went to plan.

He glanced back up the alley. Patterson and Roth stood ten yards behind in a doorway. Driscoll waited an arm's length away, half hidden behind a pile of rubble. Again he looked down the street. There was no sign of the man, but it was early. He should not be long. He felt the familiar brittle taste in his throat, but no spittle. His mouth was dry, and yet he knew better than to attempt to swallow. It was not important. Once the operation began he would not be thinking about dry throats.

He stiffened as he saw Bergner turn a corner and walk toward him, the four guards ten yards behind. It was a good sign; had they been efficient they would have had one man in front, one flanking and two at the back, but they probably did not care. Everything was coming to an end; there was little point in caring too much. Gresham hoped they continued to think that way.

He glanced back up the alley, nodded to Patterson, took a breath and stepped out into the street, waiting until Bergner was almost at his shoulder.

"General Bergner, sir," he said, clicking his heels and saluting crisply.

Bergner stopped and returned the greeting while the guards caught up and clustered around him.

"Hauser, sir," said Gresham. "B Company, Seventy-ninth Division."

Bergner grunted, looking blankly at him.

Come on, thought Gresham, remember your lines. Remember what this is all about. Remember the letter.

"Stalingrad, sir," he offered.

The smallest of the guards moved to Gresham's left, looking curiously at him as Driscoll stepped out of the alley, saluted and moved forward, placing himself between Bergner and the guard.

"Leutnant Schmidt, Herr General. You remember? B Company."

"Of course," said Bergner, but still he looked blank as if trying to recall names and faces.

"We have some schnapps, sir," Driscoll said, taking Bergner's arm and leading him toward the alley. "We would be honored if you would accept a drink from us. In memory of the old days."

Bergner allowed himself to be led as Driscoll gently shouldered the little guard to the side and Gresham moved behind him, jockeying him into position, like a runner boxing in the opposition at a curve. Then Gresham turned and smiled at the three guards who were following. "Please join us, gentlemen," he said. "A couple of drinks. Won't take a moment."

And now they had turned into the alley and were only five yards from the doorway where Patterson stood waiting.

"Stop." The small guard slipped round to the front at a trot and stood facing them, his gun held high, pointing at Driscoll's chest. "Enough of this," he was saying, and Gresham cursed. There had to be one, he thought; in a group of four there had to be one who was loyal, a stickler, one who wouldn't leave his charge for a moment just to have a friendly drink. It was just as well that they had anticipated such a possibility. Patterson moved forward, embracing the guard from behind, grinning over his shoulder at him, almost spinning him off his feet.

"Just a little drink, soldier," he said. "For the Führer's birthday tomorrow."

And even then it would have been all right if one of the guards had not stumbled. Gresham, turning, saw it happen and could not stop it. The man was moving forward, staring at Patterson as if he recognized him, when his boot struck a pebble. He lurched sideways, grabbing at Bergner's arm to steady himself, stumbling for a couple of paces, not enough to fall, but Roth decided not to take any chances. As the guard clutched at Bergner's sleeve, Roth stepped from the doorway, his rifle held by the barrel. Two-handed he swung it, breaking the man's jaw and dropping him senseless in the rubble. Gresham was the first to react, swinging his gun round on the remaining two. He motioned them up the alley and one of them did as he was told, walking slowly forward with his eyes fixed firmly on the gun barrel as the other dropped to one knee and brought up his automatic. Gresham acted instinctively, pushing Bergner into the doorway, turning fast so that the first bullet hit him in the shoulder and spun him back against the wall, where he stood motionless. He gazed dumbly ahead as Roth opened up on the two guards, while Patterson threw the small man to the ground, took aim and shot him once through the back of the neck.

Gresham could not move. He watched fascinated as Roth sprayed the two men with gunfire, blasting the unconscious man for good measure. But still the one man kept firing, his finger dead now but still rigid on the trigger, the gun set to automatic, the bullets still pumping, even after the life had been smashed from him.

Gresham blinked and yelled at Roth to stop, and together they stood back to survey the damage. Patterson was squatting against the wall, his left leg smashed below the knee, the calf a mess of bone and attached only by fragments of cloth and skin.

Now there was silence. Roth moved across to Driscoll, who had pitched forward onto his face, his head resting against one arm. Gently Roth touched his shoulder and Driscoll toppled to one side, staring upward out of a dead eye, one socket shot away, his nose torn off, his lips pursed in what seemed to be a disapproving scowl.

Behind Gresham, Bergner came slowly out of the doorway and wandered among the bodies, making tutting noises with his tongue and shaking his head.

Gresham knew what had to be done. He called Roth over to him. They took hold of Bergner and pushed him up the alley. So far the pain had not started and Gresham could move as fast as any fit man. Roth took a quick glance behind him. He could hear shouts and the sound of footsteps, the clattering of boots against the rubble.

As they ran past Patterson, Gresham looked down and smiled. There was nothing to be said. Patterson grinned back and tried to wink, but it was a feeble effort. Gresham remembered him saying once that he had tried, years ago in school, but he could never wink, and the girls had made fun of him.

They reached the end of the alley and looked back. Patterson was setting up his position, moving farther back against the wall, a lonely figure among the dead men.

He probed his tooth with his tongue as he waited, running the tip around the spot where the cyanide capsule had been implanted by the medics. A quick bite, they had said, press hard down and it would be over quickly; just a matter of seconds and he'd be joining his Maker; virtually no pain. That's what they had said. But how did they know? No one had ever come back to describe it. Perhaps it hurt forever. Maybe you kept rolling around in agony for eternity while people passed you by and the city was razed to the ground and rebuilt and people made love and died, and still you rolled around invisible, screaming in agony forever and ever, waiting for the thing to take effect. He smiled and reached for his pistol, snapped open the holster, drew it out and gazed down the barrel. So perhaps it was going to be of use after all. It would be better than cyanide, anyway. At least with a pistol you knew what you were doing. He wouldn't roll around for eternity if he used the pistol. He placed it on the ground beside him and tilted the barrel of the Sturmgewehr toward the street. He could hear voices now. He squinted up to his left, but there was no sign of anyone in the buildings above.

He glanced down at his leg, at his foot sticking out at a strange angle, the blood flowing like a stream in spate. The artery must have been severed, he thought calmly. It would not take long for him to bleed to death. How long was it? He had been told once, at a training course, but he could not remember. They'd said that it was just like falling into a deep sleep, like drowning on dry land; but how did they know? Maybe you spent eternity clutching at your leg and trying to keep it attached . . . no one had ever come back to tell. . . .

He squinted down the alley and focused on Driscoll lying in a grotesque heap. It was strange. He had seen many men die. One moment there was life and the next a pile of manure. He remembered asking Driscoll why he kept pushing himself, all that training and fitness. What was it for? What did he want? The answer was one word: "Perfection." He had grinned at the little man and slapped his shoulder. Perfection indeed; but in the end he had not fired a shot in anger and now his perfect little body was bent out of shape. All that hard work and he ended up like manure; he need not have bothered, if he'd known.

Patterson shifted position and the pain jolted through him, so that he had to take a firm grip of the rifle and bite into his lip until it eased. He saw the first of the soldiers run into the alley, framed perfectly between the buildings, and two others a yard or so behind him, coming at a run. They were not acting like soldiers, just running at him as if they were racing in the park. They were probably not expecting any trouble; maybe they just thought that somebody somewhere was acting the fool, but in a moment they would see the bodies. As he fired the first burst, the recoil thrust him against the wall and he felt the shock travel through his body, stopping at his waist. He could no longer feel anything in his legs, and the sound of the rifle shots was faint. It was strange, he thought; normally the din of the gunfire kept you going, kept the nerves jumping and the heart pumping, but this seemed more like a dream, muffled and blurred as if someone had plugged up his ears and drawn a veil in front of his eyes.

He laughed aloud as the soldiers crumbled, two diving neatly forward onto their faces and lying still, the third splayed backward against the wall, his arms and legs thrashing like some cartoon character, like Felix the Cat or somebody. He giggled; whenever they were thrown through a wall in the cartoon cinema they left an impression of themselves in the bricks. The soldier looked like that; a cardboard cutout of a German soldier, smashed into the wall.

As he watched, the body began to slip down until it slumped into a heap, the head back, staring at the sky, like an old drunk asleep in a doorway.

There was silence now, punctuated by a few muttered grunts from the street. They would split up, he thought; they would slip into the buildings and up the stairs so that they could get at him from above. There were four windows they could take; if they had done that in the first place they wouldn't have lost three men.

They were shouting something at him now but he could not hear properly, just a faint scrabbling noise from the walls, like mice, and their voices, far away as if they were shouting through cotton wool. It was strange. He had always thought that your sight was the first sense to go. He settled back against the wall and thought about it, blinking and shaking his eyes to focus better. Would it be a blackness that descended over him, or would it be red, like lying too long staring at the sun? Maybe death would be green. They would be surprised when he told them that it was green; when they came back for him and he told them what it was like.

If only he could hear properly. He did not want to die deaf. It wasn't dignified.

He did not hear the soldier who first reached the window, treading carefully on the blackened boards, but he must have sensed something because he turned and looked upward as the shot was fired, so that it smashed directly onto the top of his head and blew away half his skull. He did not move; just sat, still as a statue, while the soldiers looked down at him, gazing silently, curiously asking themselves questions but coming up with no answers.

Gresham heard the shots as he ducked down into the cellar and along the tunnel, his hand tight round Bergner's wrist. He did not look back. They were walking fast, almost at a trot, Bergner murmuring incoherently, Roth half a pace behind. Gresham was conscious only of the urgent need to find the exit to the tenement block across the street before the blood seeped through his tunic to leave a trail. He pushed Bergner ahead of him and held his arm with his right hand, hastily ripping at the material and working a rough tourniquet, twisting the torn ends into a knot. It would hold. The arm was still numb, but he knew that soon the pain would stab at him and that he needed to get to the flat without delay.

He found the staircase and guided Bergner up to the back court of the block, took his elbow again and pushed him through the lobby to the street. He looked out, waited until an old woman had tottered past, then ran across the street, pulling Bergner with him into the alleyway. At the end he turned into Christa's street, dragging Bergner roughly behind him until they reached the building, then stumbled upstairs, still clutching his arm in case the man would suddenly take off and run, like a child scampering away from its parents.

At her door he leaned against the bell until, at last, the pain throbbed through him, the landing seeming to sway as if in an earthquake. He fell through the door when it was opened, still grasping Bergner like a terrier with a rabbit, stumbling and half crawling along the passage, heedless of her cries, determined not to faint until everything was settled, hoping to God she would not turn out to be one of those women who swooned at the sight of blood. Only when he reached the mattress in the kitchen and heard the door close did he loosen his grip and collapse, letting Christa lean over him and work at the torn tunic. She was deftly pulling the material away to expose the wound. Then Roth appeared, standing above him, looking down, a worried frown, gently easing Christa away.

Gresham closed his eyes and thought of all the years of training, the sweat and the blood, the fear and the pain, all for nothing, just because some little soldier stumbled on a pebble and it was all gone in a matter of seconds. And for what? For one crazy old man mumbling in a corner. Gresham shook his head, and cursed beneath his breath.

Roth was probing now, and Gresham clenched his teeth, fighting the nausea, thinking of his first night on the beer when he was a boy. The room had swayed like this even when he had closed his eyes, still swaying even as he had tried to sleep, the walls coming in on him; they had called it the airplanes, he remembered, and it had not stopped even when the vomiting began.

Now he could hear a voice in the distance and a cool hand on his brow, a lilting female whisper, cooing gentle, meaningless words at him while he grunted and groaned and fought against the blackness. Think of it as a foxhole, he told himself . . . the enemy is approaching and you have to keep the machine gun working . . . if you sleep, you die; the will is in control of the body, the mind is stronger than the flesh . . . remember that; the first law of the jungle.

"Got it." Vaguely he heard Roth's voice and he could see the piece of lead he held in his fingers. It was over. He could give in to the blackness now. And so he did. Quite deliberately, Harry Gresham passed out.

The night seemed to last forever. Roth slept fitfully, dreaming of broken bodies, thrashing his head from side to side on the pillow trying to muffle the choking sounds of the dying. Each time he awoke he imagined he was back in the alley; each time he lay back and sighed with relief. By rights he should be dead. At least fifteen rounds had been fired at close range. He only hoped that he had not used up his supply of good fortune.

He glanced across at Gresham asleep on his back, his breath rasping from his open mouth, his face damp and pale. Roth stood up and moved to his side, checking the dressing. It would hold. There was no need to change it until later. As he turned away he heard Gresham mumble in his sleep, and briefly he wondered why the man was talking German; he was probably having nightmares, only for him they would be worse because the pain was real.

He moved down the passage, unlocked the bedroom door and checked that Bergner was asleep. He was lying on his side, his hand under his head, sleeping peacefully. Bergner would be all right, thought Roth. He had crossed over into the land of the happy people. When the time of reckoning came, he could plead insanity and spend a blissful convalescence in a room with white walls. It was a simple means of escape; just give in to the horror and allow others to take over. As he closed the door Roth was scowling contemptuously. Just one chance, he thought, and it would be a bullet for Bergner.

As he made his way back to the bed he felt the building shudder from the concussion of a bomb which had exploded nearby. He thought of Christa sheltering beneath him in the cellar. It was going to be a hard few days until Gresham was fit enough to carry on. Certainly he could not be moved into the cellar at night, and it would be a dreadful irony to get blasted by one of your own bombs.

He settled himself again on the bed, idly wondering how Patterson had died. He hoped that he hadn't fallen into the hands of the SS, but he would not have allowed that; not Patterson. He closed his eyes and drifted reluctantly back to the nightmares of his imagination.

All that morning Gresham thrashed around on the bed, mumbling incoherently, and it was all Roth could do to hold him down. Even unconscious the man possessed a terrible strength. At noon when he finally calmed down and lay still, Roth was exhausted and he scarcely bothered to move when he heard the rattle of the door handle.

Christa flinched when she came in and saw the gun pointing at her waist. She smiled apprehensively as Roth lowered the weapon. He stared over her shoulder as she closed the door.

"No one around," she said, anticipating the question. "The place is almost deserted."

"No searches?" he asked. "No one doing house to house?"

She shook her head. "I expect they've got other things to do," she said.

"Maybe so," said Roth.

"And today is the Führer's birthday."

"Congratulations," said Roth. Christa turned away and went toward the kitchen. She was not quite sure how to react to him, never could tell whether he was joking or not. And the other one, so calm on the surface, yet so crazy . . . she would simply have to accept them and let them take charge; and speak only when she was spoken to.

At odd intervals through the day, Bergner knocked on his door and was allowed to walk round the flat. He said nothing. He did not ask any questions or offer any help. If he was curious as to where he was, he gave no indication. He ate and drank what he was given, thanked Christa civilly and returned to his room.

When they had eaten, Roth stretched out on the sofa and Christa took her turn to watch over Gresham. She sat for a while in silence, then leaned across to the table and switched on the wireless.

Again it was the high-pitched voice of Goebbels. The Führer, he reminded her, was fifty-six today. As if she could ever forget. She turned down the volume so that Gresham would not be disturbed.

"Never before have matters been on the razor's edge as they are today. I can only say that these times, with all their somber and painful majesty, have found their only worthy representative in the Führer. We have him to thank and him alone that Germany exists today and that the West, with its culture and civilization, has not been completely engulfed in the dark abyss which yawns before us. . . ."

She glanced at Gresham and saw that his lips were moving. Vaguely she wondered what was going on in his mind, but again she was distracted by the wireless.

"Wherever our enemies appear they bring poverty and sorrow, chaos and devastation, unemployment and hunger. . . ."

She listened enthralled, the voice still gripping her as it had always done. She shivered slightly as Goebbels admitted that the war was almost over but that soon things would improve.

"The ravaged countryside will be studded with new and more beautiful towns and villages inhabited by happy people. We shall be friends with all nations of goodwill. There will be work for all. Order, peace and prosperity will reign instead of the underworld."

Again she thought she heard Gresham say something. She crouched by the bed and leaned over him, touching his forehead with the back of her hand. He seemed to be on fire, the perspiration running from his scalp into his eyes and into the corners of his mouth. As she touched him he moved violently, kicking out and turning his face to the wall. Instinctively she moved onto the bed, and pulled him toward her, holding his head against her breast and cradling him like a baby, crooning softly to him. He muttered something and pushed himself against her as she stroked his chest, so that she felt the heat of his fever scorching into her. She held him closer, drawing the fire out of him, listening to him muttering the same words over and over while in the background Goebbels was shouting from the wireless.

"If history can write that the people of this country never deserted their leader and that he never deserted his people, that will be victory. . . ."

Gently she rocked him, whispering in his ear, feeling maternal, smiling to herself and wondering if maybe, after all, she had missed her vocation; maybe she should have been a nurse. She chuckled aloud at the thought, but the smile froze as Gresham's eyes opened. He yelled something unintelligible at her, tore himself free and lashed out with his left hand, backhanding her across the face and sending her sprawling onto the floor. She heard herself scream as she scrambled away from him, half crawling toward the door.

She reached for the handle, but the door was pushed open and Roth stood framed in the doorway, looking past her toward the bed.

"It's all right," he said, putting his arm round her. Together they gazed at Gresham, unconscious now, sprawled across the bed on his stomach, his mouth open, his eyes staring sightlessly at the floor.

Roth drew away from Christa and went to the bed, turned Gresham over and pulled the sheet up to his chin.

"What did he mean?" Christa whispered in a small voice. "He kept saying 'They must escape,' over and over."

Roth shrugged and shook his head. "It's the fever," he said. "Don't take any notice. It's only the fever."

In the bunker beneath the Chancellery, the leading members of the Reich had arrived to pay their last respects to their Führer on the occasion of his birthday. In the afternoon he decorated a number of members of Hitler Youth and told his guests that soon the Russians would be destroyed.

The military conference in the evening demonstrated that the Reich was almost dead. The British were in the outskirts of Bremen and Hamburg, Patton was making for the Alps through Bavaria, the French had reached the Upper Danube. The Russians were in Vienna and knocking on the back door of Berlin.

The generals looked at the map and said nothing, but Hitler seemed unconcerned. He had a plan which called for SS General Obergruppenführer Steiner to attack the Russians through the southern suburbs of Berlin. But the generals knew that the battalions he was sending to Steiner existed only in his mind. And so they sat and listened, many of them getting up only to repeat their advice that the Führer leave the city and go south to Obersalzburg. But Hitler said nothing. And so they left in a convoy of lorries; Göring, Speer, Himmler, Dönitz.

From her office door, Angela Müller watched them go and muttered to herself: the rats, she grumbled, were leaving the sunken ship. There would be much work to do now that only a few were left to guard the Führer and defend the city. She would get down to it and show how much she could do. There would be no time to visit that whore of a cousin, that was for sure. She turned back and began to arrange papers in piles around her typewriter.

That day the first shells from the guns of the LXXIX Corps of the Russian Third Army smashed into the city.

◀18▶

Cambridge, April 20, 1945

Alan Francis was having difficulty explaining his point.

"You see, I'm not sure what it is about Robertson that fascinates me. I can't exactly pin down what's bothering me, which in turn adds to the fascination. Do you see what I'm getting at?"

"No," said Julie.

"Oh, well, never mind." If he could not explain it to himself, there was little point trying to explain it to anyone else.

In the two months since he had last visited Cambridge he had worked almost constantly, and he was due two days' leave. When he had called up, Julie had been pleasantly surprised. It was a compliment. From what she knew of Alan Francis, it was usually the women who did the running and issued the invitations for him to accept or reject as the mood took him. He was an arrogant man and it was unheard of for him to invite himself somewhere. He might be rejected, and he would not have understood that.

What she did not know was that he had phoned Peter Dawson before he called her.

He told her about Dawson after they had made love. He had almost made the mistake of glancing at his watch as they lay curled around each other on her narrow bed; almost but not quite. Years ago he had learned never to check the time after making love to a woman. It made them feel like a train that was late in arriving, so one had said; Susan, he thought it was.

"When are you seeing him?" she said lazily.

"Four thirty."

"Well, you'd better hurry then." And she turned her back on him. He shouted good-bye as he let himself out, but she did not answer. He thought perhaps she had fallen asleep.

At first Dawson was rather aloof, shuffling around his study stoop-shouldered, never looking Francis in the eye, always seeming to be hunting for something, a file or a book. Francis had met his type before and he knew that he would need patience.

First he had to overcome the sense of superiority, that feeling among academics that they had won the early races, the educational prizes and could therefore discount all the others; then came the second stage when their natural curiosity took over, reluctantly at first, as they tried to find out what went on outside, in the world.

"Yes, but what exactly do you mean by intelligence work?"

At last Dawson's eyes locked on his and Francis knew that the preliminaries were over. Now the incessant questioning would begin.

He spoke for half an hour, telling him little details about his work, and the occasional anecdote. Dawson was fascinated, sitting at his desk, his chin on his hand like a small boy in front of an old seaman. He had never met anyone actually involved to such an extent, he said, as he rose to make a pot of tea on a tiny one-ring stove.

While he was busy, Francis slipped the name Harry Gresham into the conversation.

"Gresham, oh, yes." Dawson turned and looked in surprise. "Don't tell me he's in Intelligence?"

"Does it seem unlikely?"

"Not really, I suppose. He was bright enough. Strange chap, though."

"In what way?"

"Oh, I don't know. Arrogant." He came back with the teapot and began fussing around with cups.

"Brilliant brain," Dawson continued, "but strange ideas. He'd lived for a while in Germany, you know. With cousins or something."

"Oh, yes?"

"Bit of a Fascist once."

"Was he?" Francis tried to appear only mildly curious.

"Yes." Dawson frowned in concentration as if he was trying to recall a conversation. "A lot of the chaps were fairly right-wing in those days as a sort of reaction against the Communists. I mean, most people with any intelligence saw Communism as the logical way ahead, but not Gresham. Mind you, I don't think his reaction was purely rational. He didn't like the Bolsheviks as people. Awfully arrogant lot, you know. And naive with it. A dreadful combination."

"Students can be like that," said Francis.

"Well, quite. Anyway I remember him cutting them up quite a few times, more by the power of his personality than force of argument. Of course there was a lot to be said for National Socialism in those days, if you discounted the criminal nature of its leaders. You could make out a good case for it as an alternative to Weimar."

"Of course."

"He almost convinced me at times, did Gresham. He would spout Nietzsche and Darwin, relate them to the particular political problem. You know the sort of thing. I mean all those Germans in that tiny space. They needed room to breathe. The desire for expansion was self-evident."

Francis sat silently, letting him talk, waiting for the right opportunity to make the connection. It came when Dawson paused for breath.

"And did he ever talk this way in front of his tutor?"

"You mean Charles Robertson?" asked Dawson.

"Yes."

Dawson nodded violently, spilling his tea slightly. "Oh, yes. It was Robertson who talked him out of it. He was the one who made him see sense."

He'd had days like it when he was a young reporter, going in almost blind to a new town with just one phone number and a whole page of facts to get by four o'clock, terrified that he would find out nothing and the readers would be greeted by an empty white space in the morning. But then one call had led to another and another, until it seemed he was talking to half the town and could have written a book by lunchtime.

He was sitting in the drawing room of a large detached house, sipping black-market brandy and listening to the academics and chinless wonders, all talking their heads off. Oh, yes, they had all known

Gresham: he was an odd-bod; and Robertson, of course, a god, nothing less than divine; did you hear about the time he applied a definition of truth to itself and discovered it was untrue?

Dawson, now that he had begun, could not stop talking. He was standing in a corner staring greedily at Julie and muttering something at her. She had decided that if there was nothing better to do she would get drunk. After all, she had not anticipated this. She had planned and cooked a meal at home. She had not realized that she would be sitting in some suburban house listening to a crowd of boring academics.

Francis found himself the center of attention, catching at the edges of conversations, picking up the pieces here and there and being drawn into three arguments at once.

"Don't you think the present policy of a war of annihilation is misguided? . . . I mean, it's one thing to win the damned thing, quite another to demand unconditional surrender. . . ."

". . . you don't really believe this atrocity stuff, do you? Sheer propaganda . . . a political device surely. . . ."

". . . in order to maintain our influence in Europe we're going to have to work with Jerry, especially as the Yanks are swarming all over the place. . . ."

Francis stepped in: "Gaevernitz," he said.

"Pardon?"

"You've read Gaevernitz on the need for a three-nation Western alliance?"

"Oh, yes. Of course."

Francis smiled to himself. One up, he thought. It was nice to name-drop in this crowd; after all, he'd been on the receiving end for long enough.

And then he found himself trapped in the corner by an intense woman with bulging eyes who said she had known Gresham for years. He glanced across the room where Julie sat, gulping from her glass and chattering amiably, her face slightly flushed, her voice loud.

"I said I haven't heard of him since thirty-nine," the woman was saying. "He went into the army, that's all I know."

"Was he attractive?" asked Francis. "To women?"

"Oh, yes." The woman blushed and giggled. "But he was odd. He never, so far as I know, actually . . ." Her voice trailed away.

"Was he gregarious?" Francis persisted. "Did he join many university societies?"

"Lots." She reeled off a number of names, mostly sets of initials, and Francis quietly copied them down on the back of his cigarette packet. He thought perhaps he had misheard one of them.

"Argentina?" he asked.

"Yes, that's right."

"Why Argentina?"

She shrugged. "I have no idea, but he was interested in South America for some reason. He was a very curious young man."

The evening ended in a pub in the middle of town. It was a small place which in the busy days had swarmed with students. It was decorated with their photographs: sports teams, debating groups. Gresham was in the center of a judo team, and no one noticed Francis take the frame from the wall and slip it beneath his coat before going off to rescue Julie from the attentions of Dawson.

They traveled back to London together early the next morning. Julie, in her uniform, was silent. He tried to cheer her up with banter about her appearance, saying she reminded him of an admiral he once knew with the same liking for brandy . . . but her smile was forced. As she had said over breakfast, it was not often she had any spare time. She had had to pull a few stunts to get the two days off, especially at such short notice. It was a pity to waste it with a bunch of intellectual Nazis. . . . He made no further attempts at appeasement. He had enough on his mind without worrying about a sulking woman.

They parted at the station, formally, pecking at cheeks and promising to keep in touch. It was one of those phrases: keep in touch, meaning perhaps yes, perhaps no. He watched her walk away, wondering if he would see her again; it was more than likely. He would have to spend quite a bit of time in Cambridge on his book. He would look her up the next time he was down there.

He got through the most urgent items on his desk, working through the lunch hour till the pile was down to manageable proportions. By three o'clock he felt he could leave his desk for a few minutes. Jeffries looked up, smiling broadly, when he came in.

"Been out in the sun, old chap?" A theatrical wink. "Down among the Wrens, I hear?"

"That's right." Francis allowed him a few minutes of chatter and playful questioning before he asked about work. Eventually he mentioned Gresham offhandedly, as if he had just thought about him.

"Oh, yes. I expect they're having a great time," said Jeffries.

"Do you know where he came from?"

"Not really, can't rightly remember, found him rotting in a guard-room. Dreadful mess."

"Do you have his file?"

He nodded and went to a filing cabinet, rummaging around among papers. "If I remember correctly it was a special signal from above that got us onto him." He drew out a file of papers and flipped it across to the desk.

Francis read aloud. "He can be found at Aldershot . . ."

"Told you. In clink."

"But where is this from?" The coded memo number meant nothing to him.

"Top brass, military," said Jeffries. "An old pal of mine filled me in, eventually."

"Could you give me his name?"

"Of course." Jeffries scribbled a name and number on the back of the file.

"And these were the people who recommended Gresham?"

"Presumably," said Jeffries. "Glad to get rid of him, I shouldn't wonder."

Francis slipped the file under his arm and moved to the window. "By the way," he said, "what's the situation about Argentina?"

"Well, since they've declared war on Germany at long last we've recognized the Farrell government."

"I know. But do we have diplomatic links again."

"They're working on it at the moment. The governor's going back to BA shortly and some of their chaps are on their way to set up the embassy again."

"Do we have names?"

Jeffries nodded. "I can get them for you."

"Thanks." Francis turned to go, hoping Jeffries would not ask why he was interested; to be sure, he hardly knew himself.

"I say, Alan."

"Yes?"

"Old Robby's been acting rather strange lately."

"In what way?"

"He's been trying to get the RAF to stop their raids on Berlin."

"When?"

"A couple of days ago. They explained that they were cutting back anyway. It looks like tomorrow will see the last raid. The Russians, after all, are almost in the city. Can't go dropping bombs on our allies now, can we?"

He raised an eyebrow, but Francis said nothing.

"Do you know what he's up to?"

Francis shook his head.

"Strange, isn't it?" Jeffries persisted. "You wouldn't expect him to go meddling around with the RAF."

Briefly Francis thought of sharing his suspicions with Jeffries but he quickly dismissed the idea. There was really nothing to tell, nothing that made any concrete sense, and sometimes Jeffries talked too much.

"I suppose he knows what he's doing," he said.

"No doubt," said Jeffries, but he did not sound convinced.

Francis smiled at him and left the office. He worked late into the evening catching up on his work, and when he had finished he opened the blank file in which he kept his notes on Robertson. He placed Jeffries's notes on the desk, picked up the phone and dialed a number. When the man answered he smiled. It was a staccato voice. Sometimes Francis wondered if military men stood to attention when the phone rang.

19

Berlin, April 27, 1945

It was the most frustrating week of Cyril Roth's life. Each day dragged interminably, to be followed by seemingly endless nights when he lay in his camp bed outside Bergner's door, listening to the whine of shellfire and snatching unsuccessfully at sleep. Each morning he gazed out at the city, and each time he looked there seemed to be less of it left standing. The place was nothing more than a rubble heap crawling with human maggots.

Occasionally Bergner would wander round the room, stop at the window and attempt to draw him into conversation. Sometimes he would talk sense; at other times he rambled incoherently. To Roth it seemed that the man was swaying on a mental tightrope, sometimes balanced, sometimes teetering toward a plunge into insanity. Roth never looked at him nor answered him. If the man was going mad, then let him. It was no concern of his.

Twice Bergner called him Rolff, then he would turn away, looking confused. "You look similar," he said once, "you and Rolff."

Roth said nothing.

"He died, you know. Tuberculosis. Another victim."

At other times he would stand at Roth's shoulder gazing out at the city, talking quietly and passionately about his guilt and that the time for atonement was imminent. Again Roth ignored him. If the man was trying to gain sympathy, it was, he thought, a crude way of going about it.

On the third day of his vigil, Roth felt a hand on his shoulder. Bergner stood smiling at him.

"Do you play chess?"

Roth said nothing. He watched as Bergner began to hunt through drawers, pulling out the contents and carefully replacing them, working quickly and eagerly. Then he left the room. Roth could hear him rummaging through the flat, talking to Christa. He turned back to the window and a moment later Bergner was back, still smiling, tapping Roth on the elbow. Again Roth turned and looked at him. The old man was nodding at him expectantly, clutching a box of chess pieces and a board.

"Don't be ridiculous," Roth said quietly.

Bergner's smile faded and he nodded, suddenly looking exhausted, like an old dog kicked by his master. He went back to his room walking stoop-shouldered, the box tucked under his arm. Roth watched him go, and for a moment he felt sorry for the man.

Maybe, he thought, hatred could only be kept alive in the abstract; meet it in person and it needs constant refueling; if only Bergner had been arrogant instead of pathetic. . . . Roth cursed aloud and told himself to be quiet, trying to force his mind to go blank, but it was impossible. He always had to be working things out, motives and reasons. It was a legacy from his family. They were all great thinkers, or so it seemed, the way they talked, the house constantly echoing with their chatter. Sometimes Roth envied the other soldiers their easy nature. The goyim seemed to flourish in mindlessness, accepting life for what it was without the need for endless analyses.

If Patterson had been the survivor he would have taken this calmly, sitting like a buddha, lost in his daydreams. And Driscoll would have done his exercises, day and night, until he came to resemble a miniature Tarzan. For them, a week of confinement would have posed few problems.

At night he thought of Christa, and occasionally he wished that she did not have to go down to the cellar each night. But there could be no repeat of the first night. During the day when she was not out searching for food, they treated each other like strangers thrown together by necessity, like travelers in a railroad compartment, making polite conversation until they reached their destination. Anything more intimate would have caused problems. Yet, occasionally, he was reminded of her face the day Gresham hit her: the fear and trembling, the tears on her cheek. She was not so tough as she pretended. Then again, she was nothing more than a whore, working her passage, doing what was necessary in order to save her skin. He had to remind himself constantly, for this was neither the time nor the place to start feeling affection. . . .

For a week Harry Gresham did not know night from day. Although he was quite capable of fighting the physical pain, he had no control over the fever which ran hot and cold through his body and turned his imagination into a treacherous enemy. Days limped into nights and stumbled back into bleak dawns, but it was all the same to him. His dreams merged with reality and he did not know which was which. He was conscious only of the continuous pain and the need to remain in some kind of control of himself. It was all too easy to slip into the darkness and allow the others to take over.

Sometimes it seemed to him that he was a child in a cot as Christa leaned over him, stroking his brow, or Roth changed his dressing; sometimes he saw them as his parents standing together looking down at him anxiously, cooing at him and tickling his chin before going off to leave him with his dreams, and he wanted to scream at them to come back and save him from the darkness. Or he would see John Patterson hopping toward him, his face a white mask of anger, the big shoulders heaving as he pressed his great thumbs down, squeezing the life out of him, cursing him for leaving him alone in the alley. Occasionally Bergner would come into focus in front of him, leaning toward him and talking about babies before disappearing once more with a strange, stiff, right-armed salute which he would try to return, but was unable to because of the pain in his shoulder. Often Christa would talk to him, always the same story, about the Russians, always the Russians, in that low melodious voice which sent him to sleep.

Only when the wound was being cleaned was he completely alert. Everything was in perfect focus. He could see and hear everything that went on. It lasted only for a moment until he collapsed once more into the blackness.

But it could not last. He had to get the job done. Recuperation was for civilians. Slowly he tried to rise, pushing his elbows into the mattress so that his head rose a few inches, but the nausea overpowered him and he slumped down once more. Again he tried, feeling the perspiration in his eyes and running down his face into the corners of his mouth, when the room tilted and he was on the floor. Vaguely he felt someone lift him back onto the bed and he could hear Roth's voice muttering something about food. He could not understand him and for once he did not care. He nodded in agreement and heard the one word: "Thanks"; but he was not sure who had spoken.

Roth stood by the door, feeling elated for the first time in a week. He knew that he could not have spent another hour in the place without going crazy. He needed a break. He had told himself that it was essential. Christa could not always forage for them. He had to go out and scavenge, but deep down he knew he was making an excuse and that it was unfair of him to have taken advantage by asking Gresham's permission. The mumbled wave of the arm he had taken to mean "Go ahead," and he could always say he had asked if he was queried later. But he knew it was just an excuse. He had to get away from the mad old man, if only for an hour. Just a breath of air and he would be back. He looked at his watch. Three o'clock. Christa would be back soon. The old man could be left alone for a few minutes. He tapped on Bergner's door.

"Herr General."

"Yes?"

"Going out on a quick trip, sir, to the mess."

"Very good, Rolff."

"The Führer asks you not to leave the billet, sir, until I return."

"Of course."

He locked the door, crossed the passage and let himself out, feeling like an animal escaping from its cage.

Once outside he could hear the thump of artillery fire, and somehow it comforted him. The Russians were gradually blasting the place into a desert, and he gazed at the devastation with satisfaction. He knew exactly where he was going as he picked his way nimbly over the rubble, turning left, right and right again until he saw what he wanted. The guard at the gate did not challenge him, nor did the group of privates at the entrance to the mess. He picked up a tin can from a pile by the door and ambled across to the counter, joining the short queue of sullen soldiers. An old woman spooned some soup into his can, and he shook it at her until she had filled it to the brim. Casually he moved to a table, picked up three loaves of bread, tucked them under his arm and walked out. At the exit someone shouted something unintelligible at him and he grinned back, giving a mock salute. Within two minutes he was back on Friedrichstrasse, chuckling inwardly, quietly pleased with himself.

As he turned the corner, he almost collided with two soldiers. It was nothing much; they did not even make contact as Roth instinctively stepped to one side so that he stumbled slightly and bumped against the wall of an apartment building. The soldiers carried on down the street without acknowledging him, strutting away without breaking stride as if Roth had been invisible. He stood against the wall listening to their voices, and a terrible rage began to burn in him. It had happened before, during periods of solitary confinement in prison; some small, unimportant incident would occur and he would see a red mist before his eyes and be compelled to destroy something.

For a full minute he stood motionless, watching the soldiers until they vanished from view. Calmly he stoked up his fury, thinking back to the last time he had talked to Christa. She had rambled on about Patterson killing the soldier, marveling how quick and clinical he had been, and now Patterson was dead and Roth knew exactly what to do.

He walked for fifty yards until he reached a doorway, then ducked out of sight. He placed the soup on the ground and balanced the bread on top, then took up a position where he could see anyone coming up the street but would not be seen himself. He waited for twenty minutes until he saw what he wanted. The man was tall and blond and had managed to retain a certain arrogance even as he made his way over the rubble; an Aryan son of the master race, broad-shouldered and square-jawed with clear blue eyes: a prototype. The Führer might have chosen him personally and presented him on the Nuremberg podium.

It would have to be quick. Roth glanced back to make sure that the bread would not topple into the dirt, then moved forward a pace. The soldier was only ten yards away now and Roth could hear the hiss of his breath. He was almost convinced that he could smell him, but he knew it was a mirage; it was the thought of the killing that heightened the senses.

"Good afternoon."

The soldier stopped and peered into the gloom, instinctively taking a step back, his hand going to his holster as Roth stepped out of the doorway. Roth took two paces, chopping sideways with his left hand to the shoulder and snapping the man's collarbone, then grabbing two-handed for his throat to choke off the scream. The soldier struggled, kicking out wildly as Roth strained backward like a dog, pulling him by the throat into the doorway, then turned him into the lobby and smashed him back against the wall. Briefly they stood together as if frozen, before Roth stepped back and brought his knee up hard into the man's groin, doubling him up. The breath wheezed out of him as Roth turned him again, gently this time, locked his elbow round his throat, placed his left hand behind the skull, took a quick breath and twisted hard, breaking his neck.

Roth bent low and hoisted the body over his shoulder, stumbled to the end of the passage, kicked open a door and dumped it down a flight of stairs into the cellar where the dustbins were stored.

The body sprawled in the rubbish, legs and arms bent at different angles. For a moment he gazed at it, then reached into his tunic for the knife and moved deliberately down the steps, grunting deeply as he thrust the blade into the center of the soldier's chest. He heard the wood splinter behind him and still he gazed unblinking. The man had turned into a butterfly, he thought, an instant metamorphosis, a big, beautiful, broken butterfly pinned to a wall. Roth placed his boot on the stomach and drew out the knife. He needed both hands to do it. That done, he began to empty the rubbish on top of him until there was no trace of the man.

The trip had been worthwhile if only for this, he thought. An eye for an eye. He wondered if Patterson had felt the same sense of satisfaction, of having done something clean, but he doubted it. There had been no malice in the big man, no sense of vengeance. He had been a gentle Englishman, someone who had to work to build up his anger.

Roth took one look at the festering heap he had created and left the building, feeling content, his rage dissipated. He had walked thirty yards before he remembered the soup and the bread.

He was tired when he reached the flat, the tension having left him bedraggled. He would have given anything now for a glass of beer and a warm bed, but at least he could look forward to the gratitude of the others. He felt like a dutiful husband returning with the provisions.

He stopped halfway up the stairs, staring horrified at the sight above him. Gresham was limping toward him, holding his arm stiffly by his side, his face white and contorted with anger. As he reached Roth he snarled at him: "Where the fuck have you been?"

The force of his words made Roth blink. He began to stammer something but Gresham cut him off.

"Bergner's gone."

Oh, God, oh, mother . . . words and phrases formed in Roth's mind but all that came out was a squeak:

"When?"

"Five minutes ago. He smashed the lock and went. It took me all this time to get the fucking uniform on."

Again the swear word, made all the more forceful because the man never cursed. Roth had never heard him use foul language.

"Where's Christa?" Gresham asked sharply.

"Due back any minute. That's why . . ." His words trailed off as Gresham stumbled against him. Roth supported him against the banister, then shoved the food at him. "Here," he said. "You get back to bed. I'll go and find him."

Gresham nodded. "Be sure you do," he said, and hobbled back up the stairs. Before he had reached the top Roth was out of the building and running, his legs and arms pumping, running blind with no idea where to turn. Five minutes, he thought; the man had gone while the killing was taking place. As he ran he cursed, a long, low string of words, some of which he thought he had forgotten. He continued cursing until there was no more breath in him.

It was not until late evening that Bergner reached the bunker. The young soldier who had stopped him for a match had become puzzled when he rambled incoherently and so he took Bergner along to his unit headquarters, where they checked his name tag against records and discovered that Klaus Lang had been reported missing six days ago; but this could not be Lang, not this old man in a private's uniform. They sat him in a corner while they tried to find out who he was, but it was not until a sergeant recognized him that they realized they were in the presence of a general. The sergeant was a veteran of the Eastern Front and said he knew Bergner better than he knew his father.

They asked him if he wanted transport arranged to Zossen. He merely smiled at them, and so they went for a jeep and drove him to the Chancellery.

At nine that evening, freshly washed and fed, and dressed once more in the uniform of a general of the Wehrmacht, he was visited by Martin Bormann.

Smiling, he took Bormann's hand and indicated a chair. The food and the change of clothes had calmed him. "Martin," he said, "how nice of you to visit." He perched himself on the desk opposite and beamed. "I've been away, you know."

"Yes." Bormann was looking carefully at him, watching his every move and trying to gauge his reaction.

"How are things progressing?" Bergner asked.

"Badly," said Bormann. "It's only a matter of days now."

"Dreadful," said Bergner. He turned and looked at the map, squinting at it. "They're closing in," he said. "The Russians."

"Yes." Bormann watched him for a moment, then placed his hand on Bergner's shoulder.

"Gerhard," he said softly, "where have you been?"

"In the snow," said Bergner, still staring at the map. "But I came back. I saw them eat horses in the snow but I came back. . . ."

He spoke quietly to himself and did not notice Bormann stand up and leave, nor did he flinch when the door was slammed shut. He just kept talking.

20

London, April 27, 1945

Alan Francis finally tracked down the man he wanted. They had dinner together in a small restaurant off Shaftesbury Avenue, one of those which still catered for the theater audiences. They talked about the military situation, made predictions, discussed what might happen after the cease-fire, and it was not until the man had relaxed and was sipping his third brandy that Francis finally put the question and received the answer he expected; that it was Robertson who had put the military onto Gresham. It was obvious; it could not have been a coincidence, but he had needed to be sure.

But the bonus was unexpected.

"Shouldn't like to be in their shoes at the moment," the man had said. "Berlin must be a ghastly place to find oneself."

Francis nodded and the man blustered slightly, coughing to hide his embarrassment. "You did know about it?" he said.

Francis shook his head.

"No, of course. It was all very hush-hush. I thought you might have known, being so close to him."

"Not really my field," he said, then smiled. "But, like a happy marriage, we have no secrets from each other. It's just not something that ever came up."

"But if it was to be mentioned?" he stammered.

"Don't worry," said Francis, "I didn't hear a word you said. You were talking with your mouth full."

They laughed together and Francis called for the bill. He needed an early night.

The earliest he could see Robertson was three o'clock the next afternoon in the Baker Street flat. As he made his way up the stairs, Francis was conscious of a certain tension and was reminded of his early days in Fleet Street when he had to confront bent policemen and con men with the results of his investigations. He smiled to himself. The comparison would hardly stand up. Robertson was no con man, that was for sure. Yet Francis needed the answer to a couple of questions. The itch had become too much to bear. It was irritating him to the extent that he could not fully concentrate on his work. Robertson would understand. He was, after all, a reasonable man.

"Come in, Alan. A sherry?"

Francis settled himself in an armchair and waited until the drinks had been poured. Robertson perched on his desk and looked at him expectantly.

"Sir, I've come about Harry Gresham."

"Oh, yes?" Robertson looked back at him impassively.

"I happened to be in Cambridge—"

"Of course," said Robertson, interrupting him. "Your girl. Julie, isn't it?"

"And I came across Gresham's name."

"Where?"

"And I discovered that you had personally asked for him to lead the special unit."

Robertson sipped his sherry. "And what conclusion did you reach?"

"And that you sent the unit into Berlin."

Francis stood up and walked round the room, waiting for Robertson to react.

"I repeat," said Robertson, "what conclusion did you reach?"

Francis turned and gazed at him. "I hoped you might tell me, sir."

"Why should I tell you?" Robertson's tone was friendly with no hint of annoyance.

"Sir, you said that the team was being sent to recover V-2 secrets." He paused. "I would suggest that you were giving me, shall I say, a false impression."

Robertson smiled. "Alan, why have you been snooping around behind my back?"

Francis shrugged. "Old habits, as they say. An unnatural curiosity."

"Your reporter's nose?"

"Something like that."

Robertson pushed himself away from the desk, moved to the cabinet and poured himself another sherry. He held the bottle up in Francis's direction but Francis shook his head.

"You'll appreciate, Alan, that there are a number of reasons why a unit should be sent behind enemy lines. All manner of things."

"But why Gresham? He has a dreadful record."

"He is a wonderful soldier. He is also slightly unhinged."

"Beats people up."

Robertson nodded. "He is not, shall we say, a complete man. Some form of sexual problem. It tends to frustrate him. A head of steam, faulty valve, you know what I mean."

"But, if you'll excuse me saying so, sir, that is not the problem. You may not have known that he was a member of the Anglo-German Club in the thirties."

Robertson smiled. "Of course I knew. I was his tutor. You must have discovered that. You must also have discovered that he was quite a little Fascist in his time and, to anticipate your next question, I did not think I was taking a risk, putting him in charge. No more of a risk, at least, than any other that one must take in wartime."

Francis tried to say something, but Robertson by now was in full flow. "Gresham was the man for the job," he said. "And it is my responsibility. No one else is involved."

"And would you care to tell me what the job is?" asked Francis.

Robertson was silent for a moment. "It will depend on your answer to an offer I will make you."

Francis frowned. What offer? he wondered. What was the man getting at?

"I hinted at it before," said Robertson. "You probably remember. It's just that, when this is over, I intend to go into politics. You know about this, of course?"

Francis nodded.

"And I am not going to be content with rotting on the back

benches putting up occasional questions and the odd Private Member's Bill. I am ambitious, Alan. I believe certain things are important." He paused. "In the near future I will need a personal assistant." He smiled and led Francis to the door. "We shall leave it at that for the moment. Unless you have any further questions?"

Francis shook his head.

"Thank you for coming to see me," said Robertson as Francis made his way slowly toward the lift.

Back at his desk, Francis flipped through the file he had made on his boss. He picked up the list of phone numbers, some with ticks against them. There was not much point calling the others. But, on the other hand, if he did not, the exercise would remain unfinished and he did not like loose ends. He would make the calls. It would not take long. And then he could relax and forget about the whole business.

21

Berlin, April 29, 1945

For the first time, Gresham awoke clear-headed. The ache in his arm was dull and manageable and the fever had left him. His throat was no longer dry and his eyeballs did not burn. He felt as if he had been purged. When he raised his head from the pillow there was no pain, and when he swung himself off the bed the room remained static. He got to his feet, aware of the weakness in his legs, but he would simply have to forget it. There was no more time; already he had lingered far too long. He could hear the others moving around in the living room, and he remembered how Christa had taken the news that Bergner had gone: the short gasp and her hand fluttering to her mouth in the immediate assumption that it must have been her fault.

He washed in cold brown water and reached for his tunic. It smelled fresh. She must have cleaned it for him. The bloodstains had been soaked away and were barely visible, and she had sewn up the torn sleeve. Quickly he slipped it on and left the room.

They were sitting on the sofa together, looking up at him silently as he came in, Christa smiling apprehensively, Roth expressionless, waiting for his reaction.

"All right," he said, "let's get this business over with."

Roth nodded, relieved. There was to be no postmortem; the past was dead and buried. Now they had to look to the future.

Gresham began pacing the room, rubbing the life back into his calves, aware of the weight he had lost. He would need to be careful and reserve his energy. He took deep breaths and gazed through the shattered window at the city below. It was almost unrecognizable, under a heavy layer of smoke and dust. He turned and cleared his throat.

"What's the situation?" he asked.

"From what we can gather, both airports have been taken by the Russians," said Roth. "There is heavy fighting in the suburbs and the Grunewald. One aircraft got in on Friday on the East–West axis, but to all intents and purposes the city is totally cut off."

"Have you been checking on Bergner?"

Roth nodded, glad that he had covered all possibilities. "There's no sign of him. No one takes a walk anymore. It would be suicide. It's almost deserted out there. Those who have not been killed have tried to make it out, north or west."

"So how do we get near to him?"

Roth had anticipated the question. He left the room and returned a moment later with a sheet of paper, which he spread on the floor. It was a map, roughly drawn in pencil.

"From what I could gather from Bergner the bunker is on two levels. You enter from the Chancellery through the butler's pantry. There's a staircase to the garden and another down to the first level, where Bergner has his room. . . ."

"Assuming he has not been moved," said Gresham.

"Of course." Roth traced the route with his finger. "From there a central passage leads to the stairs to the lower level, which they call the Führerbunker."

"So the best way would be through the garden?"

"Looks like it," said Roth.

For a moment there was silence. Roth wondered what the man was planning. Surely he would not attempt to raid the place? Surely not. As if to answer his thoughts Gresham said, "If he doesn't come out, we'll have to go in."

Christa had been silent up to now. She coughed to gain their attention. "I could get a message to Angela," she said.

Gresham nodded. He had forgotten all about the woman. The fever had affected his brain. He was not thinking straight. He snapped his fingers. "Good. Let's go," he said.

As they trooped down the stairs he stopped briefly.

"By the way," he said, "what day is it?"

"Sunday," said Roth.

"Not that it matters much," Gresham said, and followed them out into the street.

Immediately he coughed and spluttered, doubling up as the dust choked him. He looked up and saw that the others had covered their noses and mouths with scarves. He reached into his pocket, pulled out a tattered handkerchief and did the same. He sniffed. The smell of burning was spiced with something obscene. He looked inquiringly at Roth, who nodded and mumbled through his scarf.

"Corpses everywhere," he said. "They're no longer bothering to move them. The shellfire is too accurate."

It took them fifteen minutes to make their way out of Friedrichstrasse and across Wilhelmplatz to the Chancellery, keeping close to the walls. Nothing moved. It seemed as though they were the only ones left in the burning city. Those who remained were underground—the living, the missing and the dead.

Gresham and Roth waited in the square while Christa scurried across the street to the shattered archway of the Chancellery building. As she approached they could see an SS guard look up from behind a pillar and wave at her to go back, but still she continued until she reached the entrance.

"Good girl," Roth breathed, but Gresham said nothing. They squatted behind the burned-out wreck of an Opel, watching as she talked to the guard for a moment. Then she turned and made her way back toward them. She was panting as she reached them.

"I have to go back in half an hour," she said. "There may be an answer."

"Then we'll wait here," said Gresham, squatting on the pavement and leaning against the car. "There's nowhere else to go."

They sat in silence, glancing at their watches every few minutes until it was time. Without a moment's hesitation, Christa again got to her feet and ran across the street.

This time she was longer and Roth could hear Gresham muttering under his breath, cursing her, and for the first time Roth felt a tremor of mutinous anger. She was risking her life ducking shells and there was no need for him to have a go at her, even to himself. But the feeling quickly passed as he saw her running toward them again; she ducked in behind the car, reached into her pocket and produced a piece of paper.

"She was too busy to see me but she sent this," she said.

Gresham looked at it and mouthed the words: "Wilhelmplatz station. Eastbound platform. Seven P.M."

He looked up inquiringly, and Christa pointed to what was left of the entrance to the underground station.

"Did the guard see this?" he asked.

"I don't think so. He gave it to me already sealed."

"Good." Gresham tore up the note and watched it flutter away along the pavement. Maybe things were going to work out after all. As they made their way back to the cellar he was in a more confident mood.

Roth did not fully understand why Gresham decided to go alone, but he did not argue. If Gresham wanted him to look after Christa, then OK, although she was perfectly capable of taking care of herself. But he was the boss. He must have had his reasons.

Gresham left them in the cellar and moved fast through the streets, spitting dust every few yards. His shoulder ached incessantly, but no longer did the pain shoot through his body. He could live with the aching. He had done it often enough before.

He waited a hundred yards from the station entrance until he was sure no one was around, then sprinted toward it, ducking down between the shattered walls and making his way down two sets of stairs into the sulfurous air. He vaulted the ticket barrier and ran down the motionless escalator onto the platform, checking the map to make sure he was going the right way. The place stank of urine and, all around, he could make out in the gloom the debris of those who had sheltered from the bombs. He patted his pocket, feeling the outline of the small torch, but decided against using it. He did not know who might be there, and for the moment he would rather not know.

He checked his watch and settled down to wait, breathing through his mouth and praying she would be on time. Even as he did so he heard the footsteps approaching along a tunnel. As she came closer he flattened himself against the tunnel wall.

"Frau Müller."

She gasped and put her hand to her heart.

"I'm sorry to have startled you," he said, moving forward to greet her.

"That's all right," she said.

"I thought you would have come from the staircase," he said.

She shook her head and smiled. "There is a route here which runs directly to the Chancellery kitchen. It is safer than running the risk of the shells."

He took her arm and drew her along the platform, letting her talk, listening to her voice as it echoed through the empty tunnels.

"It's madness in there," she said wearily. "There are times when there is no light, and you never know if there is to be any food. And the Führer, poor man, he is so sick, always perspiring. He looks so old now, and he dribbles his food . . ."

"And Bormann?"

"I scarcely get to see him, he is so busy. They were drinking the other night, right through until dawn—him, Krebs and Burgdorf. You could hear them arguing all night. It is terrible."

Gresham glanced at her face, but in the dark he could not tell whether she was showing disapproval.

He stepped in front of her and forced her to stand still. "I want you to give Herr Bormann this," he said, handing over an envelope.

"Herr Bormann?" she repeated dumbly.

"Yes. I understand that the general is quite mad."

"Demented," she said.

"Then I need to get in touch with Herr Bormann."

She shrugged and took the letter.

"How close are the Russians?" he asked.

"On the doorstep. Potsdamerplatz, as close as that."

"Then there's not much time."

"Two days at the most, so they say," she said. "The Führer keeps talking about Wenck's army coming to relieve us, but no one seems to believe him. It's very sad."

She lowered her head and seemed to be sobbing, but when she spoke again her voice was steady. "I have to get back."

Gresham allowed her to turn and make her way back the way she had come before shouting after her. "How many are left in the bunker?"

She stopped and began counting to herself, but he did not let her finish. "Can you get me in," he asked, "through the tunnels?"

She turned back to face him and shook her head. "You would soon be questioned. Everyone knows one another. We are like a family. A new face would need an explanation, and you would never get out."

"So," he said, "you will have to get Herr Bormann and General Bergner to meet me here."

"I'll try," she said.

"There's not much time."

"I'll try. I'll do my best. That's all I can say."

"And I'll wait here," he said.

"Of course. It's the safest place." She moved away and turned left into a smaller tunnel. Gresham waited for a moment and followed her, moving quietly, almost on tiptoe. She was not difficult to track, her shoes clattering on the concrete. He followed her until he saw the shaft of light, and watched her climb a set of iron ladders to the trapdoor, then went back the way he had come.

It was not until he was back on the platform that he realized how tired he was and how much the fever had taken out of him. He sat down heavily and within moments he was asleep.

He was awakened by a scratching noise. Slowly he opened his eyes, keeping his body perfectly still. The rats were nibbling at his shoes and they did not stop even as he slid his hand along the floor, searching for something to throw. Cautiously he scrabbled in the dark until he felt something under his fingers. In one movement he hurled it and the rats scampered away up the tunnel, squealing in fright.

Breathing heavily he wiped his brow and smelled the excrement on his palm. Grimacing to himself he got to his feet, looking for something with which to clean it off. There were food wrappers and pieces of rag lying around, the remains of the civilians who had sheltered there. He smeared his hand against a fragment of a scarf and sat down again, hoping that the foul odor was animal and not human. Not that it mattered much. It was all the same now. They were all animals.

He glanced at his watch. Eight thirty. In other places in the world, people would be coming back from church or having family suppers. Quite suddenly he wanted to discharge his rage at someone, but there was nothing except rubbish to attack. Silently he squatted in the filth, letting his anger smolder inside him like a cancer.

At the sound of the first explosion, Christa leaned forward into her pillow and heard the others snicker in amusement. She did not care. It was an automatic gesture now. She had been doing it for so long that it had become a reflex; first the bombing, now the shells. It was all the same. As the dust filtered through the ceiling she heard a man curse and a woman begin to cry. She glanced around her. The tribe, as they called themselves, was diminishing; only those whose apartments were still untouched came down now, and many of them had left for the suburbs. It was only the stubborn and the insane who remained. She closed her eyes and the Russians crept back uninvited into her mind; there had been a new story that day, of babies being thrown against walls. But perhaps it was not true. The old woman who had told it had seemed pleased with herself, triumphant even, as her listeners reacted in horror. Perhaps she was just making it up. No one knew what was true anymore. The fear affected everyone. It was an epidemic without a cure; there was no vaccination against the Russians.

She pulled her coat around her shoulders, conscious of the little knob of bone protruding at her shoulder. It would take a month of good diet to get the weight back on. Peter might not recognize her, but she could remember everything about him, every line and wrinkle. It was not true what they said, that faces blur through time. Again she pictured herself with him, strolling in the London parks. They would live in Knightsbridge or Kensington, somewhere like that, and she would look back on all this as if it were another life. Maybe she would talk about it to her children and reluctantly be pressed into describing it to the English matrons; it would give her a certain mystery and they would think of her as someone with a terrible past to whisper about over their teacups. She drifted into a dream of English fields and scarecrows, except that the scarecrows had twisted human faces and cards round their necks saying, I am a traitor.

She awoke to the feel of movement; people were stretching and yawning. She blinked and looked across at Roth, who winked at her. She smiled back, glad of his presence. The other women were just meat for the Russians, but she at least had her protectors and the knowledge made her feel like a queen.

"I'm sick of living like a rat. I'm going out." The fat woman got to her feet and moved to the stairs. It was the signal. She had adopted the rank of leader over the past few weeks; every morning she would say the same thing. It was like the all clear. She would waddle up the stairs and open the door, the others following her.

"Sick of it," she grumbled, as she reached the door and pushed. For a moment she stood as if transfixed, then turned and stared back down the stairs. Even in the gloom they could see the horror on her face. Roth was the first one behind her, pushing hard at the door and grunting an oath. Quickly he turned toward her, coughing to hide the English words that had exploded from his lips. But if she had heard she gave no sign; she simply stood motionless, her eyes bulging, her lips moving soundlessly. Roth swore again, this time silently. Again he glanced at her. She had not reacted. But he knew he could take no chances.

He shoved again and a single shaft of light zipped into the cellar. He could smell the harsh stench of burning timber. He leaned back, poked the barrel of his rifle through the gap and twisted, listening with satisfaction as a piece of masonry fell away from the door. He pushed again and the crack widened. It was all right. It would be a long job but they would get out. They were not buried alive. Not this time.

It took the men half an hour, working in shifts, until the door was prized open sufficiently for them to squeeze through. Roth was the first one out, and he gazed straight up into the gray sky through the shattered ruin that had once been an apartment block. He coughed and spat, and gazed upward at the wallpaper peeling in the sunlight; tattered penants that had once decorated bedrooms and kitchens. Two stories up he could see the remains of Christa's room, just a lone wall and, incredibly, a picture still hanging tenaciously at an angle. If it fell, he thought, it would probably kill someone. That would be a strange way to die.

He was pushed to one side as the tribe emerged, stumbling into the daylight. They stood bright-eyed with shock, then began to wander in the rubble, staring upward, mumbling to one another. An old woman shook her fist at the sky and squealed obscenities at the top of her voice, while Christa reached for Roth's hand and held it tightly.

He stroked her face and led her to the remaining wall.

"Stay there," he said softly, and went over to the fat woman. She was standing alone, looking at a piece of broken fireplace.

"Yours?" asked Roth.

She nodded. He put an arm round her shoulder and led her away, over the rubble to the alleyway, looking around him and speaking in soft tones, searching for a place where the job could be done quickly and quietly.

Christa watched them go and looked at the remains of her flat. All she could think was how she could climb the smoking wall to get her picture down, and she scarcely reacted when Gresham tapped her on the shoulder, hardly listened as he explained how he had waited all

night for her cousin; she had not turned up and they would have to
go back together.

"What?" she said as he stared into her face.

"I said, where is our friend?"

"I don't know."

He slapped her face hard and she blinked up at him. "I don't know,"
she repeated. "He went over there somewhere." She waved an arm
toward the alleyway.

Gresham looked up to see Roth clambering over a pile of timber.
He looked ill, his face white and strained. Gresham frowned as he
went to meet him. Surely Roth was all right? He must be. He would
be needed. Roth couldn't crack, not now.

"She took a terrible time to die," was all Roth said. Gresham
watched him wander away. He would ask later what he meant. Right
now there was work to be done.

22

Berlin, April 30, 1945

The heart of the Reich was shrinking by the hour as the Russians moved into the Potsdamerplatz in the south, the Weidendammer bridge in the north and the Tiergarten in the west. From each position they sent mortar fire into the remnants of the city center.

Gresham no longer attempted to hide his frustration, and paced the cellar like a caged beast, close to despair, feeling useless and foolish, the initiative long since lost to him. Silently Roth and Christa watched him. Now they had the place to themselves. With the apartment block a ruin, no one had bothered to stay. All morning they sat in silence, conscious of their hunger and thirst, waiting for him to come up with a miracle.

Roth brooded. He fingered the gray cloth of his tunic, which was stiff now with sweat and grime. Perhaps, he thought, it might be soiled enough to be bulletproof. Soon he would need armor plating, the way things were going; and all because he had taken time off to kill a Nazi he was in danger of being blasted to pieces by the Russians. It was ridiculous. He only hoped that he would have time to explain in the event of capture, but he thought it unlikely. Even if he managed

183

to tell his story he would probably be shot by the time they had bothered to check it.

His thoughts were interrupted as Gresham suddenly stopped pacing and looked down at him then at Christa.

"We'll try once more," he said. He squatted low and looked into Christa's face. "I want you to go back to the Chancellery," he said.

Roth caught the look of fear on the woman and he spoke up for her. "Is there any point?" he said. "They are not going to let her in and her cousin already knows the situation." He looked away, his voice fading as Gresham glared at him. He remembered his words all those weeks ago; no rank here, not unless you disagreed, then there was rank, plenty of rank.

Christa looked down at her feet. "Must I go out again?" she asked in a small voice.

Gresham stood up and turned his back on them. "Perhaps you are right," he said. For a moment he was silent, and then he spun around once more. "We'll go," he said, looking at Roth. "We'll try to talk our way in."

"Whatever you say," said Roth. He knew that Gresham was clutching at straws. There was little they could do. It was out of their hands now, but he could understand the man's need to attempt anything rather than sit around and wait to be buried alive. He checked his rifle and picked up his pack. Gresham was bent in the rubble drawing a rough map in the dust with his finger and motioning Christa toward him; vaguely Roth heard him muttering a set of names, talking quietly like a priest intoning a litany:

"Tiergarten Railway Station, Kantstrasse, Masuren Allee, Reichsstrasse to the Sportfeld and on to Pichelsdorf . . ."

Christa was nodding and Roth came to her shoulder and listened.

"There will be boats at the Havel," said Gresham. "You sail to the west bank between Gatow and Kladow and then on to the American lines. They cannot be far by now."

Gresham stood up and stepped backward, leaving Christa on her knees staring blankly at the floor. Roth turned to him and saw him take the pistol from his holster, and just for a moment he thought the worst. He stiffened, ready to spring; whatever happened he would not let him kill her. But he was holding it out to her by the barrel. She turned and looked up at them, her face grimy with dust, the tears tracing a pattern down her cheeks.

"You'll be back, though," she said in a whisper.

Gresham said nothing. Roth bent low and wiped her eyes with his sleeve. "Of course," he said. "This is just for emergencies." He took the gun from Gresham and laid it on the ground, winked at her and stood up. Gresham was already making his way up the stairs.

Roth shouldered his pack and followed him. At the door he looked down. Christa was still on her knees, touching the gun with the tips of her fingers.

"See you later," he said, but she did not look up. He went outside into the smoke, gently closed the door and had to sprint to catch up with Gresham as he ran doubled up, shimmering ghostlike in the flames that lit up the whole of Friedrichstrasse. They would come back for her, Roth thought; he would make sure of that.

Twice on the way to the Chancellery they were forced to throw themselves flat as the shells exploded close to them. The Russians had got a fix on the building now, and soon it would be nothing but a mess of broken stone. But still the archway remained. As they dashed toward it, they saw two guards raise their heads and yell at them to stop.

Gresham crouched low and yelled back at them.

"Hauser, Leutnant, B Company, Eighteenth Division. Message for General Bergner."

They thought they could hear laughter as Gresham yelled again. "Personal from Obergruppenführer Steiner."

"Go back," the guards shouted. "All messages by telephone!"

"Personal!" shouted Gresham, but the SS man stood up and waved a machine pistol at them. "Get back," he said; "there's no refuge in here."

Gresham hissed a curse between his teeth, rose and sprinted back toward Wilhelmplatz, motioning Roth to follow him. As they reached the station entrance a shell blasted onto the road, the concussion sending them staggering through the entrance. They did not stop running till they reached the barrier.

Gresham made his way purposefully to the platform and stopped at the far end.

"We'll wait here," he said. "She must come eventually."

Roth squatted in the dirt wondering who he was talking about; not that it mattered much. At least this place was safe, even though it stank. He placed his rifle on his knees, closed his eyes and fell instantly asleep.

It was late in the afternoon when Gresham looked up, his head cocked to one side, listening. The footsteps grew louder and he got to his feet, silently uttering a prayer of thanks. But Angela was alone and walked past him as if he was not there; even in the dark he could see that her face was ashen pale. Roth stirred and looked up.

"Stay there," said Gresham, moving after Angela and taking her arm. "Where are they?" he hissed.

But she said nothing. She pulled herself away from him and carried on along the platform. Gresham followed her, content for the moment to let her lead him wherever she wished.

At the exit she walked straight out into the square, heedless of the smoke and the sound of artillery fire. She crossed the street, moved a few paces north until she came to a clearing in the rubble, and stopped, staring into the Chancellery garden. Gresham caught up with her and stood by her shoulder.

"What is it?" he asked, following her gaze. Silently she pointed to a column of smoke which curled thick and black.

Again he asked, "What is it?" Insistently this time.

"It's the Führer," she said in a monotone, "They're burning him."

Eventually she turned and looked at Gresham, but there was no expression, nothing that she could recognize: only that he had gone pale as if in shock. She looked back at the smoke, oblivious to everything else; even when a shell burst fifty yards away, sending shrapnel zipping into the brickwork, she made no move. It was Gresham who reacted, shaking himself as if he had just awakened. He took her by the elbow and steered her back across the street.

"What of Bergner?" he asked.

"Mad. Quite mad."

"And Bormann?"

"I don't know. They're all busy." As they reached the station entrance, she looked at him and sneered. "They had a dance last night, you know. In the canteen. Can you imagine?"

Gresham ignored her. "Did you give the note to Bormann?" he asked sharply.

She nodded. "I gave it to one of his secretaries. She would have passed it on."

"Have you spoken to him?"

"No."

"Christ!" shouted Gresham. "We might just as well have turned up half an hour ago in a puff of smoke."

"What?" Angela frowned at him. She did not understand his fury and he frightened her a little.

"Look," he said softly, staring into her eyes, "I want Bergner and Bormann out in the tunnel within the hour. Do you hear me?"

She shrugged. She heard him all right. But what could she do? She could not command the Reichsleiter to follow her, a mere typist.

But she would not tell him that. He might hit her. The man looked capable of anything, and so she nodded her head, agreeing with him.

"All right," he said. "Now go."

She scuttled away from him down the stairs, glad to go back to the bunker where it was safe.

Gresham waited for an hour and a half, occasionally glancing down at Roth, envying him his ability to sleep. Eventually he looked at his watch and cursed. He got to his feet and moved down the tunnel. It seemed to lead only to a brick wall, but he knew where he was going, turning to his right at the end and moving deeper underground, the air becoming more and more foul so that he had to breathe through his handkerchief. He scrambled along the tunnel for thirty yards, then hoisted himself onto a narrow ledge, crawling forward, his hands wet with slime. Every few yards he stopped and shouted so that the rats would move off. He could hear them scampering in front of him. As he stopped to spit out the phlegm that rose in his throat, a small rat, a baby, scuttled past him, its eyes wide with terror, scrabbling over his shoulder and losing its grip for a moment before digging its claws into his tunic and running down his back. Gresham shivered and moved forward until he reached the end of the ledge, and jumped down three feet into a vault. Above him he could see a crack of light. He closed his eyes and counted to a hundred. When he opened them again he could vaguely make out the shape of a set of iron rungs. He reached for the first and hauled himself up until he reached the trap-door, then took a deep breath and pushed. It did not move.

Briefly he hung motionless on the ladder, then began to batter on the door with the butt of his rifle, the sweat pouring from him as he swung his wounded shoulder at the door. The dullness of the echo suggested that it must be a foot thick. Again and again he smashed the rifle against it, the noise echoing through the tunnels like thunder. He swore at the top of his voice, and it was not until he stopped lashing out that he realized that he had been screaming.

He dropped to the floor, both shoulders racked with pain. For a moment he thought of doing a crazy thing. He raised the rifle and aimed at the hinges, then dropped the gun to the floor. In such a confined space he would have been killed by the ricochets. It would be a strange form of suicide, he thought, to die among the rats, a victim of his own stupidity; but perhaps in the circumstances it would be appropriate; the operation had been a disaster from the beginning and cursed with ill luck. He looked up at the crack of light; so near and yet . . . but there was no point in self-pity.

Wearily he dragged himself back onto the ledge, this time ignoring the rats and the slime that dripped through the roof. He had never before felt so defeated and so utterly useless.

Roth was on his knees on the platform, retching noisily onto the tracks, and he scarcely bothered to look up as Gresham approached. Finally he stopped, wiped his mouth and coughed, then lay back, sprawled out, his face white. When he spoke his voice was a broken croak of a sound. "It's the air," he said. "The smell of piss."

Gresham nodded. He had felt sick constantly and it did not help that they had not eaten for twenty-four hours.

"We'll move up to the next level," he said. "The air's better up there. We can always come back here later."

Roth rose unsteadily to his feet. It was a small mercy, but in the circumstances it was like a reprieve; anything to get away from the smell. As he followed Gresham out of the platform he noticed that the man was walking stoop-shouldered, dragging his rifle as if he no longer cared what happened next. If Gresham had given up, thought Roth, the game was over. All that was left was to wait for the Russians and pray.

23

Berlin, May 1, 1945

Gerhard Bergner did not look up when the soldier entered his room, nor did he appear to notice the man's voice.

"I said, did you sleep well, Herr General?" The man persisted until Bergner nodded absentmindedly.

"You are lucky. Not many of us got much rest last night; a lot of activity, you know." He spoke slowly as if to a child as he helped Bergner out of his chair.

"What time is it?" asked Bergner.

"Three o'clock."

"In the afternoon?"

"Yes. Hard to be sure these days, isn't it?" He led him to the basin and watched as Bergner splashed water on his face, spluttered and coughed up phlegm, retching into the bowl. He turned, wiped his face on a grimy towel and smoothed back his hair, brutally pressing his fingers into his scalp as if he were trying to polish his skull. That done he went across to his cot and stretched out, closing his eyes.

"Herr General," said the soldier impatiently, "don't go to sleep."

"Too late," said Bergner, smiling. He began to snore loudly.

"Reichsleiter Bormann wants to see you, sir."

"Martin?" His eyes opened. "Is he not dead with the others?"

"No, sir. He sent me for you. He would like to talk to you."

"Don't want to," said Bergner, pouting.

The soldier sighed, bent forward and gently lifted Bergner from the bed, dragging him by the arms to his feet. Bergner did not protest as he was propelled from the room, but the pout remained on his face.

Bormann was bending over a map table as Bergner was pushed gently into the office. He turned and smiled, his face lined with fatigue, deep circles under his eyes, and held out both hands to greet Bergner.

"You look rested, Gerhard," he said, waving the soldier away and leading Bergner to a chair.

"Oh, yes." Bergner sat down and studied the map, frowning as he took in the latest positions, only half-listening as Bormann's voice droned above him.

"We are leaving tonight, Gerhard. All of us. There is no advantage in staying. The Russians are virtually on the doorstep . . ." He paused. "Are you listening?"

Bergner nodded.

"Last night I sent Krebs to negotiate with them. He returned at noon empty-handed. So, we have no alternative."

"The Russians," said Bergner.

Bormann leaned forward until he was inches from Bergner's face.

"Gerhard. You have friends outside."

"Yes," said Bergner doubtfully.

"You remember our talk in the garden?"

Bergner shrugged, narrowing his eyes as if trying to focus some part of his memory.

"In February. You remember."

"Ah, yes."

"Good." Bormann drew back, stared at Bergner for a moment, then snapped a button on his desk, leaned forward and spoke into it. "Frau Müller, please." As he waited he patted Bergner's shoulder. "I never dreamed it would come to this," he said.

"You didn't?" Bergner looked up, a smile on his face, the look of a conspirator.

Bormann shook his head. "And we can trust your friends?"

Bergner shrugged and lapsed once more into a slouch, his eyes glazed. Bormann stared at him for a moment, shook his head and leaned over the map.

Angela knocked sharply and entered. "Herr Reichsleiter," she said, standing to attention.

"You have been in touch with the general's friends?" Bormann asked.

"Yes, sir. You will remember the note I sent you."

"Quite. And now I want to meet them." He reached across his desk and handed her a piece of paper. "This will authorize their entry. Can you do this?" He looked up for the first time.

"Of course, sir."

"Good." He waved his hand at her and she turned and left the room. Quietly he turned again to Bergner. "That's all, Gerhard. Why don't you go back to your room? We have a busy night ahead of us."

Bergner stiffly got to his feet, shook Bormann's hand and followed Angela into the corner. "I would wrap up well if you are going out," he whispered to her, but Angela ignored him, leaving him standing by the door, an old man talking to himself.

She hurried along the corridor to the kitchen. It was empty. No longer was there any bustle or the shout of the cooks. The pots stood empty on the stove, and the place had been scrubbed spotless as if they were leaving it intact for the next tenant. Angela bent to the floor and tugged at the metal ring, stepping back as the heavy trapdoor swung slowly upward, creaking on its hinges. She smoothed down her skirt, turned and made her way gingerly down the rungs, grimacing as she went. She hated the journey through the tunnels. If it were not for Herr Bormann she would never have dreamed of slithering around in the slime.

As she crawled through the blackness she recalled the old days in the house in Bavaria with her parents, when there was sunshine and peace. As a rat scuttled past, she pretended it was one of her mother's cats. That's all it is, she told herself, just a pretty cat; nothing to worry about.

As she lowered herself from the ledge she slipped and felt the heel of her shoe snap off. She stamped her foot and permitted herself a discreet little oath, then bent forward and took off her shoes, padding forward soundlessly on her bare feet.

He was not there. She looked around, peering into the gloom. There was no sign of him.

"Sir," she whispered, but there was no reply. Again she muttered a gentle swear word. Perhaps he had been annoyed that she had not kept last night's appointment, but she had been too busy and could not get away. He was probably sulking in the cellar with Christa. She would need to go and hunt him out. A small tremor of fear passed through her. It was too bad for the man, but she could not wait for him to return. Herr Bormann wanted to see him immediately.

Slowly and silently she made her way along the platform. She climbed the stairs, and in the gloom did not see the two men asleep on the landing.

As she reached the top she felt the air becoming warmer; it was a dry heat, as if it were the height of summer. When she reached street level she felt the gust of hot air, and stepped back from the flames. The whole place seemed to be on fire. She blinked and glanced nervously out into the street, looking to left and right like a nervous pedestrian in heavy traffic. The noise was deafening, the crackle of the flames mingled with the cough of mortars and the sound of masonry crashing to the ground.

For a moment she hesitated, wondering whether she could go back. Maybe Herr Bormann would not mind waiting for an hour or so. It would surely not make all that much difference; maybe he would understand. But on the other hand he might look at her in that manner of his, that silent, strained expression of disappointment, an understated reproach meaning that she had not done quite enough for him. He never shouted at her as he did at the others, and he never scolded her. Sometimes she wished that he would. But she did not want to see that look on his face, not at this stage; he had enough to contend with. He needed her to do what he asked without question.

And so she stepped out of the station and made her way across the square toward Christa's place. It was not far, at least that was something. It would not take very long. Then they would come back and do whatever had to be done, just to get out and away until peace came. Maybe she would go back to Bavaria, at least for a while, a holiday, to recuperate. Her mother would be so proud of her having done so well. There was so much she had to tell her. Quite deliberately she began to conjure up pictures of her home, making a mental inventory, trying to recall the smell and the sound of the place, anything to take her mind off the destruction that surrounded her. . . .

Bergner awoke for the second time that day, to find that his door was open. He frowned, rubbed his eyes and drew himself to his feet, trying to remember when last he had slept in a room with the door open. It seemed to him that doors had been locked on him all his life, and always locked from the outside. He tiptoed toward it and gently pulled it open. There did not seem to be any guards.

"Strange," he whispered. He looked out into the corridor and peered to his left and right; no one. So, maybe it was true. Maybe Hitler was dead, as they were all saying. He had not believed them. It did not seem possible. He listened carefully for footsteps, and from above he thought he heard gunfire: two pistol shots. He glanced at the ceiling, his head cocked like a bird.

"So," he said aloud, "the Russians." He drew himself to his full height and ran his hands down the creases of his trousers. He would meet them in a dignified manner. At last he would come face to face with an enemy he had seen only through the lens of a pair of binoculars. He would not turn his back on them this time. He would go out to face them, walk out into the snow and hand over his sword. He cleared his throat, marched into the passage and bumped into someone.

"Herr General," the man said breathlessly, "we thought you had gone."

"I am about to go," said Bergner pompously.

"We are setting fire to the bunker. Everyone is in the new Chancellery. In the cellar."

"And the Russians. Are they here?"

"No, Herr General."

"But the shots?"

"Dr. Goebbels and his wife," the man said quickly.

"I see." It meant little to him. He had never liked Goebbels, but his wife was pleasant enough. Why would anyone want to shoot her? Now the little man was tugging at his sleeve and pointing down the corridor.

"I believe Herr Bormann wants to see you."

"But I have my books," he said as he moved.

"There is no time, sir. And no one to carry them."

What on earth was he talking about? Bergner wanted to go back, but the little man was insistent. He allowed himself to be led away. He would come back later for his books; meanwhile he would let them play their little game. He looked at his watch: eight thirty. He would come back later.

As he turned the corner he looked back to see the first flames leap up the walls, and then he was being pushed unceremoniously to safety.

* * *

The face of Bormann shocked him. In the few hours since their previous conversation he seemed to have aged years. He was jumpy and irritable and seemed to have shrunk inside his uniform.

Bergner was reminded of a bad-tempered tortoise peering out from its shell. Bormann took his arm and led him into a corner away from the others, who were standing around in groups talking busily together. Some were staring at street maps. Some of them were smoking, and this struck him as odd until he remembered. The Führer hated nicotine. He had forbidden it. So, it was true after all. The madman was dead. And he had never been told about the man with the heart of a baby. It was bad. He should have known what he had done.

"Frau Müller is dead," Bormann was saying.

"I am sorry," said Bergner, trying to remember who she was.

"We waited for an hour but she did not return. I sent a guard to look for her and he found her. She had been hit by mortar fire."

"Terrible," said Bergner.

"So we are on our own."

"Yes."

Bormann wiped his brow with the back of his hand before speaking. "You will come with me," he said. "We are splitting into groups. The first will leave shortly and we will follow. Are you prepared."

"Yes," said Bergner. Prepared for what? he wondered. Where was everyone going? There was nowhere to go. But he did not ask out loud.

He settled himself in a chair in a corner while Bormann went back to the center of the room, gesticulating as he spoke. He did not look well, thought Bergner; none of them did. They all looked as if they had done a lifetime in solitary. Now they were making plans to leave; it was all very strange.

The preparations seemed to take forever. There was always something else to be seen to, papers to be collected, routes to be checked, good-byes to be said, before finally the first group left. Bergner shook a number of hands; General Mohnke, Admiral Voss, Günsche, others he did not know, and four women.

He watched them go and then felt a tug on his sleeve. Bormann was smiling at him and asking if he was ready. Of course he was ready. He had been ready for over two years. Automatically his hand dropped to his belt. He caressed the holster containing the pistol and began to hum a song he had learned as a boy. Bormann was leading him from the room, and as he left he looked over his shoulder at Krebs, Burgdorf, and Schedle. They had refused to leave, saying they would wait for the Russians, and suddenly it seemed to him that he should do the same. Someone had said that they were being taken down tunnels. He would not go down a tunnel to meet the Russians. Why a tunnel?

"What are you doing?" Bormann asked brusquely.

"Krebs is right," he said. "It is undignified to leave."

"Krebs is planning to shoot himself," Bormann whispered, pulling again at his sleeve. "Come along."

Hesitantly Bergner moved toward the kitchen. "Perhaps it would be better if we went out the front door like men, instead of rats," he said, but Bormann shook his head. "The area is a sea of flames. We would be dead within minutes, like Frau Müller."

"Ah, yes, Frau Müller." He let himself be dragged along to the kitchen down a ladder and along a series of evil-smelling tunnels. This is ridiculous, he said aloud, but there were people in front and others at the back. He could not turn back now. As they entered the station platform he was so concerned with wiping the slime from his jacket that he did not see the two men in the shadows, nor did he notice them follow him all the way up the line to the next station.

Cautiously they peered out into what remained of the great Friedrichstrasse boulevard; every building appeared to be on fire and the black night air was lit by tracer bullets, so that they could see the masonry crumble under shellfire from the north. Bormann squinted up the street toward the junction with Unter den Linden and beyond to the Weidendammer bridge. The place was deserted, empty of soldiers but filled with the sound of gunfire as if the battle were being fought by invisible armies. He shuddered, then slowly moved out of the doorway, running for the nearest wall, the others following him in a ragged file. In this manner, with Bormann in the lead, they slowly made their way north, stopping every few yards and pressing themselves against the brickwork at every explosion.

Gresham and Roth came fast out of the station, running stooped and throwing themselves into a doorway. Looking out they could see the shadows of the men in front, thirty yards ahead, as they scuttled from door to door. Gresham's eyes were bright, his face flushed; he was conscious only of the others. He had crashed against a doorway with his injured arm but felt nothing. As he swung his rifle to check the safety catch his eye caught the dials on his watch. It was two o'clock.

Again they looked out into the street, and saw the group scampering toward the crossroads, where it stopped like a crowd of schoolchildren looking for a policeman.

Nervously they glanced left and right before dashing over, one of them stumbling as if hit but scrambling to his feet again and running after the others.

Gresham and Roth followed thirty yards behind and waited until the group had reached the south side of the Weidendammer bridge before they sprinted across the boulevard, running zigzag at a crouch, their knees almost at their chins, Roth uttering little clucking sounds as he ran, strange mechanical noises, like a sleepwalker. This was the worst bit, out in the open, away from the protection of the walls, but they reached the north side safely, throwing themselves again into a shattered doorway and breathing deeply, feeling their hearts pound against their tunics.

Gresham glanced out. There were too many at the moment. It was too early to make a move, but soon they would be certain to split up. The group was too clumsy, too obvious a target. He only hoped that they would divide the right way, the way he wanted. . . .

He stiffened as he saw a movement from a building by the river, the Admiral's Palace. Another group was moving out toward Bormann.

Gresham cursed, gripping the stock of his rifle. "Christ, Jesus, they're shaking hands." He swore under his breath. "Decide, damn you, don't just stand there . . . move!"

He turned as Roth tapped him on the shoulder, and looked back to see three tanks slowly approaching them, turning north at the crossroads. Automatically he shrank into the doorway, squinting, trying to focus through the dust and smoke.

"Tigers," whispered Roth. "The last of the panzers."

Gresham nodded. "Thank Christ," he said.

Roth wiped the palms of his hands on his tunic and grinned up at him. "They're on our side," he said, and laughed as if at some private joke. He was still giggling when the big tanks moved past, heading toward the bridge.

Gresham waited until they had passed the doorway before looking out. The men ahead were moving to and fro like headless chickens, uncertain what to do but keeping on the move as if to stay still would invite instant burial. But now they had seen the tanks. Two of them separated themselves from the others and began to move toward them, gesticulating. Even over the din of the mortar fire he could hear them shout, squealing like schoolgirls.

The first tank slowed and stopped, and Gresham could hear the exchange of conversation, but not clearly enough to understand whether the tanks were going to try to cross the bridge. He stepped from the doorway and stared across. At the far side he could see a solid barrier, and behind it he thought he detected movement. So they were this close, the Russians, just a bridge away.

The others were grouping round the tanks now, ducking behind them.

Roth grunted in surprise. "Amazing, isn't it? Look at them, the fools. No sense."

To Roth it was madness. The bigger the target, the more chance of being hit. To Roth and Gresham it was an example of inexperience, the thing that distinguished the fighting soldier from the deskman, the confidence to go off alone, away from the herd.

And there they were, the top brass of the Third Reich, acting like recruits when it came to the crunch. But it was no surprise; their war had been fought behind trestle tables, and the most aggressive thing they had been forced to face until now was a map.

"We got it wrong," Roth was saying. "They're not going west."

Gresham nodded. He had assumed that they would head toward the American lines, but obviously they were taking the chance of protection to go north; perhaps they planned to swing west later, once they had crossed the bridge. Perhaps they were making for the Rechlin air base. Perhaps they did not know what they would do.

He tapped Roth's arm, ran toward the tanks and ducked in behind the last vehicle as it slowly came to a halt, the tracks tearing strips from the road like divots from a golf course, the sparks flying.

They could hear the turrets creaking open and the angry shouts and questions as the soldiers leaned out, scanning the bridge and yelling obscenities. They would not like this, Gresham thought. They would not enjoy stopping as if in a holiday traffic jam and presenting themselves as an easy target. He could imagine the grumbling that would be going on inside the hot steel shells. But now they were on the move again. Gresham spluttered as the exhaust fumes belched in his face, and he glanced out and forward. The others were clustered around the first tank, walking carefully in its shadow like small ducklings behind their mother.

It took them fully two minutes to cross the bridge, one of the front group stopping halfway over to retch noisily.

Gresham frowned and glanced over the parapet. The river was sluggish and black, swollen with rubble and filled with human flotsam, bloated bodies drifting and heaving in the swell. Someone had been sick. It was probably the first corpse the man had seen throughout the whole war.

The grinding of metal on concrete caused him to duck back again as the first tank came up against the barrier. It stopped for a moment, then reared up again, the tracks seeming to grab out for a hold before crunching downward, smashing the barrier aside. The tracks creaked briefly before the tank took a grip and then moved forward, pushing the rubble aside, the others following through the gap while the coughing of the mortars continued, louder now that the river was crossed.

Gresham could see the group signaling to one another, deafened by the noise, waving like bookmakers at a racetrack, as the big tank forced its way northward once more.

They had been lucky, Gresham thought, very lucky. By rights they should have been shelled into eternity on the bridge. He hoped that they had not run out of their share of good fortune.

Slowly they made their way toward Ziegelstrasse and the great bulk of the huge hospital on the left.

"Blast," said Gresham aloud, and Roth turned to him, wondering what was wrong. "If they're headed for the hospital, we've lost them," he said. "Once they get in there, we'll never winkle them out."

Briefly Roth wondered why Gresham had used the plural. Why "them"? But it was nothing, just a way of talking. Gresham had moved forward now alongside the tank, his brow furrowed, thinking hard. It had to be done soon. He could not take the chance of getting lost in a crowd. He nodded to himself, closed his eyes for a moment, took a deep breath and turned and gestured to Roth to follow him. He stepped out away from the shelter of the tank and ran forward, bent double. The leading tank was thirty yards ahead and he could see the backs of the men crouching behind it, but even as he tried to distinguish the figure of Bergner the decision he had made became irrelevant. A bazooka shell exploded on target, tearing into the leading tank, hurling men to the right and left, their bodies suspended briefly in the glare. Gresham was sent sprawling. He landed heavily on his shoulder, screaming with pain as the wound took the force of his fall, and he felt himself rolling onto his side and tightening into a ball, trying to escape, fighting to get out of himself, away from the pain and the noise. His mouth opened in a silent scream as Roth bent over him, supporting him, gazing anxiously into his face.

"Are you OK?"

Gresham read his lips, deafened for the moment by the blast. He nodded and moved into a crouch, feeling for cuts. He was astonished to find that he had not been hit. His shoulder was bleeding again and the pain traveled down the left side of his body, but he ignored it and got to his feet.

"You?" he mouthed at Roth, and the man was grinning, shrugging his shoulders; twice now he had been unhurt. Roth's luck was holding.

The two tanks were trying to turn, their tracks grating against the roadway, their great hulks exposed by the glare coming from the burned-out shell ahead. Gresham and Roth moved toward it. They could see a soldier running in circles, his back and legs on fire, running fast at first but gradually slowing up as he came toward them. His legs buckled and he fell forward, arms thrust out as if in prayer, his face blackened and unrecognizable. As he lay twitching, Roth stepped forward and fired a round into him.

Gresham searched the faces of the men as they rushed past him, running blind, the horror fresh on their faces, sprinting back toward the bridge. He tucked his rifle in the crook of his arm and squeezed his shoulder, cursing as the blood trickled through his fingers, trying to force the pain from his mind. Pain is something you live with, he told himself. Pain is part of your kit. If you can't live with pain you'll die with it; everyone knew that. He talked to himself aloud, mouthing the slogans, driving the agony from his mind.

Roth helped him forward toward the tank, the pair of them ignoring the salivation in their mouths caused by the dead man, and they ducked away from the flames as they reached the burning tank. Three men lay on the ground, one unconscious. A few of the group were starting to crawl away from the wreck, while others scrambled to their feet and stood swaying like Saturday-night drunks. Roth peered into the faces of the three on the ground, turned to Gresham and shook his head. He stood up, grabbed one of the others and yelled into his face, "Where's Bergner?"

The man pointed to the pavement and Roth turned to see Bergner standing by a lamppost, gazing serenely around him.

He ran up to him.

"General Bergner!" he shouted, amazed with himself, greeting the man as if he were an old friend.

Bergner smiled at him and nodded, allowing Roth to take his arm and lead him away back toward the bridge as the shells burst close to them. They could feel the gusts of air from the explosions and hear the singing of the shrapnel.

Glancing behind, Roth could see Gresham with the others, shepherding them along, his arm round the shoulders of a squat, dark man. Briefly he wondered what he was doing and why he was bothering, but he thought no more about it as Bergner muttered in his ear, mumbling some meaningless phrases. Roth pulled him along faster now, dragging him as if he were a stubborn pony until they reached the southern side of the bridge. He pushed him behind the parapet, diving after him, panting, waiting for Gresham to catch up so that he would know what to do next. Gresham would have the answer. For the moment Roth felt a sense of relief that Bergner was back with him, and was quietly pleased that he had found him; it atoned slightly for having lost him in the first place. He was reminded of his schooldays, when he had scored a goal against his own team and then later equalized. Roth laughed aloud. It was absurd, thinking about soccer in this situation, lying in the rubble in a German uniform with a German general, ducking Russian shells and thinking about football. He was going crazy, there was no doubt about it.

Bergner was looking back across the bridge, but Roth paid him no attention, although he kept a tight grip on his sleeve. He would not wander off this time; there was no chance of that. Gresham slid in behind him, followed closely by three others. Roth grunted as he heard one man whisper to another, addressing him as Herr Reichsleiter. So that was Bormann, thought Roth, the swarthy one in the SS uniform, the one who never appeared in the newsreels. Herr Reichsleiter indeed. Roth felt a shiver of anticipation run through him. Now he understood what Gresham was up to. They were going to kill two birds with one stone. Or maybe more than two: the more the merrier. He'd always suspected that there was more to this job than met the eye; why get a specialist team together for one defecting general? Why, indeed? So, they had been after bigger fish all the time. It was just a pity that Gresham had not chosen to let them all in on the secret, but perhaps he had his reasons. He must have had his reasons. Gresham would not do anything without a good reason.

And if he had the chance he would do the killing. It would not atone for much, but at least it would be something, to dispose of such scum. An eye for many eyes. He licked his lips and spat on the ground as Bormann knelt beside him. He could smell the sweat and the fear of one of the Reich's most powerful men, and he was happy; at that moment Cyril Roth would not have changed places with any man.

He listened as Gresham explained to the others that they should go west along the railway line. No one disagreed; they were content to leave the decisions to someone who knew what to do, a soldier in a stained uniform who seemed to know all about action in the field. Under the Russian bombardment, crouched under a parapet, the common soldier had become the general, and all roles were reversed.

Another group slid in beside them, and Bormann told them in guttural grunts that they were to follow the lead of the lieutenant. They nodded dumbly, looking at him, wondering who he was and where he came from, but no one was prepared to doubt him.

Gresham peered above the parapet across the bridge, counting the reports of the mortars, then sprinted across the road, shouting at the others to follow. Roth waited until they had gone and ran fast, dragging Bergner with him, across the street and down a set of steps to the railway lines, where there was some kind of cover.

Gresham vaulted a wall, landing on the tracks, his boots crunching on gravel, and waited until the others had grouped round him. Roth counted heads. The group totaled eight. As they began to move off down the track he thought of doing it just here, opening up on them, spraying them with the big automatic. But it would not be the best way; far better to wait until he could get them where he wanted them, up against a wall somewhere and facing them so he could savor their terror. The first volley would be belly-low so that they would pitch forward onto their faces, and he could finish them off at leisure with the pistol. He could feel the weight of it in the holster. It would come into its own after all, as if it were designed for that very purpose, and it would be a nice irony that it would be a German bullet which would do the job. That decided, he felt happier, knowing what he was going to do. He only hoped that Gresham would not raise any objection. But he would not object, not Gresham.

"I'll leave you behind with the spare ammunition," he had said. "You can personally mop up the Third Reich."

And that is precisely what he was going to do. He winked at Bergner as he dragged him along, and Bergner smiled back at him.

It took them fifteen minutes to reach the shelter of Lehrter Station at the south side of Invalidenstrasse, where Gresham called a halt in the ruins of the building. Here there was a certain measure of protection. Only a direct hit could trouble them and it would have to be massive. They could spend some time here working things out. Bergner wandered off to join the others and Roth dropped to his knees. He stretched out between the tracks, looking through the shattered roof at the sky, convinced that he could see the stars through the smoke and the dust. He felt at peace with himself, ready for anything, his body tense and his mind relaxed as he tried to recall the route to the west that Gresham had outlined. It should not be difficult to get through. The Americans could not be far away by now, and once the Nazis were disposed of they could make good time. Only a stray shell would worry them, but a stray shell could come at any time; if it had your number on it . . . et cetera et cetera, the old story. Nothing to worry about; like they used to say, you could get killed falling out of bed. There was no point in worrying; so long as you had done your homework you were as safe as could be expected. And Gresham had done his homework, there was no doubt about that.

Roth sat up, leaning on his elbows. The others stood huddled together in a group, gesticulating and chattering like a bunch of chimpanzees squabbling over a bag of nuts. Gresham and Bormann stood slightly apart, watching them, and at first when the large group began to move away, Roth assumed they were merely going across to the platform wall for better cover. But Gresham was calling Bergner across to him and Bergner obeyed, walking with one other man away from the group to join Gresham and Bormann while the others made their way along the platform toward the exit.

Roth frowned uncertainly. What was going on? Surely they were not splitting up? It could not be. They could not be leaving; it was impossible. He jumped to his feet and swung his rifle, shouting to Gresham, but the man did not appear to hear him. He was only about ten yards away but he was deep in conversation with Bormann. The others were fifty yards down the platform by now. Roth looked from one group to the other and began to run, shouting again to Gresham, roaring the obvious: "They are getting away!"

"It's all right!" Gresham yelled back, and Roth stopped, turned and stared at him. What did he mean, "It's all right"? It certainly was not all right. Gresham was holding his hand up, palm outward, half-smiling as if to calm him, the sort of expression you might use to an overexcited dog. "It's all right," he said again, and Roth shook his head in disbelief. He turned. The others were almost out of sight now, heading west. In a moment they would turn the corner and be gone. Once more he looked at Gresham, who was beckoning him to come near, to join them. There was something about him, in his expression. What was the word? Condescension, that was it. To hell with him, Roth thought; to hell with the man. The Nazis were not going to escape. Whatever else happened, they were not going to slip away just because of some plan of Gresham's. He turned and began to run after them, ignoring Gresham's cry to come back, not even aware that the man was calling him by his own name: "Roth," he was shouting, "Stop!"

He heard the shot and felt the sky tilt at the same time, and thought it must have been Bormann. In front of him, a couple of inches from his nose, he could see a footprint in the dirt; it was a big foot, probably one of the Nazis. He sighed and decided to get up again and get after them; to hell with Gresham, he would worry about Gresham later. He placed his hands hard against the dirt and pushed, raising his head and shoulders no more than an inch. The effort exhausted him and he collapsed again, his nose within an inch of the footprint. As the nausea rose in his throat and he retched bile into the dust, he thought that Gresham would make Bormann pay for this, one way or another. It had to be Bormann. Bergner would not have done it, or the other man, whoever he was; it must have been Bormann. Gresham would sort him out, then they would go to the American lines. But the first thing to do was to get this uniform off. It would not be comfortable to be caught in such a position when the Russians turned up. He might not have time to explain. Slowly he moved the fingers of his left hand toward his neck, working them inch by inch across the rubble, watching them; they reminded him of five little fat slugs crawling through the undergrowth, grimy and slimy, moving slowly through the bile. He coughed again and tried to retch, but he could no longer move. Even his fingers stopped. He gazed at them; only another couple of inches and they would reach the button at his collar; once that was done he could think about the next button, and the next. He was concentrating hard on moving his fingers when he felt himself being turned over.

There was no pain, only a sensation of movement, and again he was looking up at the stars with Gresham's face above him, peering down.

He opened his mouth to speak, to tell him to help him off with his tunic, but he could not seem to get the words out. He tried to shake his head when he felt the cold barrel of the pistol at his temple. No, he thought, he's got it all wrong. He wants to put me out of my misery or some such nonsense. He's making a mistake; all that needs to be done is to undo the button at the neck and then . . .

Gresham looked down at the body as it twiched once and lay still. He stepped back from the blood which continued to pump from the skull and turned back toward Bormann, who stood in a corner of the station looking uncertainly at him but saying nothing.

He glanced over his shoulder at the others. They were a hundred yards away and had paid no attention to the shots. There was enough of a cacophony for them not to worry about a couple of single rounds being fired.

"Come," he said to the others. They followed him obediently up out of the station into Invalidenstrasse. As he turned right, heading east again, he heard Bormann mutter in surprise, but he kept going. There was no time for explanations. The shells were coming in fast now and they were forced to stop every few yards and crouch in doorways, to hide in the corner of shop fronts and shelter beside the carcasses of tanks.

At the bridge over the railway line, Gresham looked to his left and right and held up his hand for them to stop. From the other side of the river they could hear the sound of machine-gun fire, echoed almost immediately by the spatter of masonry above them. They had been spotted. Gresham grabbed Bormann's arm and pushed him against the bridge wall, grabbing his head and forcing it down beneath the line of fire. Bergner stood above them, gazing north like a tourist, seemingly unaware of the shots which sang above his head, while the fourth man crouched in terror at his feet.

"Bergner!" shouted Gresham.

The general blinked, unaccustomed to such an improper form of address from a lieutenant. He bent down and peered into Gresham's face as if trying to remember where he had seen him before. Vaguely he was aware that he should be incensed by the man's insubordination.

"Take off your cap and jacket."

"All right." He did as he was told, flipping his cap onto the pavement, unbuttoning his jacket, stopping only when his companion stepped between him and Gresham, his face a strange mixture of fear and anger. "What on earth . . . ?" he spluttered.

"Who are you?" asked Gresham sharply, and it was Bormann who answered. "It's Dr. Stumpfegger," he said.

Gresham nodded, and pushed the man to one side so that he stumbled and fell against the wall. He started to rise but decided against it, and watched as Bergner stripped down to his shirt. He continued to watch as Gresham helped Bormann off with his jacket. When the two men had changed, Gresham prodded Bergner forward.

Gresham stepped back a few paces, dropped into a crouch and brought up his pistol, holding it two-handed at arm's length. He called out to Bergner, and at the sound of his name the general turned. He looked down at the gun and along the barrel into Gresham's face, cocking his head to one side like an inquisitive puppy.

Gresham spoke so softly that Bergner had to strain to hear him.

"Gerhard Bergner, you are a traitor to the Reich." The words were delivered in a monotone, emotionless, a judge about to pass sentence.

Bergner frowned, then shook his head and began to laugh. He rubbed the knuckles of both hands into his eyes, then gazed upward, shaking his head and laughing at the sky. Slowly he turned and walked away from the pistol, chuckling to himself, and when Gresham fired he pitched forward neatly onto his face as if he were diving into a pool.

Briefly there was silence, then Gresham turned to Bormann, ignoring Stumpfegger, who slowly made his way to Bergner's side.

Bormann stared wide-eyed at Gresham. He was shivering uncontrollably and did not react to the questions. Gresham turned in annoyance as Stumpfegger began to wail.

"Be quiet," he said sharply, but still Stumpfegger, kneeling beside Bergner, screamed obscenities at him. With a sigh of irritation Gresham again brought up the pistol. Stumpfegger turned away. He had just enough time to cover his ears with his hands before Gresham's bullet blasted through his spine and tore the life from him.

Again Gresham turned to Bormann.

"I said, did you have any ID in the jacket?" he asked.

"No." Bormann's voice was a squeak. "But the testament, the Führer's testament. It's in the inside pocket."

Gresham walked across to Bergner's body, turned it over, felt inside the jacket and came back clutching a bulky envelope.

"All right," said Gresham, "one more thing. Did you get my note?"

"Yes."

"And you told the Führer?"

"Yes. But he would not come. He had made up his mind to die."

Gresham turned away. For a few moments he stared at the two bodies. Bergner smiled back at him with dead eyes, and Stumpfegger gazed sightlessly at the stars.

Again Gresham turned back to Bormann. "Time to go," he said. "Once we reach Stettiner there is a tunnel. With a bit of luck our friends should be at the other end."

Bormann nodded and allowed Gresham to lead him away. He did not know where he was going or with what kind of man. However, he had no choice but to follow. His future was out of his hands. . . .

Christa waited alone in the cellar, accompanied only by rats and a half-mad cat that stared and hissed at her from a corner. She felt silly now, squatting with her pillow over her face. It had not seemed so bad when the others had been around, even those who laughed at her. During a lull in the shelling she stood up and wandered around the dark cavern, touching the walls and running her fingers over the damp bricks, picking at the moss that grew in the mortar. She thought that she could feel the heat of the flames now, but they had told her that she was in no danger of being burned alive; the door was too old and heavy and the rest of the cellar was stone and brick. The worst that could happen, they said, was that the door might crack and fall apart, but at this late stage such a thing did not matter.

They had been so reassuring, even at the last when they could not keep the worry from their faces. Again she looked at the map drawn in the dirt. It had been a gesture, nothing more than that, and she knew it; she could never make it on her own, but nonetheless she appreciated their consideration. She reached into her coat and drew out the pistol, holding it out in front of her, posing, her finger lightly on the trigger. And then she smiled. The gun was just like the map, another gesture.

When they had gone this time, they said it was for the last attempt. If they failed it would be the end, no second chance. They would come back for her one way or the other, with or without the general, and the dark one had joked that it was a long way to come just to pick up a woman. And then they had gone and she had watched them until they vanished. She would keep her promise not to move.

The shelling began again, but this time she continued pacing the floor. The noise seemed to be closer now and there were strange sounds like car engines, only deeper in tone with more of an echo, and the coughing sound of exhausts. She thought of going up to the door and peering out, but she stayed where she was. Whatever it was, it was better not to know. She looked at her watch: three o'clock. There was no need to worry. Hadn't he said that the job would take awhile?

She slumped to the floor and closed her eyes, drifting into a broken dream of strange images, of explosions and nameless faces, until a scuffling sound at the door jerked her awake.

So it was time. She rose to her feet, picked up her bag, patted her hair and smoothed down her skirt. At last they were on the move.

Despite her better judgment she thought of Peter and the London parks, permitting herself a moment of self-indulgence, then she moved toward the door.

At first she did not realize that they were Russians. It was not until she heard the laughter and the strange nasal sounds that she knew. She sighed and reached into her pocket again for the pistol, then backed against the wall as the two men came down the steps, laughing at her and coaxing her.

And still they moved toward her, even as she raised the pistol and placed the barrel in her mouth. They did not even break stride. She could taste the metal. It was a nasty taste, not something to put inside your mouth, she thought, as she dropped it to the floor.

It had been a gesture.

They grinned as she stepped toward them, her head held erect. At least she would not grovel, she told herself. Whatever happened she would retain some sort of dignity. . . .

Part
FIVE

24

London, May 2, 1945

Charles Robertson worked through his speech carefully, crossing out words and inserting others, polishing it until he was certain that he had got it right. It was good; not only good, it was excellent. He sat back, content with a job well done. Swinging round, he peered through the slats of the blind into Baker Street, where the newspaper seller was roaring at the top of his voice. The *News Chronicle,* with a banner headline announcing the death of Hitler, was selling as fast as the man could turn the copies over to his customers.

Robertson gazed at the people scurrying beneath him, little clockwork toys moving at a brisk pace; now that the ogre was dead they seemed to have rediscovered their energy; soon peace would be announced and they would all go crazy for a while. Little did they know it would be a temporary respite. Robertson grunted audibly and turned back to his desk. He tidied up the papers of his speech, then picked up the latest RAF report on Berlin. The city was a burning desert. He put it to one side and flipped through the day's messages, stopping briefly when the phone rang.

"Good morning, Audrey," he said.

"Good morning, sir. Alan Francis has just looked in. He says he is on his way to see you."

"Has he an appointment?"

"No, sir."

"Thank you, Audrey. I'll be in the office before noon."

He placed the receiver gently on the cradle. Strange, he thought. Francis was normally a man who kept strictly to form. It was unlike him to barge in unannounced. Still, if he was coming, then he was coming. Meanwhile there was work to do.

Twenty minutes later, the doorbell rang. Robertson opened the door and stood back.

"Hello, Alan."

"Sir."

Francis made straight for the study and stood with his back to the window. Robertson followed him, and gestured toward the cabinet.

"Sherry?"

"No thank you, sir." His voice was cold and formal. There was something about his manner that made Robertson uneasy.

"Well, what can I—"

"Sir," Francis interrupted, "I have come about Harry Gresham."

"Again?" Robertson sat by his desk, in the seat normally used by his visitors. "I thought we'd just been through all this."

"Has there been any word of him?" Francis's voice was hard and insistent. Robertson looked up at him, but could not make out his expression because of the sunshine slanting through the blinds behind him.

Robertson blinked. "Look, Alan, I believe I told you that Gresham was none of your concern."

Francis reached into his jacket, pulled out an envelope and handed it over.

"What is this?" asked Robertson.

"If you'd be good enough to read it, sir. It's quite clear."

Robertson drew out a single sheet of paper, a carbon copy of a letter. He frowned as he saw the address: Conservative Party Headquarters, and the name of his agent.

"Congratulations, Alan. Most people forget the silent *p* in his name."

"The first law of journalism, sir. Get their names right."

He read the letter slowly, aware that Francis was studying him. He could feel the perspiration run down one arm, and fought to disguise an involuntary shiver that threatened to make his hand tremble. When he looked up, his face was impassive. "But this is absurd," he said.

"No," said Francis. He moved away from the window toward

Robertson and stood looking down at him. "I think you will appreciate that, whatever else I may lack, at least I am thorough. I have been talking to a lot of people. The Argentinian was the last. I finally got to see him yesterday."

"But what he says is nonsense," Robertson snapped.

"I'm afraid not. He has a list of undercover agents in Europe working with Nazi sympathizers in South America. Had Argentina entered the war earlier, we would have known sooner. Their diplomatic staff has only just moved back into town. But they are cooperative enough." He paused. "It's understandable, really, under the circumstances, now they know who the winners are. My man was very friendly. It didn't take much persuasion to get him to let me see his files."

"But I can't believe . . ." Robertson said.

"He didn't have Gresham's name, of course," Francis continued. "But he had a photograph. And certain facts tallied. There is no doubt."

"No," said Robertson. "It is impossible."

"Sir," said Francis, leaning close and staring into Robertson's face, you sent a Nazi to Berlin in charge of a British patrol."

Robertson pushed his chair back and stood up, turned away and began to pace the room, tapping Francis's envelope against his teeth. Francis sat and watched him. Eventually Robertson turned and looked back at him.

"Does this Argentinian know anything?" he asked. "About the Berlin operation."

"No."

Robertson glanced again at the letter. "And I suppose this is your way of getting me to let you in on it. . . ."

"Not really," Francis said, but Robertson was pacing again. Francis was content to wait. He sat back against the desk, saying nothing, watching the little man as he moved around the room. At last Robertson stopped and leaned against the door. Francis studied him. He seemed to be in complete control of himself. If there was any inner turmoil, the effects did not show on the surface. When Robertson spoke, his voice was steady.

"This letter. It has today's date."

"I wrote it this morning," said Francis. "The ink is scarcely dry. And, to anticipate your question, I have not posted it yet."

Robertson nodded. "But you think the party should know about all this, that I supposedly sent a Nazi to Berlin?"

"They have a right to know. If the story were to come out . . ."

Francis let the sentence hang in the air, then continued. "Besides, I don't want the responsibility of sharing the knowledge of such a blunder."

"Rather cowardly, don't you think?"

Francis shrugged, ignoring the sneer in the man's voice.

For a moment there was silence, then Robertson continued. "Let us say you may be correct about Gresham . . ."

Francis grunted in annoyance and Robertson held up his hands in mock surrender. "Very well, let us *assume* you are right, that Gresham has been a Fascist all these years. It is no easy thing for me to admit. I thought I had talked him out of it years ago. But, as it happens, in the long term it is unimportant."

Francis raised an eyebrow in surprise and Robertson moved past him, settling himself in his chair. "As you do not like sharing my secrets, I will tell you only what you need to know about Berlin. There was an embarrassment in the city, someone who had to be disposed of, someone who could not be allowed to fall into the wrong hands. Any conclusions you wish to draw are your own, Alan."

Francis said nothing and waited for Robertson to elaborate.

"The circumstances dictated the events. I had to arrange the job myself and I needed to have someone I could trust implicitly, a rogue elephant, as it were. Gresham was the obvious choice." He smiled, "Strangely enough, I was also giving him a chance to redeem himself." He leaned back and gazed up at Francis. "It's ironic. It turns out he was perfect for the job. He would have carried it out to the letter even though his motives were hardly those I envisaged."

Francis frowned, his mind racing with questions, but Robertson sat forward and clapped his hands together, an indication that the subject was closed. He picked up some papers and handed them to Francis. "Alan, I have read your little offering. Now, I would be obliged if you would glance at mine."

Francis read the speech carefully. It was detailed and precise, outlining a terrible future with the democratic forces of the West aligned against Russia and her satellites, both sides armed with increasingly powerful weapons. When he had finished, he tapped the title page with his finger.

"The Cold War," he said. "A neat phrase."

"Thank you," said Robertson. He folded his arms and gazed through the window. "So you see, Alan, the last six years have been little more than a skirmish. The real work starts now. The danger cannot be overemphasized. We can't let any past embarrassments mess up the future."

He glanced at his watch, took Francis's arm and led him to the door.

"I have to show you out now, Alan," he said, and the smile was back on his face. "We'll talk later." He patted Francis's shoulder. "You won't do anything rash in the meanwhile." He opened the door, ushered him out, closed it behind him, took a deep breath and returned to his desk.

Francis walked slowly up Baker Street. It was a warm day and he decided to take a stroll in the park. As he made his way north, he went over Robertson's speech, paragraph by paragraph. It was certainly convincing enough and he knew that he, Alan Francis, would be part of Robertson's future. He had no doubt that the man would offer him a job now. Perhaps he would be proved right, but Francis could not quite believe it. Surely things would not reach such a stalemate. There would not be such global distrust, not between two groups who had so recently been allies; the idea smacked of—what was the new word? —paranoia, symptomatic of an exaggerated fear.

He stopped by a pillar box, reached into his pocket and took out the letter, the original, with Conservative Party Headquarters typed on the envelope and the stamp already in place. No, he thought, I am not convinced. Besides, the Gresham story could well resurface anytime. There would be war trials. There would always be bright young reporters ready to dig things up. Too many people knew about Gresham: Jeffries, the Argentinian, even Audrey Stevens. And if Alan Francis could find out, so might anyone. It was too great a risk and he knew that he had neither the essential cynicism, the political idealism nor the ambition to take it.

For a moment he stood motionless, the envelope gripped firmly in his hand. He did not want to share Robertson's secret and his responsibility. To do so would result in sleepless nights, and he had already had enough of those.

That the letter would signal the end of Robertson's career, he had no doubt. Even if the mandarins at the Tory HQ accepted his explanations, they would be unable to run the risk of the Gresham story becoming public.

Poor Charles, he thought. So admirable, yet in a way so naive. He had only one weakness. He chose the wrong men. First Harry Gresham, then Alan Francis. Quickly he slipped the letter into the box and moved off toward the park. There would be pretty girls in the sunshine. He planned to sit on a bench and gaze at them, maybe for the rest of his life.